QUILLER SALAMANDER

ADAM HALL

OTTO PENZLER BOOKS
NEW YORK

**OTTO
PENZLER
BOOKS**

Otto Penzler Books
129 West 56th Street
New York, NY 10019
(Editorial Offices Only)

Simon & Schuster
Rockefeller Center
1230 Avenue of the Americas
New York, NY 10020

Book design by Richard Truscott / PIXEL PRESS

Manufactured in the United States of America

10 9 8 7 6 5 4 3 2 1

Library of Congress Cataloging-in Publication Data
Hall, Adam.
Quiller Salamander / Adam Hall
    p.   cm.
ISBN 1-883402-40-9
        1.Quiller (Fictitious character)—Fiction.   2. Intelligence
    service—Great Britain—Fiction.   I. Title.
PR6039.R518Q5117   1994
823'.914–dc20

94-17372

To Dan Hagen

QUILLER
SALAMANDER

1

TARANTULA

The man came down the steps of the Hôtel d'Alsace.

He was alone.

He came straight across the sidewalk to his car without looking around him. There was another car standing in front of his, and a Pakistan Airlines minibus behind. There was nobody near him; nobody nearer, at least, than fifteen or twenty feet.

It was early morning, not long after first light, judging by the length of the shadows across the pink marble wall of the hotel.

The man reached his car and opened the door and got in and the blast blew the roof off and the light was dazzling for a second or two and then there was a lot of redness in the middle of things and one of the man's arms went sailing across the sidewalk and a long shiny red tendril began streaming out of what was left of his body—presumably the large intestine—as he went on flying upward, a leg coming off and starting to fall, turning over and over. Then the main part of his body came down too, and the smoke began clearing.

"Run it again," Shatner said.

The man at the VCR put it into fast rewind and we waited.

Shatner was sitting on my left in a rickety deck chair, not smoking but smelling of stale nicotine. The only other man in here apart from Shatner and the one working the VCR was Holmes. He hadn't said anything since we'd come in here, but then Holmes never says much anyway. Shatner was fidgeting with a pencil, wishing he could light up, I suppose, but in the screening room it's strictly verboten.

I still didn't know what they wanted me here for.

The tape hit the stop and began playing again, and the man came down the steps of the Hôtel d'Alsace without looking around him.

"We want you to tell us," Shatner said, "if you think any of these other people in the picture look as if they're surveilling the DIF."

Director in the field. His name was Fane, and he'd directed me once in Murmansk, had rigged a bomb like that one in a truck I was going to drive, did it on orders from Control in London because I'd become expendable, a danger to the mission. But I'd smelled the bloody thing out and my large intestine was still where it should be, while his was snaking all over the video screen, a bit embarrassing for him when you think about it.

He came across to the car again but I wasn't interested in him now. There were seven people in the frame apart from Fane: three Europeans standing together talking, identical suits, identical briefcases; two bearded Hindus shading their eyes and looking down the street for a taxi; and a woman in white holding a rose and waving to someone in a car just leaving, *après tout, c'est Paris.* And the man reading a paper.

Kerboom.

"They must have all been killed," I told Shatner. The screen had been going blank a couple of seconds after Fane's leg began coming down, but the blast had obviously started to reach the other people.

"Yes," Shatner said, and tugged at his rumpled trousers, a nervous habit I'd noticed in him before—he'd been my control for *Solitaire.* "They were all killed. The camera operator got clear with the tape and some minor injuries. We're working, you see, with nothing much to go on. We want to know who placed the bomb. It obviously wasn't one of the people in the picture, but we just thought one of them might have been surveilling him, not knowing the car was hot."

The rickety chair creaked as he shifted his weight. The screen went blank again and the operator hit the rewind button. "All we can hope for," Shatner said, "is to find a recognizable face and try to trace things from there."

The tape was running again, and after a bit I said, "The man with the paper. Just a possibility, that's all. No one—"

"I wondered."

"Right. No one else."

"Freeze it," Shatner told the operator. "Then make a still and we'll blow it up and send it to the field to work on."

"Good luck," I said.

He turned to me then, and I saw the worry in his eyes. "Yes, quite. He's standing in profile, isn't he, and the picture's foggy anyway. But we've got to try."

His worry was understandable. We've lost only two directors in the field—including this one—during the whole of my time with the Bureau, compared with God knows how many executives. The DIFs don't take an active role in a mission; they just hole up somewhere safe, usually a hotel, and direct things from there, keeping the executive in signals with London. The only other time we lost a director was when his executive blew him to the opposition under interrogation, the sin of sins: we're expected to pop our capsule if we can't trust ourselves, before things get too rough.

Now there was Fane, and the same thing could have happened.

I said, not looking at Shatner, "You're the control for this one?"

"Yes." The way he said it, I wish I hadn't asked.

"Do it again?" The operator was rewinding.

Shatner looked at me and I shook my head and he told the man no, and we got up and Holmes switched the light on.

"I appreciate your time," Shatner said, and pushed his deck chair against the wall.

"Anything else I can do?"

"No."

"Who's the executive?"

"Kearns."

"He's out there now?" In the field.

"No."

As we left the screening room I said, "He was doing a routine check, was he, the cameraman?" Sometimes the support people in the field run some film over the DIF's base as he goes in or comes out, to make sure there's no surveillance on him. The DIF is the queen bee of the mission, protected and held precious.

"Yes," Shatner said. "Of course he'd no idea what was going to happen."

"So where's Kearns?"

We stood together in the corridor, the three of us. Shatner was obviously finished with me and wanted to go. Holmes was just hanging around, I didn't know why. I'd been called in simply to give an opinion, as a seasoned shadow executive who spends his whole life watching to see if he's being followed or surveilled.

"Kearns," Shatner said, "is still here in London." He was fumbling in his worn tweed jacket for a cigarette.

"The DIF was sent out ahead of him?"

I felt Holmes touch my sleeve, but didn't take any notice: I'd been inactive for six weeks and the nerves were getting a bit strung out. I needed a mission, would steal one if necessary.

"Yes," Shatner said, and looked at his battered wristwatch.

"Why don't you send me out," I asked him, "now this has happened?" Kearns wasn't a senior shadow, would have his own nerves on edge now that his intended DIF had been blown all over the front of the Hôtel d'Alsace in Paris.

Holmes touched my arm again, and this time I looked at him and got the message in the dark of his steady eyes.

"Oh," Shatner said, "I don't really know what's going to happen next. We might call the whole thing off." He ducked his shaggy head and went hurrying along the corridor before I could say anything else.

"Spot of tea?" Holmes asked me.

"Not in the Caff."

"Why not?"

"I've seen enough of that bloody place in the last six weeks."

"Let's go and see a little more," he said gently. I suppose Holmes knows better than anyone in this beleaguered backwater of the keyhole game that I can be led but not driven.

There were three other people in the Caff, a couple of them wearing club ties—down here from Administration to show how terribly democratic the Bureau is—and Kearns, sitting alone in a far corner staring into his teacup, legs crossed and one foot swinging the whole time, understandably. He hadn't looked up when we came in; I don't think he would have looked up if a herd of buffalo had come through the door; all he could see was his very own director in the field going through the roof of his car—they would have shown him the tape, of course.

"Bun?" Holmes asked me.

"Are you serious?" They're like overdone concrete in this bloody hole.

"Tea, then," Holmes said courteously, and signaled to Daisy. This man's courtesy is one of his many strengths, and guaranteed to drive you up the wall at times when you're ready to strangle the first person who's got the nerve to say good morning.

"Relax," he said, "old horse." He watched me from under his thick black eyebrows, his eyes intent.

"Look," I said, "it's been six weeks."

"I know." He asked Daisy for some tea and she limped away with her arthritic hip, her red wig wobbling.

"Let me tell you," Holmes said quietly, "about friend Kearns. He—"

"They shouldn't send him out there, for Christ's sake, after what happened. How many missions has he been on—five, six?"

"The point," Holmes said with careful emphasis, "is that he needs to go out there more than ever, if in fact they don't call the whole thing off, as Shatner says." He lowered his voice, keeping his rather hypnotic eyes on mine. "He didn't do terribly well the last time out, went much too fast into the end phase and left his support people behind, wanting to impress London with a race to the finish. He brought the mission home, but—"

"This was *Bolero*?"

"Yes. But of course he nearly came unstuck, and his control had him on the carpet when he got back to London. He—"

"Who was his control?"

"Mr. Loman."

"That *bloody* man. Kearns is a neophyte, wants nurturing, not kicking."

Holmes looked down and said nothing, didn't agree. I heard the door of the signals room slam as someone came out; the Caff was right next to it in the basement.

"So Kearns *needs* this one," Holmes said at last, "if they push ahead with a new director." His eyes were on me again. "You could probably twist their arm and get it for yourself, since you're more experienced and everything. But—" He left it with a shrug, didn't take his eyes from me.

Then the door opened and in came Baker, one of the shadows, and dropped into a chair and tilted it back, one hand on the stained plastic table. "Jesus Christ, they'll never get him out at this rate." He must have been the man who'd just come out of Signals.

"Vereker?" Holmes asked him.

"Yes. Support can't get near him, radio contact's gone, and his DIF hasn't got a clue where he is. Caffeine, Daisy old dear, for the love of God."

Vereker had been on all our minds for the last sixteen hours. When you're mission-hungry you spend half your time in the Caff and the other half in the signals room listening to the stuff coming in from the various fields, so I knew what the score was with

Vereker. He was in the thick of a sticky end phase in Bosnia and had started asking for help at one o'clock this morning, GMT, the transmission fading and coming back, and his director had been signaling through the mast at Cheltenham for instructions every hour from then on.

It's the worst place there is, the signals room, when some poor bastard's got a wheel off out there in the field; it's like sitting in the waiting room at the dentist's listening to a drill going next door.

"He'll be all right, love," Daisy told Baker as she brought him his tea. "Don't you worry."

She always says that, but often the truth is different.

Holmes was still watching me, waiting. He'd made an appeal to my hypothetical better nature: let Kearns keep his mission, try and do things better this time, earn his stripes.

I was aware of anger simmering. A mission where the DIF was already a dead duck before the action had even started was the kind of thing I could handle better than most.

"That man Vereker," I said, "is in the shit. And you want to see Kearns in the shit too?"

"It's not quite like that," Holmes said.

"What is it quite like?"

He spread his fingers on the table. "The first few times you went out, things didn't always go well. But you had to push through with it, like a rite of passage. And you're still here. Give him his chance too." He lifted his fingers, let them drop. "Not much to ask."

I looked across the room at the man in the corner. He was still sitting with his legs crossed, one foot swinging, his eyes on his empty cup: I'd seen him finish his tea minutes ago. He looked so bloody young—but then they always do, the neophytes, it stands to reason.

"He's cannon fodder," I said. "You know that."

Holmes nodded quickly. "Yes. But that's only part of it. If you didn't want his mission for yourself you wouldn't mind so much, would you? You'd let him go out, take his chance."

It took away the feeling of anger, and immediately, because it had been against myself, for wanting to steal the mission from Kearns over there; and Holmes had put it on the line for me.

"Point taken," I said. "I withdraw."

He flashed his quick white smile. "I rather hoped you would." He was more pleased than he wanted to show: he'd expected a tussle. But that's the way he fights, Holmes, for what he wants: he goes in and picks over your conscience and when he finds what he wants he gently pricks it for you. The only way to thwart him is not to have a conscience for him to pick over, but of course in this trade the very idea is hilarious.

"Now let me offer some good advice, old fruit." He looked around him, back at me. "For the last few weeks you've been prowling the corridors like a bear—not to put too fine a point on it—with a sore arse, looking for a mission. One of the reasons you haven't got one yet is that there aren't many available, and another reason is that not every control is willing to suffer—not to mince matters—your notorious pigheadedness."

I sat listening. I always listen to Holmes. He's probably the only man I trust in the whole of this treacherous hellhole. He also keeps his ear to the ground and therefore knows the score before anyone else has started the game.

"So the risk you're running," he said softly, "is that before very long someone is going to drum up an excuse for sending you out to some remote and benighted region of the globe just to get rid of you."

"More tea, loves?"

Daisy stood over us with a chipped enamel teapot, the brave colors of King George V's coronation emblem still half-visible under the stains.

"That would be nice," Holmes said cheerfully.

Daisy poured for us, slopping the tea over as an expression of her generosity, and limped away with her arthritis. She dispenses her undrinkable tea and uneatable buns, does our Daisy, with the clumsy grace of a benediction, and if she ever got tipsy and fell into the Thames the entire staff of the Bureau would be there before she hit the water. Cloistered as we are in a covert haunt of sub-terfuge, we prize the presence of this single innocent soul.

"So what do I do?" I asked Holmes. He'd mentioned good advice.

He looked around him again, at Baker, at Kearns, and back at me, his voice softer than ever. "You know Mr. Flockhart?"

"Not well." Flockhart was one of the controls, but he'd never run me through a mission.

"He's quite good," Holmes said. "Some people find him a bit on the enigmatic side, doesn't give much away. He also comes and goes, runs a mission or two and disappears for a while. Of course, he's fairly senior, he can pick and choose." He spread his fingers on the table again, keeping clear of the pools of tea. "My advice, then, is that you should perhaps cultivate his company in the next day or so, and see if he's got anything interesting for you. Don't push it— just listen, and remember that one must handle Mr. Flockhart with the tender care demanded by—shall we say—a tarantula."

2

· ·

LINGUINI

It was gone eight in the evening when Flockhart came out of his office. I'd been hanging around in the corridor since five and was getting fed up.

He shut the door, locking it, his back to me. He hadn't seen me yet, so I started walking toward him, casual pace, and we met near the stairs.

"Were you coming to see me?" His face was square, bland, expressionless.

"Not actually," I said. "I thought Loman might be with you." Loman had left here an hour ago.

"I haven't seen him." Flockhart studied me with faint interest. "No luck yet?"

"No." He knew I was looking for a job; everyone did.

He wasn't moving on, was still watching me. "Have you eaten yet?"

"No."

"Come and have some macaroni." He turned toward the stairs, and I followed.

It was a ten-minute walk through fine drizzle to a pasta place called the Cellar Steps, a basement room with red-checked tablecloths and a mural of the Coliseum in Rome and one or two ceiling fans stirring the smell of garlic around. Flockhart chose a corner table under a signed framed photograph of Sophia Loren with an arm round the proprietor, Luigi Francesco.

There weren't many people here: the theaters had gone in ten minutes ago and half London had gone home.

We chose linguini.

"So how long has it been since you came back?"

"Six weeks," I said.

"Care for some wine?" I shook my head. "Six weeks is a long time, for someone like you." He sat watching me, his face a mask, his eyes attentive.

"Someone like me?"

"You like to keep up the pace, from what I hear."

"Lose momentum and you've got to deal with inertia."

"How very true." He broke some bread, looking past me, nodding to someone. I couldn't see who it was. "Let's see, you were on *Solitaire*, weren't you?"

I didn't care for the "Let's see" bit; it was meant to sound casual, and didn't. Everyone at the Bureau knew damned well I'd been on *Solitaire*: it had ended with quite a bang.

"Yes," I said.

"Thought so. Who directed you in the field on that one?"

"Cone." I waited. If Flockhart knew his facts about that mission he wouldn't let it go.

"Cone, that's right." He dug some butter for his roll, and the light of the little red-shaded lamp on the table reflected off his knife, flashing across his eyes. He was looking down, busy. "But wasn't Thrower directing you at first?"

He knew his facts, yes, and wasn't letting it go.

"At first," I said.

A faint smile came, put on for the occasion. "Not often we see two directors in the field on one mission. What happened?"

I could smell the dampness on my jacket left by the drizzle, was aware of the heated exchange of Italian going on behind the doors to the kitchen. My senses were tuned, alerted, because this man

Flockhart was putting a probe into me and I didn't know why. But of course he hadn't asked me to join him down here to discuss the cricket scores.

"What happened," I told him, "was that Thrower wanted to do things his way and I wanted to do things mine."

He put his knife down carefully. "So you had him replaced, is that it?"

"Yes."

"In the middle of the mission?"

"Pretty well."

"And Bureau One agreed to do it, is that right?"

"Yes." Bureau One was the head of the whole organization.

"So you must have had good cause."

"I had good cause whether Bureau One agreed with it or not."

He took it easily enough, but looked down quickly. In Berlin I'd demanded the immediate attention of Bureau One to get rid of Thrower, and it had meant waking him up at two in the morning in Washington; it was the closest I've ever come to being thrown out on my neck.

"Linguini Francesco for the gentlemen," and there was Luigi himself with the dishes, lowering them to the table with a flourish. "But no wine? I have some Chianti Risadori that arrived—"

"We're working, Luigi," Flockhart said, and this time the smile had surprising charm. "Perhaps later."

"There is time for work and there is time for Chianti Risadori," Luigi said with nicely feigned indignation, and went away folding his serviette with another flourish.

"You get on well, normally," Flockhart was asking, "with your controls and your directors in the field?" I didn't answer right away, and he said, "I hope you don't mind if we dispense with small talk while we're eating?"

"Not my language."

"Jolly good." He waited for my answer.

"I get on well if they're effective and don't try to bitch me about. Croder knows that, so does Loman."

"You've crossed swords, is that it?" Offered with a slight smile, but not the charming one. It was the smile, bearing in mind what Holmes had said, on the face of the tarantula.

"We understand each other. I probably respect Croder more than any other control, and not just because he's Chief of Signals."

Flockhart moved the shaker of Parmesan toward me. "How is the linguini?"

"First-class."

"Croder, yes, is quite formidable, isn't he, in terms of effectiveness. What about Loman?"

"He's effective," I said. "He ran me well in Singapore."

"But?"

"I think it's the bow tie."

Flockhart actually laughed. "The bow tie, yes, I know what you mean. What about Pepperidge? Ferris?"

"Both impeccable. They could take me through hell and back." Had done so, in a way, and more than once.

"You know Pepperidge lost his sister, do you?"

"Yes." I'd met her at his little house in Hampstead, a pretty woman with gaunt eyes and sallow skin, dying of cancer as gracefully as she could.

"What about Pringle?"

"He's never directed me."

"Less experienced, perhaps," Flockhart said in a moment, "than the directors you're used to."

"I don't know. Bit young, isn't he?" I'd only run into Pringle a couple of times in the signals room. "Wasn't he on *Switchblade?*"

"He was," Flockhart said, "and he brought it home rather well. Pringle is young, yes, but he has style." He was watching me intently now. "Which is something you'd understand, I rather think."

"Who was his control on that one?"

"I was."

He looked past me as some people came down the steps, and I watched his face as he carefully checked them out. Quite a few of Luigi's clientele are spooks of some sort from DI5 and DI6, and some of our own people come down here.

I wasn't ready to think that this man Flockhart had a mission for me but it looked as if it could be on the cards; what he'd actually been asking me since we'd come down those steps was: *How difficult are you to control in the field?* And if you think I ought to have been blowing my fuses at the thought of a new mission after six weeks of wearing my bloody shoes out along those dreary corridors, the reason is quite simple. I had a question of my own: Did I want to work for a tarantula?

Flockhart had finished checking out the people who had just come in, and was watching me again as I put my fork down and pushed my plate away an inch and sat watching him back.

"The thing is," he said in a moment, "I need someone to go and take a look at certain things in Cambodia for me."

I waited. It was obvious I'd want to know more than that.

Someone gave a sudden laugh behind me, and I recognized it. It was Corbyn, that bloody fool in DI5. He was one of the people who'd just come in, and that was the first of the series of laughs we were going to hear at regular three-minute intervals if we stayed long enough: Corbyn treats counterespionage as some sort of tiddlywinks, absolutely ripping fun.

Then Flockhart said, "It's the sort of thing I wouldn't ask just anyone to take on." He pushed his own plate away. "It requires a rather high degree of discretion."

That threw me. The Bureau is a strictly underground outfit that doesn't officially exist: we answer directly to the Prime Minister without going through those hysterical clowns at the Foreign Office, and one of the reasons for this is to give us the freedom to do things that no one else is allowed to do, and I'll say no more. And if *that* doesn't already require "a rather high degree of discretion," then what in God's name does?

I didn't say anything. Flockhart was fly-fishing with me, flicking his lures across the surface waiting for me to rise; but I wasn't in the mood: if he had a mission for me I'd look at it and if I liked it I'd take it—but I'd have to like it an awful lot if this man was going to be my control in London.

"Discretion," Flockhart said carefully, "is of course our daily bread at the Bureau. But this—"

"And for dessert, *signorini*, we have an excellent *gelati di Napoli*, anointed with just a soupçon of Punt e Mes—"

"For you?" Flockhart asked me as Luigi took our plates.

"No."

"Just espresso, Luigi. For both—is that right?"

I said yes.

"The linguini was acceptable?"

"Your best, Luigi. Your very best."

A small dark boy with eyes by Michelangelo swept the crumbs from our bread into a scoop and darted away.

"Discretion," said Flockhart again, "is our stock-in-trade, yes, but what I need would be discretion *within* discretion, if you follow."

"The ultimate clam."

"How well you put it." He waited, then said, "But you haven't asked any questions yet. Lack of interest?"

"Not really. Just put the proposition on the line for me and we'll take it from there. I don't like piecemeal information."

"Quite so." He looked down for an instant.

Behind me that clod Corbyn laughed. You can set your watch by him.

"I need, then," Flockhart said carefully, "someone capable of total discretion to look at certain things in Phnom Penh for me, leaving tomorrow and reporting back to me personally through my private lines at the Bureau and at my home."

In a moment I said, "I'm actually looking for a *mission*. The real thing."

The espresso arrived and Flockhart dropped the sliver of peel into his cup. "Yes, I understand that. I didn't bring you down here to waste your time. Let me put it this way: if you are prepared to follow my instructions with reasonable fidelity, and to work—at least for the moment—with no signals board or transmissions through Cheltenham, and with no supports, couriers, or contacts in the field, I can guarantee you a mission. The real thing."

I suppose it's the way it goes, isn't it—if you lust after something a bit too long you're not sure whether you want it after all when it lands in your hands. But it wasn't really that, I think, this time. I didn't trust this man, and if I let him run me through a mission I would have to trust him with my life.

"I would be operating, then," I said in a moment, "under a total blackout."

"Yes."

That too was suspect. I'd never known it to happen before at the Bureau, and that could simply mean that none of the other shadow executives had ever told me about it, but I didn't think so. There's a grapevine in that place, as in most organizations, and this was something I'd never picked up.

"Why?"

Flockhart was ready for it, and said at once, "You would learn why as the mission progressed."

His eyes watched me steadily, their pale blue ice reflecting the red-shaded lamp but gaining none of its warmth. It didn't worry me too much that he wouldn't answer my question: at the outset of any mission we are told only as much as we need to be told, on the sound principle that the less we know of the background the less we can give away if the opposition should ever bring us down and throw us into the cell and get out the bamboo and the shocking-coil and the rest of the toys.

"When you say you can guarantee me a mission," I told Flockhart, "there would have to be a director in the field. At least that."

He gave a nod. "Pringle."

The man he'd been trying to sell me. *Pringle is young, yes, but he has style. Which is something you'd understand, I rather think.*

I dropped my own sliver of peel into the cup and watched it floating, saw one of his ice-blue eyes, Flockhart's, reflected there on the dark surface.

Corbyn laughed, behind me.

When I felt ready I said, "When do you want my decision?"

I looked up as I said it, to see if I could catch any reaction in Flockhart's eyes: I wanted to find out how much it meant to him to know that I was actually considering the mission, how much he needed me, how indispensable I was, whether I could dictate terms. But of course his eyes didn't show anything.

Except the anger.

"I want your decision now," he said evenly.

I didn't say anything right away, partly because I wasn't sure of the answer, not at all sure, with a man like this as my potential control.

But I'd placed it at last, the vibration I'd been picking up since we'd started talking down here, the faintest whisper of something in the tone of his voice, in his breathing, the way he sat, his chin tucked in by the smallest degree and the head down, the attitude—on a minuscule scale—of a bull preparing to charge. And yes, perhaps it was also expressed in the very iciness of the eyes, which I hadn't noticed in the past, the few times I'd run across him. There was anger here, and of a high order, finely controlled, barely contained, as Flockhart sat watching me across the table.

"That's rather soon," I said, simply to give myself time. Because this anger of his was also something I should take into account, perhaps, before I made my decision. It wasn't directed against me: we were virtual strangers, had had nothing to do with each other before tonight. But anger in a man like this, directed at no matter whom, was a potent form of explosive.

"Time," he said evenly, "is of the essence."

I heard that idiot Corbyn laugh again, but the sound was faint this time; the hum of voices in the room had seemed to die away as I let my mind fold into itself to seek guidance. I wasn't worried by the instant deadline Flockhart was giving me; with comfortable time to make any kind of decision we tend to cloud the issue with pros and cons, and are never quite sure, when we've cast the die, whether we've done right or wrong. Whereas intuition is as fast as light, flashing up from the subconscious with all the facts marshaled and the answer ready, if we're prepared to listen.

"All right," I said.

Because the only fact that really mattered was this: when I'd been prowling those dreary corridors for weeks on end I would have taken on *any* mission for *anyone*.

And nothing had changed.

"You'll do it?" Flockhart sounded, if anything, surprised.

"Yes."

He left his eyes on me, leaning forward a little across the table. "You'll do well," he said quietly. "You'll do very well."

The next morning the drizzle had given over and a pale sun was trying to show through the clouds, with a March wind rising.

Flockhart saw me in his office not long after nine, giving me a chair and going behind his desk again, throwing some papers to one side. They fell across a silver-framed photograph, and he left them there; I couldn't see it clearly at this angle because of the reflection on the glass, but it looked like a woman's face.

"You can do your medical clearance," he said, "with your own doctor, or mine if you prefer. Your expense account is open as of now, and I shall be personally responsible."

He looked much the same as I'd seen him last night: cool, very controlled, expressionless. But the anger had gone. His speech and the movement of his hands were faster; anger had gone and left room for energy.

"Fair enough," I said. "What about briefing?"

"None, officially." He turned his head to look from the window on my left, where a pigeon was waddling on the sill; then he looked back at me and said, "There's nothing official about this *at all*, you must understand. Let me put it this way: your mission would not necessarily meet with acceptance by Administration if I proposed it to them. That is why I didn't." He watched me carefully. "Does that bother you?"

"I've spent most of my career," I said, "doing things totally un-acceptable to Administration."

"Yes, I've heard it rumored. That's why I selected you."

"There was a chorus line?"

"Only in my head," he said quickly. "I've spoken to no one else, be assured. No one."

The pigeon flew off the sill, and through the gap in the window I heard the soft beating of its wings. "All right," I said. "So if there's no briefing, what about instructions?"

"You'll find them at the office of Trans-Kampuchean Air Services in Phnom Penh; I've already sent them on ahead of you. Here's their address. Your sealed envelope also contains rather substantial funds in U.S. dollars and local currency, together with your hotel reservation and identity papers as an agent for Trans-Kampuchean."

"Are they Bureau?"

"Shall we say, associated. Totally secure, but not a safe house."

He pushed his chair back and got up, taking an envelope from a drawer and handing it to me. "Air tickets and visa. You're on Air France Flight 212, routed through Kuwait and Bombay. Departure is 1:05, which will give you time for the medical and packing. Any questions?"

"When will Pringle be there?" I asked him. In Phnom Penh.

"Not for a day or two. You won't need him. He'll contact you when he arrives." He let his eyes rest on mine for a moment. "Pringle is young, as you say, and hasn't carried out as many missions as you. But I have the utmost confidence in him and I want you to treat him accordingly. He's shown himself capable of resourcefulness, imagination, and cool-headedness in difficult times. We're clear on that?"

I heard the warning. Pringle was Flockhart's man, and I wasn't expected to bitch him about if things got rough.

"Quite clear," I said.

Flockhart came with me to the door. "I'm not opening a signals board for you at this stage, as you know, but for the purposes of identification, the code name for the mission is *Salamander*."

The sky was still clearing when I went through the door behind the lift and into the street, with Big Ben chiming three quarters of the hour at the far end of Whitehall. I'd committed myself and the die was cast and all that, but I wasn't feeling any regrets. I suppose it was just Flockhart on my mind, and the question of whether I could really trust him, trust him with my life, because when I walked across to the car and pressed the door button there was a sudden flash of memory and Fane went through the roof again and left his blood all over the video screen. Then it was gone, and I opened the door and got in.

3

GABRIELLE

We came down through black overcast across the Gulf of Thailand with a glimmer of light below us to the east of the mountains where the city of Phnom Penh lay sprawling across the land. A cloud of water vapor started filling the cabin as the Tupolev-134 settled into the approach path and the landing gear went down with a thump.

"Tout va bien, vous croyez?"

I said yes, everything was fine, you often got fog on board these things, par for the course. He was a jeweler from Paris, out here to look at some silver, and was actually wearing, he'd told me, a bulletproof vest.

There was the normal chaos inside the main hall at Pochentong and it was gone eight in the evening when I walked into the Trans-Kampuchean Air Services office, my shoes squelchy from the puddles in the street. Office? Call it a shed, tucked against the wall of what looked like a maintenance hangar.

"I'm here to pick up an envelope," I told the man behind the chipped plastic counter. "Name of Jones, David."

"Jones, David, yes. Righto." But he didn't move yet, just sat looking at me with his head turned slightly as if he were deaf in one ear, English, pale, sweating—touch of malaria? I waited.

A phone was ringing somewhere but he didn't seem interested.

"Jones," he said, "now that's a good old name. All the way from the valley, are you?" He'd put on a Welsh accent, not a very good one. He was pissing me off a little by now.

"I'm in a hurry," I told him.

"But of course you are." He dropped the magazine he'd been reading and got up and went across to a dented metal filing cabinet and hit it with the palm of his hand to get the top drawer open. "The same with all of us, isn't it? Always in a hurry. How's Daisy?"

"She's fine." I'd got it now: he hadn't just been chatty; he'd been fishing around for a code introduction because I hadn't given him one. And he wouldn't give me the envelope marked David Jones until I'd done that. "Arthritis still bugging her," I said. Not quite your traditional code intro, but it was telling him I knew my way around that rotten dump in Whitehall and must therefore be strictly kosher.

Why hadn't Flockhart given me a code intro to use? Because *Salamander* was so ultra-clandestine that the normal routines didn't apply? But that was plain bloody dangerous.

The man started whistling tunelessly as he went through the top drawer and fished out a manila envelope and came back and dropped it onto the counter. "Jones, David."

"Thank you."

"When were you out here last?"

"Couple of years ago."

"Things have changed for the worse since the UN cleared out, if that sounds possible, but the basics are still there. Don't drink the water or go with the girls or eat anything raw, and if you need medical attention keep clear of the hospitals: they still haven't heard of sterilization and if you ever needed an operation you'd have to take along a can of diesel fuel to run the generator for the lights." The telephone began ringing again, and again he ignored it. "We've still got one doctor for twenty-seven thousand people, so the thing is to play it safe. And watch out for trip mines: the Khmer Rouge are still blowing up whoever they can find—military, civilians, women and children, you name it, they'll kill it." He gave a sudden bright smile. "Enjoy your stay in exotic, sunny Cambodia."

I stowed the manila envelope into my flight bag and walked down the steps into the street.

The black cloud cover was still spread across the sea to the west, but above the mountains there were starfields clinging to the night sky. The air was pale gunmetal-blue as the lingering heat of the day pressed down across the boulevards, and I felt the tension here in Phnom Penh, dangerous and oppressive, as I splashed through the puddles to the Peugeot 604 that Flockhart had left for me to pick up at the airport. I pulled a door open and threw the flight bag in.

"Did you come through Bombay?"

"Yes."

"I have friends there." She gave the menu a token glance. "It never changes, the food in this place."

Her name was Gabrielle Bouchard, and the most notable thing about her was her dark, deep-water blue eyes. Flockhart hadn't mentioned them in his instructions. *When you reach the Royal Palace Hotel, ask for the room number of Gabrielle Bouchard, a French photojournalist from Paris, and phone her to say you're there. Then let the evening take care of itself. She is a friend, but ignorant of my work; therefore maintain strict cover.*

"What will you have?" she asked me.

"Anything with shrimps."

She looked for them on the menu. I suppose she was early thirties, efficient-looking in her paramilitary khaki slacks and tunic, short sleeves above thin bare arms, the muscles of the left one a degree more developed, presumably because she carried her cameras on that side. French nationality, perhaps, but her looks were Eurasian, had the best of both worlds.

"Sizzling shrimp cashew with lobster sauce?"

"Fine." She'd asked me to have dinner with her; she was in Mr. Flockhart's debt, she said.

There were thirty or forty people in here, most of them in the dining section, the rest lining the long canvas-canopied bar on bamboo stools. Two of the ceiling fans were wobbling on their brackets, and if we'd been sitting under either of them I would have suggested moving. All the serving boys wore rubber-soled flip-flops, and they made the loudest sound in the room as they moved among the tables. There was a television set at one end of the bar but the volume was turned right down; I couldn't see the screen from this angle. Even at the bar there was no talking above a murmur; it was as if someone had just died. They had, of course, somewhere or other in the city. *And watch out for trip mines: the Khmer Rouge are still blowing up whoever they can find.*

Gabrielle ordered in Khmer, rapidly and with ease, and the boy took the menus away, his eyes dull, distracted by things on his mind.

"You speak Khmer?" the Frenchwoman asked me.

"*Please, thank you,* and *your prices are too high.*"

"You've been here before?"

"Yes."

"As a tourist?"

"Yes." Or sort of, but I hadn't been able to look at the temples the last time I was here because I'd been trying to locate three of our agents-in-place who'd disappeared after a small hotel had been blown up and the left hand of one of them had been taken along to the police station for identification, a signet ring still on a finger. I'd signaled London, *Wilson got it.*

"Mr. Flockhart is well?" Gabrielle Bouchard asked me.

"In very good form." The smell in this place was obtrusive, a mixture of rotten fish, kerosene, mangoes, and disinfectant. "He sends his best regards."

"I took some pictures for him in Paris, and he was generous. He told me you were to arrive here and asked me to settle you down." She meant settle me in; I'd started speaking to her in French when we'd met in the lobby, but she preferred English, perhaps for practice.

Well now, that had been nice of Mr. Flockhart to ask Gabrielle Bouchard to look after me, but in point of fact there must be more than one agent-in-place and a sleeper or two in Phnom Penh who could brief me on local conditions if I needed that; it wouldn't normally be left to a Parisian photojournalist who wasn't Bureau.

The thing was, then, he didn't want even the local a-i-p's or the sleepers to know I was here.

Invisible man.

"Who do you work for?" I asked Gabrielle.

"*L'Humanité.*"

"Are you covering anything specific for them?"

I got a very direct look from the dark blue eyes, as if I'd said something offensive. "Just Phnom Penh," she said.

"What have you got so far?"

"Nothing. I am waiting. We are all waiting." She looked away, around the big shabby-ornate room, as a boy brought the sodas she'd ordered from the bar. In a moment she squeezed the lemon into them, her thin strong hands moving automatically, her eyes abstracted. "But meanwhile"—her mouth tightened—"I might be lucky and get a shot of a little girl being blown to pieces in the sunshine, something like that. Something to make the world pay attention, if it will ever open its eyes." She passed me one of the sodas. "Where is your identity bracelet?" She'd followed the thought train from the little girl.

"I'm getting one made." The bracelet she wore on her left wrist was stainless steel, the standard issue, fireproof and even percussion-proof, within limits.

"But you've had your shots?"

"Yes." My medic in London had thrown the book at me: tetanus, diphtheria, meningitis, and gamma globulin.

"It's very important," Gabrielle said, "in this—" She broke off as the bulbs in the grimy-looking chandelier in the center of the ceiling flickered for a bit and went out.

"Is the power station under attack?" I asked her.

"No. The power station does not work very well." The serving boys were lighting small kerosene lamps, one of them giving a giggle as he hung his lamp back on the wall; the sound was as shocking as laughter at a funeral. As the flames burned brighter the room took on an unearthly glow. "You are in the media?" Gabrielle was asking.

"No. I'm on a roving commission for Trans-Kampuchean Air."

A man came up to our table and dropped a Kodak bag in front of Gabrielle. *"Et voilà!"*

"Jacques, tu es un ange, mais vraiment!" She reached up and he stooped to receive a kiss, tall, painfully thin, his stubbled face ravaged and his eyes deep in their shadowed sockets, his long mouth creased in the pleasure of the moment.

"Pour toi, n'importe quoi . . ." He straightened up, the clown's smile lingering as he dipped his head to me and walked away, one shoulder drooping.

Gabrielle took some of the small yellow boxes out of the bag, turning them over to read their printing in the dim light of the lamps—"Fast film, 1,000 ASA—almost impossible to find in Phnom Penh . . ." She followed the leaning Don Quixote figure for a moment with her eyes. "He has been here for twenty years, and has seen terrible things. He saw the Killing Fields."

She put the boxes back and pulled the drawstring tight at the neck of the bag. "He's a photographer too?" I asked her.

With a quick, tight laugh: "Jacques is many things, but yes, he takes brilliant pictures, frightening pictures." The draft from the ceiling fans was fretting at the wicks of the small kerosene lamps, and shadows fluttered across her face. "He goes sometimes into the jungle, for days on end."

When the food arrived we stopped talking for a while and Gabrielle forgot my existence, eating only occasionally and without appetite, deep in her thoughts; in this light she looked as if she slept little, and not well. I took the chance to glance around the room; most of the people here were men, Cambodians; most of the rest were Chinese and Vietnamese, with only a few Westerners in plaid shirts and jeans or crumpled white tropical suits, one or two in khaki with shoulder flashes ripped away.

"*C'était bon?*" I heard Gabrielle asking.

"Excellent. How was yours?"

"*Pas mal.*"

"Would Jacques liked to have joined us?" He was at the bar, his untidy head touching the fringe of the canopy.

"No. He never joins anyone." She looked for the boy.

The lights came on again, flickering and then steadying, and I said, "Is Pol Pot expected to make a final try for power?" It had been in the news for a while.

Gabrielle's eyes had widened at the sound of the name. "Everyone thinks so, here. Everyone is afraid."

"But you're more informed than most."

"I think the same as everyone does. It is not just fear, although we all feel that. From my . . . sources of information, yes, I believe he will make a final attempt to seize power, now the UN has left. And if he does that, we'll have the Killing Fields all over again." Our serving boy came for the dishes, and it occurred to me that Gabrielle preferred not to use French in public places because it was the second language, though English was catching on fast among the students. "Would you care for some *li-chee?*" she asked me.

"Just coffee."

She told the boy, and when he'd gone I said, "You believe Pol will launch an armed attack on the city?"

"Perhaps, but no one knows. The UN took its intelligence services with them."

"Has the Khmer Rouge got a base here in Phnom Penh?"

"Yes, but we do not know where it is anymore. Pol has moved it, and taken it underground. But we know it is still here. We see his agents."

She'd turned her head as she said that, looking toward the tables near the grandiose archway of chipped plaster and gilt that led to the hotel lobby.

"One of them is over there?" I asked her.

"Yes." She turned her head back. "The man at the corner table, sitting alone."

I'd noticed him earlier, simply because I knew his type, recognized his attitude, his body language, his stillness, the way he moved his head, always slowly, his eyes moving with it, passing across the target without stopping, passing back. I had also identified the target, the man he was keeping under surveillance.

"You know his name?" I asked Gabrielle.

"No. I only know he is an agent of the Khmer Rouge."

The boy put down two small gold-crested cups and poured coffee for us; I could smell the kerosene on his hands. He looked very young, was probably not long out of school, was possibly still at school, one of the children Gabrielle hoped to photograph one day being blown to pieces in the sunshine, so that the rest of the world would wake up.

"And who is the man sitting near the far end of the bar?"

"With the gold-rimmed glasses?"

"Yes."

"He is the Minister of Defense, Leng Sim."

"It's safe for government officials to move around in public?"

"Not very. But he is known for that. He openly defies the Khmer Rouge. There are others like him, but not many, now the UN has gone."

"Do they blame the UN for pulling out?"

She gave a little shrug. "The UN began its peacekeeping operations with good intentions, and the conference in Tokyo was also well-intentioned, but no one wants to go on protecting a country like this one, where there is no oil, no industry, no economy after twenty years of war and bloodshed at the hands of the Khmer Rouge—a country where poverty and disease and pollution have brought down the average life expectancy to thirty-six years, even without a shot fired. But we *have* to get help from *somewhere*, from *someone*. That is why I take my photographs." She leaned toward me, her small, calloused hands clenched on the table. "I have the blood of these people in my body. My grandfather was an administrator here as a young man under the French rule, and he married a Cambodian girl. So I understand them, from a source deeper than the intellect. I feel for them. I cry for them in the night. And I have to believe that if I and people like myself—like Jacques— work hard enough we can stir the compassion of the rest of the world, so that our little world out here won't be bled to death again in the Killing Fields."

She leaned back, toying with her coffee, not meeting my eyes anymore, regretting, I thought, having given herself away like that, exposing her fears, her anger—this was my impression. As a photojournalist in what amounted to a wartime theater she was expected to keep her nerve, control her emotions, let nothing show but what she intended to show through the lens of her camera. But what she'd told me explained her coloring: she would be called by the people here—her own people, to a degree—a "round-eye," but she had the raven black hair and the ivory skin of a native.

"You say Pol Pot has moved his base in Phnom Penh," I said in a moment, "and gone underground. What about his guerrilla forces?"

"He has moved those too. They used to be in the southwest jungle, near the Thai border, but they've gone from there, according to reports."

"Reports or rumors?"

She gave a shrug. "One cannot always tell the difference. The reports often come from long-term foreign aid workers in the outlying provinces, but no one in the capital can really trust their word—Pol is quite capable of spreading disinformation, old Soviet style, without their realizing."

The Minister of Defense over there was paying the bill.

"Pol's forces are well armed?" I asked Gabrielle, and turned my head slightly the other way. The Khmer Rouge agent was beckoning to his boy, also wanting to pay.

"Very well armed. He rebuilt his forces after the government attacked his jungle hideout in August."

I finished my coffee and looked at my watch.

"It's late," Gabrielle said.

It was just gone eleven. "I've got to make a phone call," I told her, "that's all. It's four o'clock in London."

"I'm going up anyway. I need sleep. How is the jet lag?" She got out a black snakeskin wallet.

At the edge of my vision field I saw the minister leaving his table and moving across the room. "It doesn't seem to affect me. You've been very kind," I told her, and took her hand. *"Au plaisir?"*

"Mais oui. Au plaisir." I left her paying the bill.

The Khmer Rouge agent was going through the lobby and I held back for a moment to keep my reflection out of the glass doors and then followed him into the night.

4

* *

MAH·JONGG

There was no moon, but the streets had the stark look of a lunar landscape, with patches of glaring neon and black shadows between where the lamps had gone out. Through the windscreen of the Peugeot I could see the curved roof of a temple, decorated with the great eye of a god outlined in red with a gilded pupil.

Nothing moved in the street; it was more than an hour after curfew. The air pressed down from a hazy sky, its sticky warmth moving through the open windows of the car; it must still be eighty degrees across the city, less than an hour before midnight.

They were waiting in the Russian Zhiguli that was parked nearer the main street, Achar Hemcheay, where it ran diagonally across the center of the town. The agent I'd followed from the Royal Palace Hotel had got into the front passenger's side of the Zhiguli; the driver had already been there behind the wheel.

The Minister of Defense had got into the black Chevrolet at the corner, nearer the hotel, less than a minute ago. His driver had started the engine and I saw the lights come on. The agent's driver in the Zhiguli had had decent enough training: he'd stationed it between two other cars and facing away from the Chevrolet, relying on the mirror to keep it in view; there was quite enough room available for a U-turn.

I was out here, really, just to keep my hand in after six weeks' absence from the field; there'd been an obvious surveillance setup in progress, so I thought I'd move into it and practice the routine. I knew now what that man Flockhart had sent me into Cambodia to do, but he must have been out of his mind. I could have signaled him from the hotel after I'd left Gabrielle, and told him to pull me out of the field, but I wanted to go through with this little exercise now it had started.

It was going to be distinctly tricky because there wouldn't be much traffic to afford cover; there'd be nothing on the streets at this hour except for police, military, or Foreign Aid Services transport. There were some lights crossing the intersection at 136 Street now, but I couldn't see what kind of vehicle it was.

The agent was armed. I'd seen him adjust the holster strap under his jacket when he'd got up from his table in the restaurant.

The Chevrolet was in motion now, pulling away from the curb. The Zhiguli started up but didn't move until the target vehicle was nearing the intersection; then it made its U-turn and took up the tag. I waited ten seconds and fell in behind at a distance of fifty yards with the lights off, turning at the intersection and rounding the Central Market and taking a side street parallel with theirs, gunning up quite a lot to come abreast until I could see their lights and keep station.

There was a problem after a minute or two because the streets converged and I was directly behind the Zhiguli again and none too distant. I'd switched on my lights when some other vehicles had shown up—two military jeeps and a van with CATHOLIC MISSION on the side—but they were out again now. The Chevrolet had taken a couple of side streets as a matter of routine and come back to the main thoroughfare—a government driver would know the rudiments of evasive action and this one might even suspect the Zhiguli by this time—and we were keeping station roughly two intersections apart, and it was then that I saw the gun.

The lights of the Zhiguli were out at the moment and it was silhouetted against the bright street background, and from the movement inside it I saw that the agent on the passenger side was reaching into the rear and bringing the gun across the seat squab, a heavy short-barreled assault rifle.

Not surveillance, then. They were running a hit.

I was still forty or fifty yards behind the Zhiguli and the distance was increasing now because it was gunning up suddenly with a squeal from the rear tires to close on the minister's car and I did the same with the Peugeot and felt it shift through the gears and hit what speed it could with the throttle wide open and the rear wheels whimpering as we shortened the distance and the Zhiguli pulled out to overtake the minister's car to give the agent a steady target at close range.

I was right behind the Zhiguli by now and took the Peugeot to the offside and swung in again and rammed the rear quarter of the Zhiguli and sent it skewing and rammed it again as the driver overcorrected and lost control and tried to get it back in a zigzag action to kill the momentum but didn't manage it, lost the whole thing and hit the curb and bounced once and rolled as a burst of shots came and some glass flew into a glittering kaleidoscope as the Zhiguli skated on its roof until it smashed against a wall and ended its run.

The minister's car was in the distance now and I let it go and gunned up again and took the first side street to get my rear number plate out of sight. I didn't know whether the agent had tried to make a last-chance hit with that burst of fire or whether he'd triggered it by accident while the Zhiguli was doing its loop, but anyway I wasn't all that interested, the thing now was to get clear of the scene.

It was just gone one o'clock in the morning here in Phnom Penh when I telephoned Flockhart.

I'd driven the Peugeot ten kilometers out of the city and left it on a smashed vehicle dump and ripped the number plates off and dropped them into the river and got a lift back in a Foreign Aid Services jeep. The police might take the trouble to look for a recently damaged car in the morning if one or both of those people in the Zhiguli had finished up in a hospital, so I didn't want to leave the Peugeot standing outside the Royal Palace Hotel and I didn't want to take it back to the auto-rental because they'd want to know why the front end was smashed in.

The line opened and I heard Flockhart's voice.

"Yes?"

"*Salamander.*"

"Good evening."

In London it was still six o'clock yesterday. The call had taken only a couple of minutes to put through because we were going via the Intersputnik satellite linkup in Moscow.

I told Flockhart, "I'm pulling out."

In a moment: "Why is that?"

"You'd need a whole battalion, you know that."

It wasn't only because he wanted me to operate out here in total isolation, unknown even to the local agents-in-place, that he'd asked Gabrielle Bouchard to meet me and "settle me in." He'd also known she was a fierce supporter of the Cambodian people and would tell me what was on her mind, exposing me to the mood of terror that was leaving this city numbed. And his message was quite clear: the objective for the mission was the leader of the Khmer Rouge guerrilla forces, Pol Pot.

Flockhart was off his bloody rocker.

He didn't comment on what I'd just said about needing a battalion; he just asked me, "How are things out there at the moment?"

"Fairly quiet." This was an open line but we weren't using speech-code, just not dropping names. "Power station's up the pole, that's all, and we've had a bit of rain."

I didn't mention the brush with the Zhiguli. I didn't want him to know I'd done anything at all against the Khmer Rouge since I'd got here, even *en passant*. It wasn't my job, wasn't in any case a job, God only knew, for one man.

"How was your evening?" Flockhart asked next.

His tone was quiet, his questions riddled with innocence. I didn't trust him, I tell you I did not *trust* this man.

"Delightful."

"A rather attractive young lady," he said. "I wanted you to start enjoying things as soon as you got there."

Bullshit.

When the silence had gone on for a bit he said smoothly, "Our friend is on his way out there as we speak. Would you feel like meeting him when he lands? I told you he'd contact you when he arrived, but it's been difficult to fix up transport." He meant Pringle, of course.

"I'll be gone," I said, "by then." The next long-haul flight wouldn't be in until the afternoon.

There were voices in the corridor outside my room, and I watched the thin line of light below the bottom of the door. It was dark in here; I'd pulled the shutters back and opened the window on the warm night air.

"Surely," I heard Flockhart saying, "you wouldn't object to amusing yourself for a few hours more, now that you're there. I'd rather like you to listen to what our good friend has to say—I really think you'd be interested."

The voices loudened outside the room and shadows moved across the line of light; then things were quiet again and a door opened somewhere farther along. I was perfectly secure here; I'd come into Phnom Penh under impeccable cover and there'd been no witnesses to the Zhiguli thing, none, anyway, who could have got a good look at my face inside the car.

"Is our friend," I asked Flockhart, "bringing a battalion for me?"

It sounded like gentle laughter on the line, a sound designed to assure me that he knew I was joking. "Wouldn't it be frustrating for you," he said, "to come all the way home and have me prove to you that you'd missed the chance of a lifetime?" His tone was silky, more dangerous than steel. He could have reminded me that I'd undertaken a mission for him and that he wasn't going to have me backing out before I'd even started. But that wasn't how he was going to play me, and I sensed he'd done an awful lot of clandestine research in the Bureau files on my track record and personality profile after we'd parted company in the Cellar Steps that night.

The chance of a lifetime. Oh, the bastard, he'd got me rising to the fly. The chance of a lifetime for an active shadow executive means the chance of bringing home a mission that will go down in the archives of the Bureau as one of the really momentous operations in its history, a model for all others to come, the equivalent, if you like, of the Nobel Prize, except of course that no whisper of it will ever pass through the walls of that phantom fortress of intelligence in Whitehall. He was appealing, Flockhart—as they all do, those bloody controls—to my vanity.

In a moment I asked him, "What flight?"

He affected surprise, didn't miss a trick. "He'll be covering the final leg with Lao Aviation from Saigon, Flight 47. The ETA is 18:53, local time."

I said I'd be there.

The Antonov AN-24 hit the runway in heavy rain, bouncing a lot and settling in its run with its lights flashing in the haze and the blast of its reversed thrust booming back from the terminal building.

Pringle had only one bag and went straight into Customs and Immigration without going through the baggage claim. They kept him only twenty minutes, so he must have been swinging a lot more clout than I had—it had taken me an hour yesterday—and this didn't endear him to me. But then, the director in the field is expected to wield the maximum clout available, and it has sometimes saved the executive's hide for him and brought him back alive. It was simply that nothing about Pringle was likely to endear him to me, because he was working for the smoothest con man in the business, and if I didn't love Flockhart I could hardly love his dog.

"It's good to see you," Pringle said as he came into the main hall. "I hope I didn't keep you waiting too long."

He wanted to shake hands and I obliged; he was young and of the new school, liked conducting the social side of the business as if it were a cocktail party, even though the social side of this clandestine trade is traditionally comparable with the scene in an underground lavatory, where the glance is carefully averted on the understanding that nobody else down here actually exists.

I took him along to the small bleak coffee shop where not too many people go because when it's raining the leak in the roof tends to flood most of the floor, making the place look like a sinking ship. I dropped the newspaper onto the table, the one I'd bought from the stands outside.

Pringle put his suitcase on a chair and ordered two *soda kroch chhmars* and sat back with his hands folded on his lap and gave me his steady gaze, a faint socially pleasant smile on his mouth. He had the looks of a junior barrister, already adept at disarming a jury with a display of visible charm; and his cool gray eyes were watchful within the smile, and I was aware of being carefully appraised. That was all right; I expected to be. If we ever decided to start *Salamander* running we'd need to know each other as well as we could for the sake of the mission, perhaps for the sake of its executive's survival. But I didn't think we had a chance of starting anything running at all, with Pol Pot as the objective.

I was here, we may remember, simply by reason of vanity, and one of the problems with vanity is that it can be lethal.

"Mr. Flockhart," Pringle said in a moment, "has briefed me that you feel your services would be inadequate for this particular mission. Is that right?"

"It's one way of putting it." I didn't like his opening move: it was obviously intended to rile me.

"How would you put it?"

"I told Flockhart that if you want to stop Pol Pot you'll need a battalion. Forgive my stating the obvious."

"It would depend on how it was done. And perhaps we should be wary of using names in public."

There were only two Chinese in here, sitting in a far corner, and they'd been there when we'd come in and the rain drumming on the roof made perfect sound cover, so I'd thought it safe enough to drop the Pol Pot name to see if it bothered Pringle. I was glad it did: it should have. He'd run a few missions but he'd never been my DIF and I needed to know his standard in tradecraft.

"How d'you expect me to stop him," I asked Pringle, "without a battalion?"

"By gaining information about him for others to use." He left it at that while the boy came up with his blue rubber flip-flops splashing across the floor and put our two sodas and half a lemon onto the table.

When he'd gone I asked Pringle, "So the specific objective for the mission is information on that man?" Pol Pot.

He squeezed some lemon juice into my soda. "That about right?" I nodded. "Yes," he said, "in the first instance."

He was so bloody *smooth*, this man. "I don't know how many times you've directed in the field," I told him, "but you can't have an objective for any mission *in the first instance*. The objective is the final goal, shit or bust."

In a moment he squeezed some juice for himself and put the lemon carefully back into the little lotus-pattern ceramic bowl and looked up at me with his very open gaze and said, "I directed Thurson in *Switchblade*, among others. I also directed MacKinley in *Whiplash*."

"MacKinley's in a nursing home now."

"But I got him back."

I left it. They'd been two of the more notable missions, one in Moldavia and the other in Beijing, where the police had given

MacKinley the works. But yes, if Pringle had run those two he wasn't a novice.

"If I decide to do anything here," I told him, "for Flockhart, I'd need a specific objective, no bullshit about first instances."

Pringle picked carefully at the label on his soda bottle. "This is an operation, you see, like no other. I'm sure that has become clear to you. You'll be responsible to one man alone: to Mr. Flockhart. This means"—he looked up at last to get my reaction—"that you won't have the usual bureaucratic red tape to worry about. Whatever you want—support, aircraft, smoke screens, money—you'll get immediately, since Mr. Flockhart won't need to go through the normal formalities. We can promise you *immediate* attention."

Watching me for my reaction, not seeing anything because in this trade you've got to keep it all behind the eyes, rage, fear, surprise, the emotions we're so familiar with after our first ten or eleven missions that we can deny them, blank them out on demand. But Pringle knew how very attractive he was making things sound, knew, I'm certain, that I don't suffer gladly those fools upstairs in Administration.

"So you must be prepared to play this one by ear. Your *first* objective is to gain information on that man. We don't think it's a lot to ask. You've operated in jungle terrain before and proved equal to its demands."

"I'm a round-eye in a slant-eyed country."

"There are quite a few of them here, what with the various Foreign Aid Services and Catholic missions and the remnants of the world media still hanging on. And you've got an impeccable cover."

"I don't understand the Khmer language."

"You've worked several missions without understanding the language—in Thailand, Czechoslovakia, Tibet. Rather successfully."

He'd done his homework. I thought it was time I put a question that had been on my mind since I'd talked to Flockhart in the Cellar Steps.

"The world in general," I said, "doesn't seem all that interested in a very minor state that's economically on its knees. There wasn't much help for Cambodia at the time of the Killing Fields—the rest of the world stood by and said what a bloody shame it was. So why is Flockhart interested in helping these people?"

Another plane came in, shark-shaped through the dirty windowpanes, its lights coloring the rain out there. Our soda bottles vibrated on the iron table and the PA system began putting out its tinny message, first in Khmer, then in French: Flight 19 from Hanoi had arrived.

"I don't know," Pringle said at last.

"If you knew, would you tell me?"

I think he would have liked to look down, or away, but didn't allow himself. The expression in his cool gray eyes was just shut off for an instant. "If the progress of the mission demanded it."

That could mean anything.

"Is it something personal, with Flockhart?" I wasn't letting it go, at least not yet. Because why had Flockhart been in such a seething rage when he'd talked to me in the Cellar Steps? Whose photograph was it on his desk, the one he'd thrown the papers over when I'd gone into his office? And why had he sent this very smooth operator here to pull me deeper into the quicksands?

"I don't know," Pringle said again. "Perhaps he simply wants to save Cambodia."

I let it go. He wasn't being offensive, didn't believe I'd take him literally; it was just his way of telling me to shut up about Flockhart's motives—they were to remain under wraps.

The rain drummed on the roof, splashing around the broken tile and sending a constant trickle onto the concrete floor. The two Chinese over there had started playing mah-jongg.

"Have you any other questions?" Pringle asked.

"Yes. Put yourself in my place for a minute. Why—"

"Questions concerning the mission."

"I *am* the bloody mission! So put yourself in my place—why

would *you* take on an operation that simply stinks of tricks before we've even got off the ground, that doesn't have official backing or a signals board or access to London except through a rogue control working on his own and for his own clandestine motives?"

The passengers from Flight 19 began straggling through the main hall past the doorway to the café.

"Because you gave Mr. Flockhart your word," Pringle said.

"I didn't have all the facts. I still don't."

I needed time, that was all. If I took on this job the first of the lives that were going to be saved out here in this stinking hole was going to be my own, and that might prove difficult if Flockhart's intention was to throw me into a fire to see if I came out cooked. To use me, in other words, for his own purposes, and certainly not the Cambodians'.

The rain hit the roof, splashing around the gap in the tiles. Why didn't someone put a new one in? Was it because you couldn't expect to live, as a Cambodian, for more than thirty-six years even without a shot fired, as Gabrielle had told me? Or was it because the photographs of your mother and two sisters on the wall of your tumbledown little room were simply the photographs of some people who were there in the Killing Fields, raped and then clubbed to death because of the shortage of ammunition? Perhaps, yes, it was because of things like that. With a broken life, how would you find the interest in mending a broken tile?

They crowded past the doorway—merchants, women with infants in their arms, soldiers not six weeks out of school, a little girl trailing a worn stuffed tiger. They would have photographs, those people. They would have photographs too.

"In London," I heard Pringle saying, "you told Mr. Flockhart that you accepted the mission. He was a little put out when you changed your mind, but felt that after I'd given you a preliminary briefing in the field you might reconsider."

Two schoolmasters or government clerks, proud of the status their glasses gave them as intellectuals, the glasses that would mark them for death if Pol Pot took over the country again and began his political cleansing.

A gaggle of young girls, twittering like birds, gaudy paper flowers in their hair.

"I need," Pringle said, "to signal Mr. Flockhart tonight with your decision."

"Do you," I said.

Two more merchants, their canvas bags clinking with tin Buddhas and cheap brass pagodas, then two cripples helping each other along with only one crutch between them, two of those who got away with it the last time but wouldn't have a hope of running fast enough the next.

A pale unkempt woman walking alone, a red plastic comb in her hair and her eyes permanently frightened, going home to look again at her photographs.

Then I saw the doll.

It was life-size, its pale porcelain face perfect and unmarked, and it was being carried by a half-starved middle-aged woman who seemed hardly to have the strength. The doll was in a worn rattan basket that concealed its legs, and as I watched, the woman made to hitch the thing higher, but her companion—younger and stronger, perhaps her daughter—took it from her, lifting it out of the basket and holding it tight against her, and I saw that in fact it had no legs—they'd been broken, I suppose, and taken off. The older woman walked beside her, stroking the hair of the doll. Both were smiling, as if they were sharing joy in having this toy to carry around with them, and then I saw the toy smile too, suddenly and sweetly. It wasn't a doll after all, with that perfect porcelain face, but a child, a little girl with a blanket wound around her hips and nothing below, no legs.

And watch out for the trip mines, the man in the Trans-Kampuchean office had told me, *the Khmer Rouge are still blowing up whoever they can find—military, civilians, women and children, you name it, they'll kill it.*

I watched the two women, their backs to me now as they neared the exit doors, the small bobbing head of the child lost from sight; but I could still see—went on seeing, would always see, forever—that sweet sudden smile.

"Yes," I told Pringle.

"I'm sorry?"

"Yes," I said again. He gave it a moment, absorbing the unexpected.

"You agree to go ahead?"

"I said yes, for Christ's sake, didn't I?"

In the corner of the café the mah-jongg pieces clicked like broken bones.

Pringle sat back from the table. "Very well. I'm glad I was able to brief you so successfully. We—"

"It's nothing to do with your bloody briefing."

He tilted his head and brought it down an inch, raised it again in a gesture of concession. "Whatever your reasons, I'll be delighted to signal Control tonight with your decision. And as your director in the field, is it too soon to ask if you've any idea how you'll start *Salamander* running?"

"You speak French?"

"Yes."

I pushed the gray, cheaply printed newspaper across the table for him so that he could read the lower headline; it was the paper I'd seen and bought on my way in here through the hall, *La Vie Cambodge*.

"Apparently I killed a man last night," I said, "so I'm going to start things running at his funeral."

5

SALAMANDER

There'd been a moon tonight, a thin curved blade of light cutting through the haze across the city. The rain had stopped in the late afternoon, giving way to a stifling moist heat as twilight came.

"Are they in trouble?" I asked Gabrielle. One of the ferries on the Tonle Sap was drifting in midstream, butted and nudged by two or three smaller boats.

"They're always in trouble." She uncorked the bottle of red wine she'd brought with the other things in the brown paper bags—a tin of smoked salmon and some *escargots,* a hunk of Brie and a loaf of *pain de seigle.* I'd asked her how she'd managed to find stuff like that in a place like this, and she'd just smiled and said she had French blood.

I'd phoned her room from the lobby of the Royal Palace Hotel an hour ago to ask if she could join me for dinner somewhere, so that I could return her hospitality.

"Tonight?" She'd sounded cautious.

"If the spirit moves you."

"Well, yes, I—I'd like that. But you don't mean here at the hotel?"

I thought that was interesting. There were good reasons why I didn't mean here at the hotel, but she wasn't expected to know them.

"Somewhere more private," I said.

The caution was still in her voice but she said in a moment, "The most private place I know is a pension along the river in Hassakan Street. I'll bring something for us to eat. Will you give me a little time?"

We'd met here ten minutes ago, and she'd said a few words in Khmer to a shy little woman with only a few teeth but a heart-breaking smile, and we'd climbed the half-lit stairs to this small room at the top of the house with its window looking east across the river.

Pouring the wine, Gabrielle said, "I didn't expect to see you again so soon."

"I haven't the patience to wait long for my pleasures."

She didn't smile, gave me a studied look in the light of the cheap brass lamp. "I think you have. You are a very disciplined man." The note of caution I'd caught over the phone at the hotel hadn't quite left her voice, or it had changed to a hint of reserve. She was different from last night in the restaurant, less open.

She sliced the bread with a plastic knife she'd brought and offered me butter, using a give-away tin opener on the smoked salmon before I could help, arranging everything with the formality the French practice even at a picnic.

"Did you get any pictures today?" I asked her.

Her dark blue eyes clouded. "Fifty or sixty. I take fifty or sixty every day, and put them on the first plane the next morning. Cripples, weeping widows, fatherless children playing at soldiers in the ruins. I think in English you call it 'sob stuff.' I call it getting the message across. Or at least trying."

I cut some more bread. "It used to be the pen that was mightier than the sword. Today it's the camera."

We both looked across at the window as a splash sounded from the river. In the glow of light from the city we could see a man overboard from the ferry. Shouting broke out as others leaned over the rail to help him back.

"He should be careful," Gabrielle said. "There are snakes in the river. They swim across at night—the light attracts them, and the rats." She drank some wine, still watching the scene out there. "Especially the hanuman—do you know it?"

"Bright green?"

"Yes, the bright green one. Quite small but more deadly than the cobra, even the king cobra. Some more wine?" She tilted the bottle, but I stopped her.

"No, it'll make me sleepy. I've got some work to do later."

She studied me for a moment. "I cannot ever imagine you being sleepy. It would be quite out of character."

The lamp began flickering and in a moment went out; below the window the streets had gone dark, and the lights on the ferry out there seemed brighter, reflecting across the black water.

"Is your husband in the media?" I asked Gabrielle. Tonight she'd changed from paramilitary khaki into a simple white dress, with no jewelry except for the plain gold ring.

"I am a widow."

Close as we were at the little table, we could hardly see each other now; we had become voices.

"For how long?" I asked her.

"Three years."

"Did it happen out here?"

The silence went on for a little and then she said with a soft roughness in her voice, "No. It happened in Paris, after we had been married only six months." I wished now that I hadn't asked about him; I thought she was having to hold back tears, or wasn't managing.

"I'm sorry I—"

"It is quite all right. It helps, to talk about him, not to make him a secret." Her English was so formal; I wished she'd use her native tongue: there was a need for its subtle nuances just at the moment. "It was cancer—'an unromantic and ungallant way of departure,' as he said. You can imagine how much I loved him."

"And how much he loved you."

The lamp and the lights in the street below began flickering, and we waited, both embarrassed, I think, by the tawdry intrusion. When the light steadied, Gabrielle said with a rueful laugh, "I didn't realize how bright it was, before." Her eyes were glistening with the tears that hadn't come, and I switched off the lamp altogether.

"It is nice," she said, "like this." We sat in the soft light rising from the street. "You are sensitive, for a man of action."

"A man of action?"

"Wasn't it you who saved the life of the Minister of Defense last night?"

This was why she seemed cautious this evening, wasn't sure now what kind of company she was keeping. In my copy of *La Vie Cambodge* they'd reported that shots were fired in the vicinity of Minister Leng Sim's automobile, but that "a mysterious and fortuitous accident" enabled him to escape harm. A passenger in another vehicle died from his injuries.

Gabrielle was waiting.

"Not as far as I know," I told her.

"*Vraiment?* But in the restaurant last night you asked me where the Pol Pot agent was sitting, and you asked me who the other man was, and I told you. Then when they both left there you went to make your telephone call." She put her hand on my arm. "You can trust me, you see, but I am not asking for your confidence if you do not wish to give it to me."

She started to take her hand away, symbolically, I suppose, but I put mine over it and she didn't withdraw. "It's not a question of that, Gabrielle. I know when I can trust people and when I can't." It was, in point of fact, why I'd phoned her this evening: to find out more about Flockhart if I could, see if it looked all right to give him my trust at last, or at least some of it. Gabrielle had seen something of him when they'd met in Paris, but in London I'd only ever passed him sometimes in the corridors, seen him sometimes in the signals room, never spoken.

"And you believe," her voice came softly in the shadows, "that you can trust me?"

"Yes." This was true: I can spot an actress fifteen miles from the footlights. What I didn't trust was what Flockhart might have put into her mind in Paris, because it could affect *Salamander*, and I didn't want to take this mission blindly into the dark. "It's more a question of my becoming a danger to you," I told her, "the more you know about me. But for the record, yes, there was a bit of a dustup in the street last night, and—"

"A dustup—"

"*Un fracas.*" I went on in French now, because for security reasons alone we didn't want any misunderstandings. "And I preferred not to let the minister get shot. But there wasn't anything political in it, I mean on my part."

"Very well, it was a 'fortuitous accident,' as it said in the paper. But if you are in Phnom Penh to take any kind of deliberate action against the Khmer Rouge, you should know that you are putting your head in the lion's den—"

"Mouth."

"*Pardon?*"

"Never mind."

She switched to French now too, taking the hint, and the stiff formality went out of her speech. "Listen," she said softly and quickly, "it's just that if I don't try to make you understand what you're taking on, I might regret it later. I might regret it bitterly."

Pringle had given me much the same kind of warning at the airport this afternoon— "We acknowledge quite freely, of course, that the personal risk you'll be taking is very high. Very high indeed."

I'd thought about that. "You mean I'm expendable?"

He hadn't looked away. "Let's say that if we didn't think you had a reasonable chance of pulling this one off, we wouldn't have offered it to you."

"All right, but if I crash, are you going to replace me?"

He watched me steadily. "For an operation like this, we believe you are irreplaceable."

"So this is a one-shot thing?"

"I think you described it just now as 'shit or bust.' I can't hope to put it more accurately."

I'd thought about that too, because this was another first: I'd taken over God knew how many missions when the executive in the field had crashed. I'd walked so many times in a dead man's shoes and every time I'd been sent out with a brand-new mission I'd known perfectly well that if I came unstuck they'd shake the dice in London and send the next man in. This was a brand-new mission but if I couldn't bring it home they'd write it off in the records: *Executive failed, mission abandoned.*

It had never happened to me before, and it gave me a heady feeling of control, of identity. I wasn't working a mission: I *was* the mission. I was *Salamander.*

Flockhart was breaking every rule in the book: he wanted me to operate with a single, unassisted control—himself—with no board opened in the signals room, no signals crew, no emergency supervision by Chief of Signals if a wheel came off, and no awareness, even, on the part of anyone else in the entire Bureau that there was a mission running at all. Just this isolated, ultra-secret triumvirate operating in the shadows behind the scenes: a control, a director in the field, and the ferret. Correction, yes—the salamander.

The lights flickered again in the streets below the small high room, bringing me back to the present with a new thought flashing through my mind—I was trying to decide whether or not I could trust Flockhart, but for Flockhart to run this operation successfully on those terms he had to rely on me to honor his confidence. *He* had to trust *me.* Totally. And that was what he was doing now. He had no choice: I could pick up a phone and go through the government communications mast at Cheltenham and ask for Croder,

Chief of Signals, and tell him that Flockhart was running a rogue operation on his own and perhaps he ought to check it out, and Flockhart could be hauled upstairs to explain himself to those soul-less ghouls in Administration and then get himself thrown into the street.

The lights steadied again and there was some shouting out there on the river; I think they'd got the ferry going again because there was a chugging noise coming across the water.

Another thought flashed across the dark and I caught it in time and looked it over, looked it over very carefully because so much depended on whether I got this thing straight or not, whether I went into the mission knowing everything I needed to know or risked crashing it through ignorance.

Did Flockhart really have no choice but to trust me?

No.

It was I who had no choice. He knew he could trust me, and totally, and we both knew why. *I needed the mission.* I'd been desper-ate for this one, for anything they felt like throwing me in London, and now I'd got what I wanted, and nothing could make me call the Chief of Signals because I'd never survive the flak. If I blew Flockhart out of existence I'd blow *Salamander* with him.

And I was *Salamander.*

I felt Gabrielle's hand stirring under my own. "I thought I'd leave you," she said, "to your thoughts."

I got up and went to the window and looked down into the street and across to the riverbank, letting my eyes roam the shadows, seeing nothing that shouldn't be there. I'd checked the environment when Gabrielle had come here, checked it again before I followed.

I went back to sit with her again at the little table. "If ever I decide," I told her, "to do anything against the Khmer Rouge, I'll remember your warning. But tell me about M'sieur Flockhart—you said you did him a service in Paris. Or is it personal?"

"Oh no. I was waiting in the street across from the Hôtel d'Alsace about a week ago—my editor wanted me to get some shots of the British delegates to the Anglo-French Conference on the Arts as they came down the steps. But something unusual happened. A man came out of the hotel, obviously English, and I thought he was one of the delegates, so I started my camera running." She just called it "something unusual," I suppose—not "terrible" or anything—because here in Cambodia she'd got used to seeing people blown to bits; she meant unusual for Paris. "But there was a car bomb incident, and I had to spend a few hours in hospital with concussion—and it was there that M'sieur Flockhart made contact with me."

"He followed you there?"

"Yes. He saw the incident himself, and—"

"He wasn't hurt as well?"

In the dim light from the window she turned her head to look at me. "I suppose he must have seen it from inside a building. I hadn't thought of it before."

Covert surveillance, yes. "Go on."

"He told me he was a security official with the British contingent, and asked if I would give him the film I'd taken. I told him he'd have to put the request through *L'Humanité*, but he said he didn't want to go through 'all that red tape.'" She was watching me again. "He's very charming, your M'sieur Flockhart."

For a tarantula. "Yes," I said, "he is."

"He told me that if I cared to have a quiet little dinner with him we might come to some arrangement. I was a bit surprised, but he was in security, so—"

"And that's what happened?"

"Yes. He promised to let me have the story, once he'd got to the bottom of the bomb incident by having the film analyzed in London." With a little shrug: "Either there was no story, or they haven't finished their analysis yet. But he gave me a very sumptuous evening, and we made a lot of jokes in 'Franglais.'"

"*A la Major Thompson.*"

She laughed lightly. "*Absolument!*"

Jesus, you've got to hand it to Flockhart. Except for him, the amount of charm you'll get out of the entire senior Bureau staff above the third floor would fit comfortably under a microdot.

"And you told him," I said, "that you'd be coming out to Phnom Penh shortly?"

"Yes. He seemed quite interested in the situation here."

So he'd asked her to "settle me in" when I arrived. Didn't miss a trick, friend Flockhart.

The sticky air moved into the little room from the window, tainted now with diesel exhaust gas from the ferry as it rumbled across to the bank on the far side.

"Are you going straight back," I asked Gabrielle, "to the Royal Palace when you leave here?"

"Yes."

"I've moved from there."

"I didn't know."

"You mustn't be seen with me again."

"Because of the man who was killed last night in the 'accident'?"

"Partly."

"There were others who might have seen you?"

"Possibly."

"You must get rid of your car—"

"There's another thing, Gabrielle. Unless I ask for your help as an interpreter, I don't want you involved in any action I might decide to take against the Khmer Rouge. That would be extremely dangerous. I know you're here in Phnom Penh to get pictures, but wherever I go and whatever I do will be strictly off-camera."

It was after curfew when she got into her car and drove west away from the river along Hassakan Street, and I tailed her far enough to make sure she was completely clear and then peeled off.

6

✳ ✳

RAIN

The air was rich with incense.

The coffin, decorated with red and gold embellishments and intricately carved Buddhas, was being carried into the temple by six yellow-robed monks, with the waxen face of the deceased open to the view of the mourners and the body enrobed in colored silks.

People were still coming into the temple, all of them Asian except for a couple of women in sunglasses and headscarves, tourists, I would have said, or Foreign Aid Services workers, here for the local color.

I was kneeling below the rough stone wall at the back, in a shadow created by two of the oil-burning lamps below the east oriels. Most of the light in here came from the rows of candles brought into the temple by the mourners, who had placed them below the gilded Buddhas along the wall.

The pallbearers lowered the coffin onto the silk-covered trestle in front of the principal shrine, and the mourners began forming a line behind the three women and two men who were standing nearest the coffin. I put them down as the mother, wife—or sister—and daughter of the deceased, and his father and brother.

It was the brother who interested me.

I'd come here straight from the house in Kralahom Kong, a narrow street leading to the jetties on the Tonle Sap, not far along from where, last night, we'd watched the ferry in trouble out there on the water, Gabrielle and I. Before I'd left Pringle yesterday afternoon at the airport I'd told him to use a local sleeper agent to keep up the daily payments on the Peugeot so that the clerks at the General Directorate of Tourism wouldn't report it as missing. I'd picked up a Mazda 626 LX from one of the black market dealers for twice the normal rate.

The house in Kralahom Kong wasn't strictly a hotel—there was no name or sign outside—but it had rooms for rent behind its scarred walls and its peeling shutters hanging at an angle above the street. It was the third place like this I'd checked out, and I chose it because there was a picture of King Sihanouk over the rickety little desk and because the proprietor was one of the hundreds of cripples in the town. A cripple with Sihanouk's picture in his house would kill Pol Pot if he ever got the chance, with his bare hands, and slowly, if he could be sure it wouldn't land him in one of the Khmer Rouge torture cells before they finished him off.

The abbot was intoning the prayer for the dead, but I understood only a word here and there—*Buddha, heaven, departed,* words like that, and only then because they were repeated so often and I was able to work out the context.

The incense lay heavy on the stifling air, filling the lungs with perfume.

The line of mourners began moving now, filing past the catafalque, many of them in robes, all of them scooping holy water from the stone basin to trickle into the upturned hand of the deceased. When his family began moving slowly toward the east wall of the temple on their way back to their places, I joined the two Caucasian women in the line of mourners, the only cover there was available. I couldn't have stayed where I was, against the wall; everyone had come in here to pay their respects to the dead, and a round-eyed observer would have stood out a mile.

The eyes of the cadaver were closed as I reached the coffin, scooping some water for its upturned hand and thinking for a moment of the life I'd taken away in exchange for the life I'd saved, a deal is a deal, shuffling past the shrine behind the two women as the abbot intoned his prayers and the flame light flickered along the walls and across the faces of the gilded figurines, a deal is a deal, my friend, in the land of dog eat dog, so rest in peace if the Lord Buddha thinks you've earned any, because you weren't the driver that night, you were the one with the gun.

There was a moment, as I reached the north wall and turned and began making my way to the back of the temple again, when I was closer to the dead man's family than I'd been before. I was looking straight ahead but at the edge of my vision field I thought that one of them, perhaps the brother, turned for a moment to watch me as I passed—I couldn't be sure. But he'd been too busy that night with the Zhiguli going wild all over him to have got a look at me, and I'd seen no one else there who could have borne witness.

One of the women in the group was weeping, the mother I suppose, the agony of her grief making a soft high whimpering against the incantations of the abbot. Weep, then, good mother, for your dear departed son, but weep also for the widows and the orphans and the cripples hereabouts, for he touched their lives too, and less kindly.

"They'd be so much better off with *Christ*," one of the Caucasian women whispered as we reached the back of the temple. "All this chanting and everything."

"Each to his own," the other woman said, "and I wouldn't have missed the experience."

A monk began beating a gong behind the shrine, and when some of the mourners rose from their knees I got up too and turned and moved through an archway into the burnished copper morning outside.

It wasn't yet nine, but the temperature would already be in the eighties, with the humidity the same on the hygrometer; the sun was a shimmering disc above the pagodas and temples and pockmarked concrete buildings to the east. The city had sounds of life, with the streets filled with the ringing of cyclo bells and the shouting of merchants, but in a couple of hours the sun would be nearly overhead and we'd be in the nineties and the siesta would begin.

I could feel the heat radiating from the row of parked cars and jeeps on the temple grounds, and barbs of dazzling light bounced off their metalwork and windows as I moved past them into the shade of a rubber tree where I'd left the steel-gray Mazda.

I got into it and sat behind the wheel, and the sweat sprang onto my skin at once, the thing was like an oven, sat there while they came slowly out of the temple, some of them walking down the path under the sugar-palm trees, the others trudging in their sandals to the row of vehicles, standing there talking for a while and then getting in, slamming the doors. At last the family came out, talking with the abbot for a minute and then moving across to the ivory-white Honda that was standing under one of the trees.

He didn't look around him, the brother, which I thought was cocky. I'd been prepared for him to check the environment, and that was why I was sitting low on the seat of the Mazda with the sun visor down; but he was simply helping the women into the car and getting behind the wheel. I thought it was cocky of him because he knew it hadn't been an accident that night, that someone had seen his brother bring the gun into the aim and had gone for the Zhiguli. He should have realized that for someone to do that, they would have had to be tailing both cars, his and the minister's. In other words the hit had been blown, and it had cost him his brother's life, and that should tell him there was someone operating in Phnom Penh against the Khmer Rouge, a lone-wolf agent who might well show up at the funeral with a bullet for him.

He'd know the hit hadn't been blown by a government body-guard: a bodyguard would have had his vehicle close to the minister's outside the Royal Palace Hotel, and the hit team would have done one of two things: they would have called the whole thing off or they would have opened fire on both cars the instant the minister climbed into the Chevrolet, going for a hit-and-run operation with a good chance of getting clear.

But perhaps he wasn't cocky, the brother; perhaps he was just untrained, an efficient guerrilla, say, but not an espion.

He'd started the car but wasn't moving off yet, and while I waited I thought of *Salamander*, thought of the debriefing signal I might be able to send sometime today, sometime tonight, so that they could pick up their bit of chalk in the signals room and scratch it across the board: *Executive has gained access to the Khmer Rouge base in Phnom Penh.* Because that was my immediate objective: they'd gone underground in the capital, Gabrielle had told me, and no one knew where they were.

But if the day went well and I got access to their base and signaled Pringle and told him, it wouldn't go onto the board in London because there wasn't a board for this one, for *Salamander*. No one in the whole of the Bureau except Flockhart knew I was out here in the field; no one even knew there was a field; no one was in the least bit interested in Phnom Penh or Cambodia; no one could care less. No one.

And for an instant I knew I'd brushed close to the truth of what was really happening in the scene behind the scenes, where Flockhart was pulling the strings.

Then it was gone, and all I was left with was the knowledge that at this moment I had as much substance for the Bureau as a phantom. So how had that bastard done this to me? But we know, don't we . . . his tone had been so silky when he'd said over the telephone, *Wouldn't it be frustrating for you to come all the way home and have me prove to you that you'd missed the chance of a lifetime?*

The Honda was moving off and I let it get as far as the road past the temple gardens before I started the engine and got into gear and took up the tail.

"You want girl?"

"No," I said.

"Want boy?"

"No."

"My sister pretty. Look."

He pushed a creased sepia photograph through the window of the Mazda, the picture of a child-woman with frightened eyes and tiny breasts that would never get any bigger before she died one of the dozen deaths her gods in their bounty had to offer her, starvation, abuse, privation, AIDS; she could take her choice but must hurry, she was already twelve years old.

"No," I told him and hit his hand away, harder than I'd meant but without regret.

09:43.

No one had come out of the building over there for the past fifteen minutes. I was using the clock on the dashboard instead of my watch because it allowed me to flick my eyes down and up again without losing time. The sign on the wall of the building said KAMPUCHEA IMPORT-EXPORT, and there was a bleached and tattered flag hanging limp from one of the windows. The man who interested me had taken the women home and then turned north and west onto what had once been called U.S.S.R. Boulevard, the route to Pochentong Airport. He'd parked his Honda at the side of the building, and I could see it in the gap between two of the market stalls, the one selling mangoes, bananas, and pineapples and the one next to it, where dried fish were hanging from poles. They and the people milling around them made adequate cover: I was hiding in plain sight.

The sun was higher now by two or three diameters, and its brassy heat pressed down through the haze, shimmering on hard surfaces and spreading mirages across the airport road.

Within the next hour six men went into the Import-Export building and four came out again. None of the four was my target.

10:53.

"Move car."

He looked down at me, his uniform ragged and sweat-soaked, his rifle slung from the shoulder, his eyes in the shadow of his peaked cap.

"What?"

"Move car now."

He was blocking my view a little and I shifted on the seat to keep the main entrance of the building in sight. The target had gone in there and would presumably come out at the same place. I could watch his car instead, until he went over to it, but I wanted to take a look at everyone else who went through those doors and came out again. At this stage I needed to watch faces and commit them to memory, because this operation could last for hours, even for days, and some of the people I was watching now could become surveillance targets too. The dead man's brother wouldn't be the only Khmer Rouge agent in that building; it could even be their base.

"Papers."

I reached for my wallet without taking my eyes off the building. I had the sun visor down but the glare from the white concrete was becoming a problem, flooding the retinas and causing loss of precise definition, making their faces look much the same, the faces of the men going in and out of the building. Sweat trickled on me; the oven I was sitting in was set higher than a hundred degrees for a slow roast.

"British?" the policeman asked. Sweat dripped from his chin onto the papers. I didn't say anything; two men were coming out of the building, and I couldn't remember seeing them go in. "British?" the policeman asked again.

"What? Yes."

He gave my papers back. "Foreigners move car. Not place here for car."

I put the papers into my wallet and got out a one-thousand-riel note and gave it to him and he went away. The two men were getting into a Toyota and I lost interest. Only one man would come through those doors and get into the ivory-white Honda and he was my target.

I'd brought nothing for an overnight stop from the house in Kralahom Kong: I might have to abandon the Mazda at some stage of the operation and wanted to travel light. But I had enough coins for a phone call, my only connection to my director in the field. I'd told Pringle at the airport that I'd found my own base, but hadn't told him where, and he'd been expectedly stuffy.

"I'd prefer," he'd said, "that you use the safe house we've set up for you in Keochea Street."

"Is it Bureau?"

Without looking down: "Actually, no. But the man who owns it has a deep hatred of Pol Pot and is in our debt."

"I'll think about it," I told him. "Deep hatreds can flare up at the wrong time, and I don't want any excitement."

In the end Pringle had said he'd be reluctant in the extreme to report to Mr. Flockhart that I refused to use their safe house and I'd said that was tough shit and when I left the airport I made sure he wasn't in my mirror.

12:31.

Another man came out of the building but he didn't go anywhere near the white Honda. The long siesta had begun, and at any moment my target should be leaving his office to drive home and be with his grieving family again. But nothing was certain, except that the sun had reached its zenith and the streets were shimmering.

A sheet of pale green paper came eddying through the open window of the Mazda and my reaction was slow because of the heat and it worried me: it could have been something else, a hand with a knife in it, or a gun. A Caucasian woman in a white T-shirt and slacks was moving away behind the car.

The heading on the pamphlet read EURASIAN ACTION COMMITTEE, CHURCH OF CHRIST. *In this report we shall address a tragic situation in Bangkok, Thailand, that has been given a token reference in the general media but nothing more. Thai and other travel agents working with the airlines are boosting the tourist trade in that country by offering package tours for men only at the equivalent of 4,000 U.S. dollars, with a promise of—and we quote—"Four days and nights of exotic entertainment that is guaranteed to satisfy any man's wildest dreams."*

Three Asians moved beyond the top edge of the pamphlet and

went into the building; they were wearing camouflage outfits and combat boots; I couldn't see any weapons. Conceivably they were out of the jungle, guerrillas from the Khmer Rouge forces.

It is known throughout Asia that at least half of the male and female prostitutes reserved for European and American tourists are below the age of fifteen, and at least half of them are carrying the HIV virus, while many are passing into the first stages of AIDS, despite spurious "medical certificates" to the contrary. This was not mentioned at the recent conference in Amsterdam on the rapidly spreading global AIDS epidemic. The Geneva-based Association François-Xavier Bagnoud, which runs a shelter for child prostitutes in Thailand, has also reported through Reuters that according to the testimony of a girl rescued from a brothel and questioned, she was constantly beaten and underfed, and that girls were taken away and shot by their pimps when they fell sick or were of no further use. We urge you to do whatever is in your power to make it widely known, beginning with your family, your friends, and your representatives, that unless the most strenuous diplomatic pressure is brought to bear on the Thai government to cease trading in tragedy, the present efforts of the Church of Christ to succor the suffering must prove of little avail. We want to see the world that God created made fit for His people to live in. Is that too much to ask? But we ask more—we ask for your help, for without it we can do so little, and with it we can do so much.

I folded the sheet of cheap, badly printed paper and put it away.

At 1:13 the young Kampuchean running the fruit stall dragged a roll of canvas down across the front and put the cashbox into his patched shoulder bag and got onto his bicycle and wobbled away, the back of his sweat-stained T-shirt proclaiming him to be a supporter of the Brooklyn Dodgers.

And then the rain came, driving across from the coast and blotting out the dark burnished gold of the temple domes and quenching the sun, bringing a false twilight into the streets.

In the middle of the afternoon the white Honda was still standing over there beside the building, half-lost to sight in the rain, and I realized that the agent must have been driven away by one of the men who had gone inside, and that his car could still be there at midnight, or in the morning. But that was an assumption, and I didn't act on it. I had no other lead: the block of apartments where he'd dropped off the women was in the center of the city, a difficult surveillance target; it could also be that he didn't live there himself, might not go there to comfort his family before tomorrow, if then.

At six in the evening, when the only moving shapes were the trucks plowing through the downpour along the airport road, I opened the door of the car and emptied the Coke bottle and filled it and emptied it again, for this relief much thanks, but it didn't help the overall situation, which was that I'd been sitting here on the bloody peep for most of the day and could be here for most of the night.

The smell of frying was coming from somewhere, seeping through the vents of the car, and I realized I hadn't eaten since early this morning, would need to take in some protein as soon as I could, but this wasn't the right time because a man was coming out of the Import-Export building now, huddled against the rain as he jogged across to the Honda and got in.

This was at 6:14 and I noted it simply because it might be a habit of his to leave there at this time of the day. It wouldn't be dark for another hour but the sky was still heavy and the headlights of the Honda came on and I waited until it had splashed through the mud beside the building and turned south before I started up and took a left and two rights and another left as fast as I could and got him in my sights again at a distance of fifty yards, closing the gap a little but leaving my lights off, keeping track of him through the rain with the wipers moaning across and across the windscreen as we kept on going south until we reached Pokambor Boulevard and turned southeast toward the Killing Fields of Choeung Ek.

7

. . . .

BOGEYMAN

The point of no return was the ninth stair.

That was my estimation.

There were twelve stairs and I was now on the eighth, watching the crack of light under the door on the landing above me. It was at eye level. It had taken me a long time to reach here, perhaps fifteen minutes; this was partly because the stairs creaked—the villa was old, with cracked plaster walls and rotting timber—and partly because the situation was so dangerous and I didn't want to hurry.

Voices came from below the door, voices and tobacco smoke creeping blue-gray in the crack of light.

I've told them so often at Norfolk when I'm roped in as a temporary instructor between missions: *Never use a staircase when you're approaching a hot zone, unless there's no other way. And even then think twice.* To help get it into their heads I throw them the statistics from a report I remember reading on safety in the home: "In dwellings of more than one floor, thirty-five percent of fatal accidents occur on the stairs. Fifteen percent of these involve the elderly, fifty-two percent occur when something bulky is being carried *down* the stairs, and thirty-three percent occur *when hurrying*."

Tonight, as I watched the light under the door, I was aware that my chance of a fatal accident on this particular staircase was closer to a hundred percent because if that door opened and I had to go down the stairs there'd be a gun at my back and all I'd have to do in my hurry to get clear was break an ankle and it'd stop my run, *finito.*

If the door opened when I reached the next stair, the ninth, the point of no return, I would have a gun in my face but there'd be a chance of dealing with it before it was fired.

There was a balcony on this side of the villa. The room where the agents were talking would open onto it; so would the rooms on each side. When I approached the villa through the last of the rain some thirty minutes ago, following the dead man's brother at a distance from where we'd left the cars, I'd seen the balcony but hadn't been able to reach it from the ground: there was no creeper, no drainpipe, nothing but the sheer wall. That was why I'd had to ignore my own warning to the neophyte espions at Norfolk and use this staircase to the hot zone, the room where the agents were talking. I'd come in through the back door of the villa; it hadn't been locked; guerrillas armed to the teeth don't think of locking their doors.

The voices behind the door rose and fell, fell sometimes to silence, then broke out again. I recognized the language, that was all: it was Khmer. They would be talking, some of the time, about the death of the hit man, a death to be avenged, and bloodily, as soon as they could find out who had killed him, so that his brother here could at least know that the score was settled.

I listened on the stair.

The way I worked things out was that if the door of that room opened at any next second and someone came out when I was still on the eighth stair my chances of getting clear would be better if I turned and crashed down the staircase and got out through the open back door before the agent had time to pull his gun and fire it with any accuracy. But once I was on the ninth stair, only three from the top, I thought I might stand a better chance of getting clear by taking the man head-on and dropping him cold and going through the vacant room to the right and onto the balcony and making a controlled drop to the ground before the fuss started.

But when I talk about one chance being better than the other I mean of course by a hair, by the tenth of a second, by the reaction time of the agent's nerves, the degree of friction between the gun and the inside of the holster, things like that, a thousand things. And there were other unpredictables: whether the room on the right was in fact vacant; whether the latch on the door was weak enough for me to smash open if it was locked or if the handle was loose and wouldn't turn fast enough to let me in there.

The talking rose again and then one voice barked and there was silence. He would be their top dog—the man, almost certainly, I would need to meet, and talk to, or kill.

I lifted my right foot to take the next step upward but froze as someone moved inside the room and the shadow of a boot darkened the crack under the door and I waited for it to come open, going over the distances and the angles that would be involved if a man came out and I had to get to him before he was ready, working against the glare of the light from the room before my pupils had time to retract but using my one advantage—the element of surprise—for all it was worth.

Waited.

Four stairs and a distance of three feet across the landing, say two seconds, two and a half, before the heel of the right palm reached the nose bone and drove it upward into his brain and dropped him, the gun in his hand by that time but too late, with any luck too late.

The boot was still close to the door. I watched the handle, waiting for it to turn, to trigger the nerves, alert the muscles.

Waited with my right foot lowered again and braced on the eighth stair with the heel raised and the ball of the foot burning as the energy surged from the brain to the muscles on hot waves of adrenaline.

Soon?

I watched the crack of light, the shadow of the boot.

Now?

The muscles burning, the organism triggered, the nerves drawn tight.

Then a voice came and the boot moved and the shadow was gone and the handle of the door remained still, perfectly still, as the talking broke out again and I moved to the ninth stair and went on climbing and crossed the landing and went into the room on the right with no impediment, the door unlocked and the handle easy to turn but the heart still racing under the whip of the adrenaline and the mouth dry, the reaction bringing sweat out, itching on my face.

It was darker in here than it had been on the staircase, because the lights had been left burning in the main room on the ground floor. I had spent a little time in there when I'd come into the villa, smelling the film of burnt cordite inside the barrels of uncleaned guns—most of them Chinese assault rifles stacked in the corners and lying around on a trestle table. I had also studied the picture gallery on the wall, a big spread of black-and-white photographs of men in camouflage dress holding weapons at the alert with dramatic look-mummy expressions, a lot of the pictures showing Pol Pot himself, carefully shot from below to make him look taller, others showing a younger man in jungle battle dress with a peaked cap and a general's pips on the shoulders, one with his name below it: Kheng San, presumably the second-in-command of the Khmer Rouge forces.

I had studied his face with particular care, going from one shot to another and letting the flat black-and-white features saturate the memory while the imagination supplied the third dimension and added color. I knew the face of Pol Pot from press photographs and the television screen, but it might be as important for me to know the face of General Kheng.

I listened now to the voices coming through the plaster wall from the room next door. One of them I had learned to recognize:

it belonged to the top dog, the one who barked when everyone else started talking at once. He could possibly be General Kheng, but I didn't think so: the forces of the Khmer Rouge were twelve thousand strong and would have the normal number of officers of all ranks.

This could of course be their secret base, the one they'd moved to when they'd gone underground. In the normal run of things a hit man is low in the echelon, but a hit man ordered to target a government minister would rank higher, and his brother might be persona grata at headquarters. Or he could simply have come here on orders to debrief, as the driver of the Russian Zhiguli on the night of the attempted assassination.

Two of the voices were women's, sharp and shrill, the voices of fanatics. In a culture where female citizens were looked upon as cattle and female soldiers as whores they had done well, these two, to have risen this far in the ranks.

I put one ear against the wall and listened. The volume was increased but it still wasn't good enough: I'd be wasting my time. I felt in the darkness for the French doors to the balcony and found them and turned the oval handle, drawing the vertical bolts clear at the top and bottom, taking time, keeping pressure against the doors with one shoulder to stop the bolts springing free with a bang—I couldn't afford to make a sound, the slightest sound, during the brief silences that came from the next room.

As I inched open the doors the night air came softly in, humid after the rain but cooler than in here. But it was the light that stopped my movements dead, the light and the sound of their voices. Through the slats of the shutters I could see the floor of the balcony in the light that came from the other room: they'd opened the shutters there and the French doors as well, possibly to let the smoke out or cool the air or both. I hadn't expected that.

The options were unattractive: their voices were clear now and I could set the recorder going and leave it running for thirty minutes and turn the tape over and run it for another thirty but there was the distinct risk that during the hour someone would come into this room and raise a shout when he saw me and before I could reach him, call it a hornet's nest.

Or I could open these doors wider and ease the shutters back and move onto the balcony, but it ran past both rooms and I'd risk being seen and if that happened there'd be no point in going back through the room and down the stairs because there wouldn't be time before they pulled their guns and put out a fusillade, *finis*.

Or I could abort the operation *now*, get out of this room and go back down the stairs while I had time, the risk factor zero unless that door opened onto the landing and someone came out within the next twenty seconds, the time it would take me to reach the ground floor.

I stood listening to the voices coming through the shutters.

There was no laughter, not even occasional. That wasn't a party they had going in there. One of their hit men had been killed and they'd be debriefing his brother on that; they would also be discussing other business, and that was why I'd bought a Sony 309 compact cassette recorder at the Marché Olympique yesterday on the chance that when I went to the funeral it would give me a lead. The objective for *Salamander* was information, and all I needed was to hear people talk.

Their voices rose and fell.

I was terribly disinclined to abort.

You'll get yourself killed if you don't.

Shuddup.

I didn't like the idea of the staircase as an escape route. I was already this side of the ninth stair, the point of no return, and even if I ignored that, the scene projected for me in the imagination was unpleasant: the shadow executive for the mission crashing down the stairs with his hands flung out and the steel-nosed slugs from the Chinese rifles going into his spine before he could even start counting. The space was too confined and once on the staircase I wouldn't be able to dodge or turn or break for cover, I'd be like a dog in a drainpipe.

Discount staircase.

One of the women was speaking, using a lot of emphasis, her eyes watching the moon for the first time not so long ago, the round white toy in the sky, while her mother told her its ancient name, the name of a goddess, told her it was much too far to touch as the tiny hands reached out for it, using a lot of emphasis now as she pulled herself to her full height, with her eyes brighter than the moon and burning with the light of the crusader, her small breasts flattened under the battle dress and the bandolier and her small hands calloused by the long hours at the firing range, a lot of emphasis, her voice chopping at the air as she spoke of the things she had learned in these few years, how to bring bloodshed back to the Killing Fields of Choeung Ek in the cause of communism for Kampuchea.

Try the last option next, then, get it out of the way: abort the operation.

Yes, because if you don't—

Oh for Christ's sake *shuddup.*

I'd come here for information and it could be a breakthrough if I got it, a breakthrough within three days of coming into the field, so the *only* option I was prepared to take was going out onto that balcony and hitting the record button and letting this thing go on running until we had a bit of bad luck and one of them saw me there or heard me there and I had to use the balcony itself as the escape route, make a controlled drop, and that wouldn't be anything new because—

You'll kill yourself—

God's sake *piss* off, will you, because I'd already allowed for it in my original plans, to make the drop and get to the corner of the building and out of the gunsights and get clear. The balcony faced west and I'd left the Mazda on the east side of the villa and that made the whole thing possible: I'd have time to get as far as the car and take it away before they set up the fusillade; *it could work*, let's put it like that, if things went wrong it wouldn't be a *certain* death.

And that was as much as I would ask: to know that the risk was calculated.

Kheng was barking again, if that was his voice in there, General Kheng San's, and silence fell and I didn't touch the right-hand shutter until the voices came in again and provided sound cover. I chose the right-hand shutter because it opened away from the other room instead of toward it and would reflect less light from the angled slats on the floor of the balcony.

As the shutter swung back by a millimeter at a time I sighted along the balcony with one eye in the gap. The other room was open to the night as I'd thought, but all I could see were a few inches of the wall inside and a rifle leaning in the corner. They weren't troubled, these people, by the thought of being overlooked, overheard, shot at by a sniper: the villa stood in its own grounds and there was no traffic on the muddy track we'd taken here tonight, the agent and I.

The night air came against my face as I pushed open the shutter far enough to let me through in the prone position, with the Sony 309 held in front of me. Then I began crawling.

On my left, the wall of the villa, with the open doors twelve feet away; on my right, the balcony rail with the sheer drop beyond it. My world had become narrowed, together with the margin of error. If one of those people came onto the balcony now it would simply be a question of my luck having run out; but on top of the chance factor, mistakes could also be made, and as I pushed the record button on the little Sony I noted the dark crescent of tape under the transparent window as it began running, because in thirty minutes the automatic shutoff would be triggered and would produce a definite click, and if that happened during one of those silences in there they'd hear it, no question. Luck was out of my control, but mistakes would need to be avoided.

Crawling.

The Sony wasn't big; I'd chosen a micro because I might have to make a run with it: there'd been no choice. But it made things trickier, because the microphone wouldn't pick up distant sound, and I had to get as close as I could to the source—the voices that rose and fell in there, punctuated by the top dog's bark and lightened by the shrill tones of the women.

Cigarette smoke drifted through the open doors, blue-gray and curling, as if someone had thrown a bomb in there.

Crawling, holding the Sony as far in front of me as I could, until direct light touched it from the open doors and I pulled it back an inch and froze. This was as far as I could go, and all I could do now was lie here to wait this thing out as the tape ran silently in the little recorder, the dark crescent narrowing on one side under the plastic window, widening on the other.

The beat of the heart against the wooden boards of the balcony, the deep slow rhythm of the breath bringing oxygen for the muscles, the adrenals producing fuel to fire the blood in the instant if something went wrong—if the toe of a boot moved into the light six feet, less, in front of me, as one of them came out to take the air.

Watch the little plastic window.

I would have liked to lie here with both palms flat on the boards, ready to push up if I had to, but that wasn't possible: I must keep hold of the Sony with my right hand, and that made things awkward. But what do we expect, we the doughty ferrets in the field, when we go out on the limb—a six-month guarantee that the bloody thing won't break?

I don't like this—

Nor do I, so shut up, I'm trying to concentrate.

If someone comes out, you won't have time.

God's sake, piss *off,* I'm busy.

The tape narrowing on one side, widening on the other through the little window, the reek of the tobacco smoke, the rough grain of the boards under my left hand, under my right wrist, the sound of a truck in the distance, its lights sending a silver spark of reflection moving across the chrome case of the Sony, watch the tape, *watch it*, we've been here fifteen minutes now, don't let that thing shut off, it'll sound like a bloody bomb, we seem, we seem to have bombs, don't we, bombs on the brain, quite so, images of violence in the mind as we lie here like a corpse, a cadaver, shall we do that if we see a boot suddenly in the doorway, if one of them comes onto the balcony, just go on lying here like a corpse, play dead with our paws in the air?

Conceivably ill-advised.

Watch the tape. Just watch the tape and clear the mind of boots and bombs and pandemonium and things that go bang in the night as they grab the rifle and bring it into the aim, *bang* and you're dead before you're even on your feet, my good friend, my good late friend with your blood all over the—*watch* the tape, that's all we have to do, we clear the mind of the bogeymen and watch the tape.

Widening on one side, narrowing on the other through the little window, the voices pitching up and falling again, the smoke drifting across the light.

Watch the tape. Twenty minutes now.

But it's no go—*look*.

Boot of the bogeyman.

8

❖·❖

PLAYBACK

I saw his eyes in the instant before I was on my feet and he was going for his gun when I hit the balcony rail and it broke as I tilted across it and began falling with the air rush against my face, pushing the Sony into my field jacket and kicking out to keep my body vertical, kicking again and tilting forward so that I could let the legs jackknife to absorb the initial impact, and when I hit ground at that angle I went straight into a forward aikido roll with my head tucked down out of the way and the right shoulder taking the worst of it, sending me spinning as the vertical momentum became rotational and I rolled twice, three times before it was exhausted and I could straighten my legs and start pitching forward into a fast run, and by this time a lot of shouting had broken out above me and in the blur of images I saw a gun come up from the hip and heard the shot thud into the rain-sodden earth a foot distant as I reached the corner of the building and rapid fire began puckering the ground.

Running flat out, the Sony in my hand now to make sure it stayed with me, running flat out for the Mazda, a lot of noise inside the villa, boots on the stairs like distant thunder as I closed on the car, twenty yards, fifteen, ten, with the air smelling sweet after the rain as I sucked it into my lungs, a night bird calling and then a burst of fire going into the roof of the car as I dragged the door open and pitched inside and got the engine going and gunned up and took the thing away with the lights still off and the rear wheels sending a mud-wave across the Peugeot standing alongside and then finding traction as I brought the power down and waited and then took it up again with the treads biting now as we headed for the crushed-stone track through an avenue of palms.

Light began flooding from behind as I reached the track and gave the Mazda the full gun and switched my own lights on because there were buildings here, call them huts, whitewashed and peeling and huddled among the palm trees, some of the windows lit by kerosene lamps inside. There wasn't a dog's chance of outrunning the pack behind me because it was less than half a mile away and closing, and the next group of shots smashed into the bodywork and I ducked and started looking for options as the rear window snowed and glass whirled inside the car from the backdraft. If I switched off my lights at this speed I'd crash, and if I left them on I'd present the Mazda as a perfect target and it was a matter of time, seconds, before a shot blew my head open, so I hit the brakes when I saw a side track coming up and put the Mazda into a controlled slide with more huts looming in the swinging wash of the lights and *then* I cut them and drove blind and used the brakes again and slid to a stop and hit the door open and pitched out and slammed it shut behind me and broke into a run as the pack swerved into the side track and their lights flooded across the buildings and the leading gunner saw the Mazda and started work on it with a burst of shots, and by the time I reached the shelter of the huts they were putting enough firepower into it to blow a tank away, and the last I saw of it was a small metal carcass standing there frozen in the glare of their lights until a shot sparked the fuel and there was a fireball turning the buildings red in a man-made sunset as I went on running for the darkness beyond, just a steady jog because it was going to take time for them to move in close enough to see there was no charred relic sitting at the wheel of the burned-out wreck.

• • •

She was standing near the ferry station on the river, leaning against the rotting timber wall, part of it in the half-dark, had done some training somewhere, I wouldn't have seen her if this hadn't been the rendezvous.

I stopped within fifty yards and waited. I'd picked up a battle-weary Mercedes 300D from another black market dealer near the airport, two of the wings bent and the air-conditioning on the fritz, got him out of bed and crossed his palm with two hundred thousand riels, enough to buy the bloody thing, but you get what you pay for and what I'd paid for was a fresh set of wheels under me and a shut mouth, he'd never know who I was unless he saw my face again and I wasn't going to let him. He could be a Khmer Rouge agent on the side, anyone could, you had to shake your shoes out whenever you put them on.

She was walking slowly toward me, Gabrielle, across the broken boards of the quay, but I didn't get out of the car: I wanted to see if she'd picked up any ticks. She hadn't. She had a camera slung from her left shoulder as usual, and I saw fatigue in her walk, fatigue from looking for crippled children to photograph, from finding them.

I pushed the door open for her and she got in.

"Ça va?" she asked.

"Ça va."

I started up and took the Mercedes past the first wharf and found cover between two trucks, one of them spilling ropes and barrels, the other listing on three wheels. Moonlight sparked off the river as the ripples reached the quay.

"What has happened?" Gabrielle asked in French; she'd remembered my preference.

"There's something I need your help with." I reached across her and pulled the Sony out of the glove pocket. There was garlic on her breath, suddenly reminding me I was starving, hadn't eaten since early this morning; it was now nearly midnight. There was also a bushfire going on in my right shoulder, touched off by all those aikido rolls. "I know you speak Khmer," I told Gabrielle, "but exactly how fluent are you?"

"Perfectly fluent."

"Fair enough." So at least we had a chance; I'd fast-forwarded the tape a couple of times while I'd been waiting for her, and things hadn't sounded too good: I'd known a mike this size would have to be moved in close to the source to pick up anything well and I'd tried to do that on the balcony of the villa, but it still hadn't been close enough: the voices were so faint that I couldn't have told what the language was if I hadn't already known. There were also squelchy patches of white sound, possibly because the heat in this place had got at the cassette.

"How was your day?" I asked Gabrielle as I ran back the tape.

"Okay. Yours?"

"Okay." I raked around in the glove pocket but couldn't find anything. "Have you got a pad I can use?"

"This." She pulled out a small sketching block from her bag. "Will a pencil do?"

"Fine."

"What will I be listening to?"

"Voices."

Lights washed across the side of the wharf and I tilted both the sun visors down.

"Are you expecting anyone?" Gabrielle asked. That is an exact translation, and I think she was mimicking the kind of dialogue you find in private-eye novels, just for fun.

"If I were expecting anyone, you wouldn't be here." The lights fanned across the river and then swung full circle and were swallowed by the wharfs.

"I can look after myself," Gabrielle said.

"Of course. But you've got enough on your plate already, tip-toeing though the trip mines all day." I hadn't wanted to bring her out tonight, but the stuff on this tape might give me a breakthrough if she could make out what any of the voices were saying.

I pressed the play button.

Light from a tall gooseneck lamp on the ferry station was bouncing softly off the clapboard wall of the wharf, faint and diffused but enough to guide my hand across the sketching block—it had to be, because I couldn't use the dashboard lamp without switching on the parking lights and I wasn't going to do that.

The voices began coming in and I rolled the volume higher, but it brought up the background too, and I rolled it back.

They sounded so bloody *faint*.

So I should have gone closer, yes, closer still, if the trick had been worth pulling at all.

You went too close as it was. You could have—

Perfectly right.

It's happened before. You work out a good trick and you calculate the odds and they look okay—or put it this way, they don't look actually lethal—so you gird up the loins and put the turnscrew on the nerves till they're as tight as harp strings and you go in with at least the thought that if something goes wrong and you end up spreadeagled across enemy terrain with a shot in the spine or a knife in the throat it won't have been your fault, it will simply have been a calculated risk that turned suddenly into a certainty, a dead certainty, *finito*.

She wasn't getting anything, Gabrielle, the voices were too faint.

And then afterward, when you've got away with it, you look back and suddenly know that you were out of your mind even to think of going in at all, that the risk was too high, appallingly high, and all that had sent you in had been an overweening faith in your own abilities, blinding you from the start. And you were lucky, just plumb lucky, to have survived.

But you can't run a mission on luck.

I was sitting here sweating now; I hadn't wanted to think about this, it had just come and hit me in the face because I'd not only put myself in extreme and inexcusable hazard but I'd done it for nothing, I knew that now, because that's what we were getting from the Sony as we sat here listening—*nothing*, just the squelch from a flawed tape and a drone of voices so faint that even Gabrielle, fluent in the language, wasn't picking anything up to give me.

Contact Pringle and debrief, wouldn't take long, would it, *Am still alive, have a nice day.*

No actual *information*, let's not be too ambitious.

"They are to remain patient," Gabrielle said.

"What?"

There was a faint barking now from the Sony, just as I'd heard it at the villa. This was the voice that had started to come through.

"They want to do something," Gabrielle said, "but he's telling them to wait, to be patient."

I hit the stop button and rewound for five seconds. "To do what, exactly?"

"I couldn't hear. I'm not even sure about this—I'm having to fill in the gaps. But the word 'patient' is definitely there."

I switched to play and she listened again while I watched the moonlight glinting along the river like a drawn blade. The barking began again and I looked at Gabrielle but she was shaking her head slowly.

"It wasn't any better. But some of them want to *act* in some way, and this man won't let them, at least not yet. He's in authority."

"You're not getting any names?"

"No."

I let the tape run on, sliding lower against the seat back, scanning the wharfside, the ferry station, the river. Light had washed across the far end of the wharf a couple of times from the main street as a police patrol had passed, a police patrol or perhaps a military vehicle: there wouldn't be much other traffic in this city now because of the curfew.

"He is a colonel," Gabrielle said in a little while.

"The one with the bark?"

"Yes."

"Name?"

"I don't know."

"Shall I run it back?"

"No." She angled the Sony nearer her on the armrest and hit the stop button. "If I need to, I'll do it myself." With her head turned to watch me: "How close were you to these people?"

"Not close enough."

"They sound like agents of the Khmer Rouge. You knew that?"

"Of course."

She gave a little shrug and pressed the play button again.

I left it to her now, and she stopped the tape three or four times and rewound, replayed, stopped it again, rolling the volume up sometimes, rolling it down when the colonel's voice came in, getting rid of the background whenever she could, and after fifteen minutes she switched the thing off.

"This is the gist of what I'm getting so far. The man in authority is Colonel Choen. He is visiting the Phnom Penh cell of the Khmer Rouge in order to give its agents their latest orders from General Kheng San."

He would be the man in the photograph I'd seen on the wall of the villa, his name below it, a general's insignia on his battle dress.

"Have you heard of him?" I asked Gabrielle.

"General Kheng? No." She waited for another question but I left it. "The local cell appears excited about something they're planning to do in Phnom Penh—or something they've been ordered to do. But Colonel Choen is telling them to hold on, to wait for the right time. This is the *gist*, as I've said, and I'm trying hard not to jump to conclusions of my own."

"I understand that." It wasn't easy for her: given a snatched word here and there, and her imagination would start inventing scenarios, and that would amount to unintended disinformation, could take us dangerously off-track. "Have you done any intelligence work before?" I asked her.

She turned her head. "No."

"You're a natural."

"Thank you."

Then suddenly I thought it might have sounded patronizing, and wished I hadn't said it; she didn't need anyone to grade her homework; she was a world-class photojournalist working in a flashpoint theater of operations. I decided to leave it, didn't apologize, it could make things worse.

"There's a date," Gabrielle said, "that's come up three or four times. The nineteenth."

"Of?"

"I don't know."

"This month, then." Today was the twelfth.

"Perhaps. Colonel Choen says they must all wait for the nineteenth."

"Big day."

"Perhaps."

White light flushed the walls of the wharf again and I watched it, some kind of vehicle on the move, sending shadows fanning out until they vanished into the peripheral dark. Then a glare came suddenly on the windscreen of a parked truck, throwing reflections like silver fish flickering along the walls. I could hear the engine now, a small one, maybe a jeep's. There'd been no vehicle coming as close as this to the ferry station while we'd been here.

"I heard another name," Gabrielle said. "Leng Sim, the Minister of Defense. The colonel was—"

"If this is a police patrol," I said quietly, "I'll just do the usual thing and pay them off. If it's anyone else, and there's any problem, I want you to get down low as soon as I start driving out. Understood?"

She turned her head to look at me for a moment, her face lit and shadowed, her eyes deep. "Yes."

I found my seat belt and snapped the buckle, and Gabrielle did the same.

There was a narrow gap ahead of us between a gantry and the

corner of the warehouse, and I'd parked the Mercedes in line with it. That was our point of exit from the scene: the gap. Beyond it was an alleyway wide enough to take the Mercedes, provided I didn't need the outside mirrors anymore, and I didn't, because in a night escape you don't need to see behind you: all you need to do is watch for your own shadow on each side of your headlight beams on the turns, see how it swings across the buildings, see how close the tracker is and which way he's moving and how far away he is, and whether he's gaining or falling back.

Echoes were coming in as the engine of the vehicle was revved a little, pulling away from a corner. The light was bright now.

At the other end of the alleyway was a stack of crates and a blind T-section, and if I managed things right we could go in fast enough to lose the rear end of the Mercedes in a sideswipe and bring the crates down behind us and provide an instant barricade. I'd arrived ten minutes early for the rendezvous and looked around, simply as a matter of routine procedure, and set up an escape route in case we needed one.

Light very bright now.

"The Minister of Defense?" I said. "Oh yes, he was the one they tried to wipe out."

"The one whose life you saved."

"So what were they saying about him?"

"I don't know. I just heard his name mentioned."

"Do you think he was the target of the orders they'd received? They're mad keen to try it again and get him this time? And the colonel's telling them to wait, be patient?"

"I don't *know*. That is absolute conjecture."

The light burst from the far end of the warehouse and flooded the environment as the jeep went bouncing across the intersection and vanished behind the buildings, its engine note fading.

In a moment I said, "Right, absolute conjecture, but I'm just trying to put things together, to see if some of the gibberish you're hearing suddenly makes sense. Sometimes it works."

"It's very dangerous."

"Yes, it's very dangerous. And if it doesn't sound patronizing, I'll say it again: you're very good."

She rested her hand on my arm and said with quiet intensity, "I just want to be sure I don't make any mistakes, that's all, any mistakes that could put you in harm's way."

"I can look after myself."

"*Touché.*"

The lights of the jeep flashed in the far distance as it turned a corner, then the darkness came down again.

"Do you think," I asked Gabrielle, "that is as much as you've got, so far?"

"Yes."

Three names, a date, and a brief scenario: Colonel Choen was in the capital to stop the local cell from jeopardizing some kind of action timed to go off on the nineteenth, a week from tonight. Not a great deal, not even enough to debrief to Pringle, but if that date was important it would mean we had a deadline, and *that* would affect things: whatever Flockhart wanted me to do out here would have to be done within a week.

And honor was mine again: it had been worth it after all, the trick I'd pulled at the villa tonight. We—

Nothing can excuse what you did—

Shuddup.

Colonel Choen was barking again as Gabrielle started the tape. She gave it five minutes and started rewinding, replaying, her eyes closed as she listened; then she switched it off.

"That was a little better. You were nearer, then." Right, edging the Sony as far as I could along the balcony, watching for a boot to show. "Colonel Choen is flying to Pouthisat in the morning," Gabrielle said. "I think he could be meeting General Kheng there, or someone else—all I can hear is that he'll be 'talking' to him, so it could mean by telephone, though I doubt it: the lines are pretty bad everywhere." I think she was waiting for me to make notes, but I didn't need to; I could keep what little we'd got in my head. "I heard King Sihanouk's name mentioned, but couldn't get the context. I think Colonel—"

An orange flash bloomed in silence across the river, spreading against the dark, and in a second or two the sound reached us, a deep thudding cough. Faint cries came keening, leaving echoes among the wharves.

"More funerals tomorrow," Gabrielle said softly, "more flowers."

"That was bigger than a mine."

"Sometimes they rig bombs in vehicles, when they're left unattended. Their aim isn't specifically to kill people, but to keep up the atmosphere of terror in the city. They do it very well."

The blaze had caught the timbers of the ferry station over there, and a siren began wailing.

Gabrielle closed her eyes. "I think Colonel Choen is flying on to somewhere else, when he leaves Pouthisat."

"Somewhere other than Phnom Penh."

"Yes."

I didn't ask her where: if she'd caught it, she'd have told me. She pressed the play button again and we sat listening to the tape as another siren started up across the river.

"Colonel Choen is cautioning the two women agents particularly against precipitate action. They sound excited, and he's getting angry with them." She started the tape again, and there was half a minute of voices and then a break and the sound of wood splintering and then nothing much more until the shot. I hadn't had time to switch off the Sony when I'd gone over the balcony rail.

Gabrielle turned her head to look at me. "They saw you?"

"Yes."

"Are you injured?"

"No." I touched her hand. "I'm very grateful to you, Gabrielle."

"It wasn't much to do for you. Not nearly as much as you're trying to do for my people." Soft red light was on her face, from the fire across the river. "Will you go to Pouthisat tomorrow?"

"I don't know."

"I'm sorry. I shouldn't have asked."

I had to make a decision, to do it on instinct, forget the book, let the subconscious weigh the risks, assess the gains, come up with the answer. "The only reason," I said, "why I can't be open with you is that the more you know about me, the more dangerous it is for you. And of course for me, if at any time you're seized by the Khmer Rouge and forced to talk."

"Yes. I understand."

"But there's also this. I'm moving into something, simply as a paid agent, that could turn out to be quite significant to Cambodia at any given stage of the game. How long have you been out here taking photographs?"

"Nearly two years."

She couldn't have sent anything sensational to Paris in the last two years: just pictures of crippled children, the elections, the UN pulling out, Sihanouk's coronation.

"And how long will you stay here?"

"Until Paris recalls me."

The blaze was getting out of control over there and the river was running red. A fire truck had reached the scene and was sending out a jet, backed up to the quayside and sucking water from the Tonle Sap. Whenever she saw a fire, this woman beside me, she was watching her home burning down again, her homeland, Cambodia.

I took the Sony from her and stowed it in the glove compartment and started the engine. "Where did you leave your car?"

"I walked. It's safer."

"I'll drop you off at the hotel."

"All right," she said.

I stopped the Mercedes in the narrow street that ran behind the Royal Palace, and left the engine running. The decision had come up for me on our way here, and I looked at Gabrielle. "In case anything happens in Pouthisat that you might want to photograph, you may decide to fly there tomorrow. If so, where would I contact you, if I needed to?"

She watched me steadily, her eyes dark. "I don't know. I've never left the capital."

"How soon could you find out, assuming you'd be interested?"

"You don't have to do this for me."

"I know."

Two beats, and she said, "I would stay at the French Catholic mission. There'll be one there."

I got out of the car and stood with her for a moment while she touched her mouth on mine and turned away and went through the gate to the hotel gardens, camera slung from her shoulder, not looking back.

9

SPOOK

"How soon can you get me to Pouthisat?" I asked Pringle.

There was a brief silence. It had taken four rings before he'd picked up the phone but it didn't worry me: it was long gone midnight and the mission wasn't in a hot phase and he needed his sleep; later there might not be too much available.

"There's no night flying," he said.

"In the morning, then."

"I'll need a little time."

I looked at the clock in the lobby. I'd given Gabrielle five minutes before I'd come into the hotel by the main entrance. "I'll call you again in half an hour," I told Pringle, "that okay?"

"It depends on how soon I can wake anyone useful. Why Pouthisat?"

"I could have a lead."

Tobacco smoke hung on the air, drifting from the bar.

There was another brief silence on the line. "Indeed. Do you need to debrief?"

"Yes." I hadn't got any real information for him, but if that date—the nineteenth—was important, then yes, I should debrief on the principle that if the executive is in a hostile field he should send in whatever information he's got and as soon as he's got it, in case he gets killed or cut off. "We'll need a rendezvous."

The Vietnamese girl by the big gilded doors took another step, another step back, glanced across me, leaned on the wall again, closing her eyes and letting her red lips part a little.

"Do I bring London in?" Pringle asked me. He meant should he signal Flockhart.

"No. All I've got is access, of a sort."

Colonel Choen.

"Indeed."

I started feeling impatient. Pringle was blowing this whole thing up into a big deal. Access *of a sort* didn't warrant signals to Control, for God's sake.

"Look," I said, "nothing's carved in stone. But I need to get to Pouthisat. I'll call you back in thirty minutes."

The Vietnamese girl took another step, drifted near me, and laced the air with frangipani as I went out through the main entrance, my head turned away from the bar.

The moon was higher in the south by now, its crescent perched with a touch of artistry on the silhouetted minaret of a temple near the river. Smoke still rose from the fire on the far side, and the sound of sirens moaned through the streets in a chorus of echoes.

I waited in the Mercedes, watching the windows of the hotel, not knowing which was hers, Gabrielle's, and not knowing, with the warmth of her mouth on mine lingering in the memory, whether I should have told her I was going to Pouthisat, where it would be even more dangerous for her to know me, contact me. Her credentials were impeccable—she'd been screened, in effect, by Flockhart himself, my control for the mission—and she had her camera, a means of freezing images in the instant, of recording reality unimpaired by the eye's reliance on the brain's interpretation, which could sometimes show the bias of its own judgment. A camera could be useful, even invaluable, at some stage of the game, and if going to Pouthisat could give Gabrielle the chance of a major scoop for Paris I wanted her to have it. Not for the credit, but for Cambodia, the country she loved, was weeping for.

But I was aware, as I waited in the car and watched the lights in the windows over there, that Gabrielle Bouchard had already stirred an undercurrent in the stillness of my psyche that had nothing to do with reasons. And that gave me no excuse for exposing her to danger.

Scruple, thy sting is sharper than the serpent's tooth, therefore shall I pluck thee from my bosom, otherwise I'll never get any bloody sleep.

Pringle picked up on the first ring this time.

"Tomorrow at 07:00 hours," he said, "there'll be a dark green Renault van waiting on the perimeter road to the south of the airport, opposite the Trans-Kampuchean maintenance hangar. It will have MINE ACTION UNIT NO. 6 on the side. The driver's name is Tucker. He'll be your pilot."

"Code-intro?"

"There isn't one. You've been presented simply as an 'observer.' Choose your own name, and whatever you want to observe."

And keep the David Jones cover intact. I liked his thinking. I would have played it that way in any case, but the fact that he'd already got it worked out for me was reassuring; he was beginning to sound more like a pro.

"I get into the back of the van?" I asked him.

"Yes. Tucker will then drive you through the freight-area gates past the guard and take you onto the plane."

An elderly Chinese in a dark silk suit and brilliant shoes came out of the bar and slowed, seeing the girl and then nodding, going out with her through the tall gilded doors, shooting his cuffs and trotting jauntily by her side.

"This is a routine flight?" I asked Pringle.

"No, it's been chartered, through discreet approaches to Mine Action Committee Headquarters." That wasn't bad either, gone midnight and with only thirty minutes to work with.

"Will you be moving?" I asked him.

"Oh yes. You can telephone me at noon at the Hotel Lafayette.

Then we'll meet and chat." Make a rendezvous and debrief.

"Will do."

"Any questions?"

"No."

We shut down the signal.

It was a Siai-Marchetti SM 1019A built for battlefield surveillance, turboprop, observer's door, with a stack of mine detectors rattling aft of the seats as we lifted into the huge red orb of the rising sun and turned to the northwest.

"The Killing Fields," Tucker called out, pointing downward as we cleared the airport, and I had a *frisson* because he sounded like a tour guide and those fields down there weren't a historic monument yet: the whole thing could happen again.

We leveled out at six thousand feet and the mine detectors stopped rattling.

"Been here before?" Tucker asked me. He was stocky, bare-armed, handled the controls in his sleep.

"Yes."

"Been some changes, right?" We were flying over rice paddies now, tobacco crops, savanna grass. "Gonna be some more." He turned his head to look at me, correction, look me over, his eyes intent. "Who are you with? Or is that—"

"I'm just observing. What's the medical situation now?"

"Situation? It's a bloody tragedy. There's one doctor for twenty or thirty thousand people in this country, so most of the health care's done by volunteer services. Call it health care, but a lot of it's a matter of sterilizing the stumps before gangrene can set in. My sister's in the Red Cross out here, Christ knows how she does it, she had a kid in yesterday, fell *right across* a mine, and my sister—her name's Mary—she just started work trying to stop the blood flow while the doctor was throwing up—the *doctor.*" His eyes were hot now, simmering. "You know what I'd do if I ever came across Pol Pot? I'd hang him by the testicles from a sugar palm and watch the crows come in."

In a moment I said, "Is he still dangerous?"

Tucker thought about that, tapping out a tattoo on the control column. Then he said, "Ask me, he's planning a final strike. Look at it this way, he's out there somewhere in the jungle with one fucking dream in his head—bring communism back to Cambodia before he dies—and he's pushing, what, sixty-five now, seventy? But he'll never do it politically, so what are his options? There's only one." He moved his head an inch to watch an aircraft below us on the starboard side, its strobes flashing as it neared. "He's done it before and he knows he can do it again, because the UN won't come back into Cambodia if things blow up, any more than it went into Bosnia."

"Do you see anything," I asked him, "of Pol Pot's troops?"

"Oh, sure. They come and go, mostly on wheels, camouflaged transports and battle dress. But we steer clear of them, be stupid not to, I mean we're not fuckin' kamikaze, you go near those bastards and that's your lot, even the government troops leave 'em alone."

"Have they got a base in Pouthisat?"

"Sure."

"Where is it?"

He turned to look at me. "If I told you that, and it got out to them I told you, I'm dead meat."

"They've got an intelligence cell in Pouthisat?"

"You could call it that. Nothing organized, maybe, it's just that wherever you are you've got to be bloody careful who you talk to. People have disappeared, you know what I'm saying?"

I watched our shadow slipping ahead of us across the savanna grass, rippling as it met groves of sugar palm and then steadying again across the plains.

"Pol Pot's main base," I said, "in the jungle. Is that still in the northwest?"

"I don't know. We get rumors every bloody day—he's moved his army here, he's moved it there. Ask me, he's putting out the rumors himself to keep everyone confused. He could be anywhere."

"You think he's planning an armed coup? At this moment?"

He gave it thought again. "I can't see him fading out gracefully in his old age, which is the only alternative. I'll tell you what one bloke says—and he knows what he's talking about because he runs dope out of Thailand, got his own air service, keeps his eyes open, has to. He says Pol is in the queue for the missiles coming out of Russia illegally and as soon as he gets enough of them he'll put Phnom Penh in his sights and give 'em the good news—either they let him walk in and take over the capital without a shot fired or he'll take it over anyway, what's left of it."

"You think he'd do that?"

"It's like what Mao said, remember? The ultimate power is in the muzzle of the gun, something like that. And Christ knows it's even truer today, with a missile leak in Russia as big as a main drain, not to mention the nukes. Certainly I think Pol Pot would do that, you bet your arse, and it wouldn't be anything new—he used a missile a couple of weeks ago, shot down a plane right after it took off from Phnom Penh one night, wheels weren't even up, blew it out of the sky, Piper Seneca, government-owned, kerboom."

"Is that why there's no more night flying?"

"Right on. It's not been officially banned, it's just that you won't find any pilots daft enough to take off. It's less easy to set up a missile shot in broad daylight."

"Why was the Seneca shot down?"

Tucker turned his head to look at me. "The one I hear most often is that it had a government intelligence agent on board, famous for putting his nose in Pol Pot's business."

"It sounds as if he was careless."

"Right on. You've only got to make one little mistake with Pol Pot, and that's your lot."

"Have you heard," I asked in a moment, "of a General Kheng?"

"Kheng? Can't say I have. But I mean this place is full of bloody generals. Why?"

"Just trying to catch up, my first day here for a while."

"Right, go ahead. I don't know too much but I hear plenty of rumors."

"Does the nineteenth mean anything to you?"

"That's a date?"

"Yes. I don't know which month, but probably this one."

"Search me, then. It's not a feast day or anything—Chaul Chhnam's next month, Cambodian New Year, that's the nearest."

"Okay. How many British nationals are there in Pouthisat at the moment, as a rough estimate?"

"Not all that many, now the UN's pulled out. But I run across them in the Food Services and the church missions and the Red Cross, places like that, all volunteers, of course."

"Would you imagine," I asked carefully, "that any of them could be undercover intelligence people?"

"Brits?"

"Yes."

Specifically, DI6. If they were operating out here they wouldn't be likely to tell the Bureau.

"Search me," Tucker said. "I mean how would I know, if they're undercover?"

"Some people aren't too careful. Like the man in the Piper Seneca."

"Right, but there's nobody," he said, giving himself time to think, "who comes across as a shadow, to my mind."

I watched the patches of sugar-palm jungle slipping below us, wondering where Tucker had picked up that particular word. Not many people outside the intelligence services use it—no one I've ever met.

"You talk to a lot of Brits?" I asked him.

"We've got one or two in Mine Action, of course. Volunteers again, along with some French and Italians, Germans, Aussies, Yanks, you name it, people left over from the UN forces. I dropped out of the Royal Engineers myself, thought I'd put my training to a bit of good use out here where it's wanted. Never thought

I'd make Cambodia my field, but life's full of surprises, isn't it?"

"How very true." Because that was another word—"field."

Standing on its own it didn't amount to much—scientists had fields, doctors, lawyers. But coupled with "shadow" it was more interesting. The problem with another intelligence service working the same field is that we can sometimes trip over each other's courier lines; it's not even unknown for an agent to find himself on another's terrain, especially at night, when a lot of the work is done—and that can be dangerous. Feldrake was operating a photo-reconnaissance assignment in Iraq at the end of the Gulf War and crossed paths with a DI6 agent in a night action, and they surprised the hell out of each other and Feldrake took the DI6 man for an Iraqi shadow and put him down, and there are still representations going on with the Prime Minister aimed at liaison between the two services. But it couldn't ever work: the Bureau doesn't officially exist, and it's got to stay that way. All we can do is check out the field as we go in, to see if there's anyone else in the shadows.

"When do we land?" I asked Tucker.

"Half an hour." He looked at me deadpan. "But if you want to get into signals, you can use the radio."

"You *bastard*," I said, and he exploded into a laugh. "Get into signals" was strictly Bureau-speak.

"Think I was DI6 or something?" Deadpan again, the tone indignant.

"Are you still active, Tucker?"

"No. I played it too wild, got sacked, went into the RE's for a bit, worked on bomb disposal, more fun, less bullshit. But I can still spot a shadow when I see one. After Pol Pot, are we?"

"I'm after information."

"On that bastard? You must be off your fuckin' rocker—you like life short and sweet, is that it?" He reached for his headset and put it on, calling up the tower in Pouthisat.

The flat white waters of the Tonle Sap lake were already spread diagonally across the plains ahead of us, and we came down with the sun three diameters high above the east horizon and the air already heating up as we crossed the dusty apron from the plane to the freight sheds.

"You need a hand with those mine detectors?" I asked Tucker.

"Nope, there'll be a crew coming. But you'll want some wheels, right?"

"Yes. All-terrain."

"We'll go and see Jimmy. And leave the talking to me, okay? He'll have the skin off your back if he doesn't know you."

Jimmy was an energetic young Vietnamese, holed up in a huddle of tin-roofed sheds on the airfield perimeter track, a flash of gold teeth and lots of nodding as Tucker spoke to him in his own language, then switched to English.

"Jimmy, this guy's a friend of mine, you know what I'm saying?" He turned to me. "Jimmy says he doesn't understand the Queen's English, but that's just so he can screw you on the deal—hey, Jimmy, your flies are undone—there he goes, see what I mean?"

"All new here," Jimmy said, blushing, "all new vehicles, cost me lot of money to buy them, what you looking for?"

"We're looking for a jeep, Jimmy, four-wheel drive, new tires—what about that one?"

"If it's in good shape," I said. It had camouflage paintwork and the springs looked even and the headlamps still had glass in them but that didn't tell us anything about the big ends or the rocker arms.

"Start her up, Jimmy," Tucker said, and we listened to the engine and I rocked the front wheel bearings and bumped the shocks and looked under the crankcase for leaks.

"I'll take it," I said.

"Okay, Jimmy, the gent's going to take it, so I'll tell you—"

"Hundred thousand riels," Jimmy said, flashing gold, "for day."

"So I'll tell you what we'll do," Tucker said. "We'll give you fifty thousand for the first two days in cash right now and we'll make it twenty thousand a day after that, start with a tankful and that tidy little dent in the rear wing, and if—"

"Hundred thousand," Jimmy said, flashing his gold assets, "for day."

"And if you can't meet those terms," Tucker told him pleasantly, "I'm going to bring in the drug enforcement guys and they'll go through this place with sniffer dogs and you'll spend the rest of your life in the torture cells in Phumi Prison and you'll wish to Christ you'd said yes to our handsome offer of fifty the first two days and twenty thereafter, you want me to repeat that, do you, Jimmy?"

I paid in cash.

There were two canvas water bags slung outboard on the jeep but I drove round to the front of the airfield terminal and picked up half a dozen sealed plastic bottles of Evian water from the concession and stowed them behind the driver's seat. I didn't know where I'd be going today, or how far, and at noon the sky would be a hot brass dome across the city and the plains.

By nine o'clock the sun was already over the mountains southeast by east of the town, and the heat waves were spilling molten silver across the airfield. In the distance the sugar palms leaned along the horizon like a broken palisade, and I saw egrets on the wing, black against the blinding sky.

There was no shade for the jeep that wouldn't block out my view of the landing strip and the tower on one side, the freight sheds and the hangars on the other. But the canvas top was up and I had my sunglasses on against the glare. The runway slanted across my visual field, broken away at the edges and streaked with black rubber, and I saw a rat as big as a pig darting across it, God knows whence or on what errand.

I began watching the sky to the south.

10

················◆◆◆◆◆◆◆◆◆◆◆◆◆◆◆◆◆◆◆◆◆◆◆◆◆◆◆◆◆◆◆◆◆◆◆◆◆◆◆·············

LEOPARD

It was an hour before a black splinter floated into the glare above
the horizon, the sun flashing on it as it began turning into its descent, becoming an aircraft, drifting on its flight path above the
foothills to the southwest with its strobe sparking in the saffron
haze as the landing gear came down and its profile tilted as it settled toward the runway, a Czechoslovakian-built L410 Turbolet flying the Trans-Kampuchean insignia at the tail.

It was a passenger plane, so I started the jeep and moved
round the perimeter track to the terminal building and
parked near the bus station and walked across to the Arrivals
wing, finding adequate cover on the far side and well clear of the
car-rental desks and the newsstand and the baggage carousel and
the toilets.

Fourteen passengers came through, one of them Pringle, none
of them Colonel Choen. I had never seen Choen, but I would
know him when I did.

Pringle wasn't looking around for me, wouldn't expect me to be
here, wouldn't expect me to approach him even if I was.

I went back to the jeep and took up station again halfway between the terminal building and the freight sheds.

The rising heat shimmered like a lake across the runway, and I
sat with my eyes closed now behind the sunglasses to protect the

retinas from the glare, checking the south horizon at intervals through the slits of my lids.

11:10, but this one wasn't coming in: it was a Beriev Tchaika amphibian, lowering across the east toward the Tonle Sap.

Noon plus twelve and a Skyvan 3M came rumbling out of the south like an elephant, and I started the jeep again and moved toward the freight sheds and was there when the crew came off, three Caucasians, one of them limping, all of them lighting cigarettes as they walked across to the office.

At noon I opened the first bottle of Evian and drank half, holding it like a trumpet and seeing beyond it the helicopter moving in from the south, lower than the other aircraft had been, tracing its path across the mountains to the southeast now and turning, making its approach, fifteen degrees high. I put the cap back on the bottle and stowed it with the others, not taking my eyes off the chopper, noting the camouflage paint, the absence of any insignia, simply the identification letters, FKYP, the strobe flashing, the fronds of the sugar palms waving under the downdraft from the twin rotors, a Kamov KA-26, touching down within fifty yards of the freight sheds as I started up again and found cover between a hangar and the loading dock as a camouflaged staff car with the fabric top raised came in from the perimeter road and pulled up, two men in battle fatigues dropping to the ground and going toward the helicopter as the rotors slowed and the cabin door came open.

I could hear his voice already, barking an order to the pilot, and his walk was as I'd expected, a militarily correct parade-ground strut as he crossed the apron, snapping back a salute to the two men and swinging himself into the staff car on the front passenger's side, barking again as the driver got in and asked him something and nodded quickly and started the engine.

Colonel Choen.

Access—of a sort. Access to General Kheng and finally to Pol Pot, if I got it right.

Your first *objective,* Pringle had told me at Phnom Penh airport, *is to gain information on that man.*

So I waited until the car was through the gates and halfway round the perimeter road and then took up the tag.

I watched the mirror.

Thirty-five minutes ago the staff car had stopped outside a white two-story building next to a temple, their walls bullet-scarred and covered with faded slogans. Colonel Choen and one of his escorts had gone into the building. The other man, the driver, was leaning against the car, smoking his third cigarette.

An hour and fifteen minutes ago I should have telephoned Pringle at the Hotel Lafayette, but that was when the helicopter was landing, and I'd had no chance since. The traffic in Pouthisat was the same as in Phnom Penh: motorized vehicles with native drivers plowed through everything else on the narrow streets—cyclos, oxen, pushcarts, bikes, dogs, and chickens, and it had been difficult to keep track of the staff car without moving in too close.

Now I sat watching the mirror.

It would have been nice to fish out the half-bottle of Evian from behind the seat, but I wanted to keep movement to the minimum. I was parked facing away from the building where Choen had gone in, with the jeep tight against the wall of a storage shed. The plastic rear window, scratched and yellowed, wasn't wide enough to let the Khmer driver see anything of my silhouette unless I moved, even if he took any interest. He was a rebel soldier, not an espion; if he'd been in our trade I couldn't have parked the jeep here at all.

The heat pressed down, and instead of thinking about the bottle of Evian I thought about *Salamander.* It was beginning to look like a full-blown mission, despite the fact that we had no signals board in London, no contacts or couriers in the field. We had, at least, access of a sort: I was keeping surveillance on an officer in Pol Pot's forces and it might not turn out to be totally a waste of time. He might well come out of that building and get into his car and be taken back to the airfield and the helicopter: the driver had been told to wait for him. But if so, I at least had a fix on the building itself and could make a night reconnaissance, given the absence of guards, or the absence of guards difficult—in terms of number—to silence and subdue.

It was beginning to seem conceivable that Flockhart, my control in London, wasn't totally out of his mind. He needed—for whatever reason—information on Pol Pot, and the only way he could normally expect to get it was by forming his own little army of military intelligence troops and sending them in—and they would have to be Asian, ideally Cambodian or Vietnamese. But the Bureau hasn't got any Asian troops, nor is it equipped to recruit any, administratively, economically, or politically.

The driver was lighting his fourth cigarette from the butt of the third, dragging the smoke in deep and holding it, not a man, you would say, with enough oxygen available in his muscles to afford him much endurance, if he were, for example, attacked. But then of course he had his Chinese-made assault rifle, if you were slow enough to let him use it.

The Bureau, moreover, hasn't got even *one* Asian on its shadow executive staff, or he would have been the obvious choice for *Salamander*. All Flockhart had had when he dined with me at the Cellar Steps was a standard-model ferret bored out of his gourd after six weeks without a mission, someone who would take anything on simply to keep his nerves in tune.

And Holmes had known that when we'd sat in the Caff drinking Daisy's undrinkable tea.

You know Mr. Flockhart? He's quite good. Some people find him a bit on the enigmatic side, doesn't give much away. He also comes and goes, runs a mission or two and disappears for a while.

For a control like that—senior, with the ability to pick and choose—I had been the perfect choice: seasoned enough to work an operation where a single shadow could conceivably get through to the objective while a whole battalion might fail, and desperate enough to take it on.

So I found it comforting, as I watched the Khmer driver chain-light his fifth cigarette in the mirror, to realize that Flockhart might not simply have chosen to set me running in a manifestly doomed mission just to find out if I had a chance in a thousand of bringing it home.

We seek comfort, my good friend, we the stalwart ferrets in the field, where we can find it.

The sun's weight pressed down on the canvas top of the jeep; its light shimmered along the bonnet and sent reflections fanning against the wall of the storage shed; the day staggered under the burden of the afternoon sky. No one was moving in the narrow angle of the street that was all I could see through the windscreen.

Three women had passed, minutes ago, their sarongs clinging to their stick-like bodies, their faces dark and featureless in the shade of their raffia hats as they pushed their cart along, piled with junk—to them, presumably, treasure, the sum of their worldly goods. People were leaving the cities, Gabrielle had told me, hoping to find safety in the countryside, in the mountains, in the rice fields, before whatever was to happen to Cambodia cut short their lives.

A cyclo driver had followed them, minutes later, bowed over his rusting handlebars half-comatose, a gaunt dog lurching after him, one eye lost beneath a black cluster of flies.

The Khmer driver lit another cigarette, took a turn, kicking the baked mud of the street with his boot, hitching his assault rifle higher, took a turn back, then looked suddenly up at the steps of the two-story building.

1:57, and Colonel Choen came down to the street with his escort and climbed into the car.

Sweat cooled on my shoulders as I sat up straight and put my fingers onto the ignition key, watching the mirror, waiting. The staff car was facing away from the town, from the airfield, and if it was going to turn back it would take the next side street and turn left again and come past the storage shed. That was all right: I wouldn't by then be visible below the windscreen; there would simply be a jeep standing here.

If the staff car kept on going in the same direction I would need to catch up, but at a distance. That was all right too, but less easy: it would need noisy bursts of acceleration in the silence of the siesta hours.

I started up and waited for thirty seconds, forty, fifty, heard the sound of the staff car fading and moved off and took a right and a right and a left and saw it ahead of me, bouncing across potholes in the distance, and we settled down at five hundred yards, heading out of the city and then taking a road south, with the foothills forming along the horizon and the sun high and in front of us, casting short shadows.

There was no other traffic and I dropped back, letting the staff car increase the distance to a mile and checking the mirror, hoping for moving cover, but there was nothing coming up behind.

A bullock cart lay on its side near the road, the beast still harnessed, lowing and kicking; I couldn't see the driver. Egrets crossed the skyline in a black skein against the glare of the sun, dipping toward water somewhere. A girl sat on a pile of rice bags near a track to a farm, nursing an infant, her round raffia hat shading it from the sun. A snake, crushed by wheels, lay across the road in the shape of a question mark.

In fifteen kilometers we were among the foothills and I closed the distance between us, reaching behind me for the bottle of Evian and draining it in gulps and dropping it back behind the seat as the road began twisting between outcrops and I had to close up again, this time to within three or four hundred yards of the staff car, less, too close, too close for comfort, dropping back again, letting its profile shrink into the distance.

Potholes suddenly, and the jeep shuddered, the tires skating across the surface, and I had to let the speed die, couldn't touch the brakes. The sun swung to the right, to the left, to the right again, and then steadied as the road straightened and I saw it running ahead, empty now, no staff car.

I didn't think they'd seen me and increased their speed. They wouldn't do that. If they'd seen me and wanted to know why I was on this road behind them they'd just slow and block my path and stop and ask questions; these were the Khmer Rouge.

They'd turned off somewhere, at a time when they'd been out of sight past an outcrop.

I swung the jeep in a U-turn and gunned up.

Access of a sort, providing I didn't lose the target—a hundred kph on the clock and then slowing through the hills, seeing nothing, the sun swinging behind me now, bringing relief from the glare.

Target not seen.

A stretch of potholes again and I hit the brakes in time and let the jeep skitter across them, one of the headlights shattering to the vibration, glass tinkling against the bodywork in the slipstream.

Target still not seen but there was a track to the left, hidden by boulders until I was almost on it, had to use the brakes and let the rear end swing through the U as I gunned up to get the traction back and then turned to follow the track, baked mud and loose stones, the surface natural, the way ahead formed simply by the passage of wheels over the passage of time.

A small leopard vaulted a rock and turned to watch the jeep go past.

Target.

The sun flashing across its rear window as it turned in the distance ahead and below me among the hills as the track descended, stones rattling under the chassis.

We were in a ravine, with rocks rising on each side, their shadows on the right, sharper now, the air less humid. I let the speed die again, losing the staff car from sight but not worrying. There wouldn't be another track leading away from this one: the terrain was too steep, too rocky.

Flash and I saw the target again, much smaller now. But even at this distance I wouldn't be safe if they looked back and saw the jeep; this wasn't a public road, and any vehicle on it would belong to the forces of the Khmer Rouge. This was their private territory. It wouldn't have been possible to get even this far if I hadn't chosen a camouflaged vehicle, but that wouldn't help me if they took an interest and brought me to a stop.

There would have to be a break-off point: at some time I would need to decide when I was as close as I could go to the target without risking exposure.

Flash and the staff car was turning again, but this time onto a side track where the rocks gave way to flat terrain half a mile across and covered with dark green foliage—scrub or short trees, from this distance I couldn't tell which.

Then the target vanished.

It hadn't turned to one side or the other: the sun had been steady on the rear window, then had gone out like a lamp switched off.

I cut down my speed, rolled for a hundred yards, and put the jeep onto a slope of firm ground that would let me turn without having to back up, give me a chance to get out fast if I had to. Then I sat looking at the flat green terrain down there, some kind of plantation except for the rocks strewn across it, no individual bushes, no clearly defined trees, just a stretch of—right, got it now—camouflage netting.

This was how the staff car had vanished like that in an instant, passing under the edge of the screen and out of sight.

The camp was perfectly placed, too far from the main track to attract visitors and too far west of the airfield in Pouthisat to be seen from the lowering flight paths. But even so, it had been decided to rig the camouflage screen to provide total concealment from the air.

I switched off the engine, because this was the break-off point. I was as close as I could get to the target, was too close, even, for safety: if there were guards mounted there at the camp's perimeter the jeep would be in sight of them.

The heat lay across the canyon, the sun burning its path through the sky to the south and touching fire from the rocks, dazzling the eye, leaving the lungs stifled. Under the spread of camouflage down there it would be cooler; perhaps that too was its purpose.

There was nothing more I could do here. I couldn't hope to infiltrate an armed camp, even by night; let it be enough that I had a fix on it; the day hadn't been wasted. But as I reached for the ignition I stopped and froze as a sound came into the silence, echoing among the rocks. Another vehicle was on the move, coming the way we had come, and I slipped across the passenger's seat and dropped to the ground, crouching, listening to the sound of tires scattering loose stones, one of them hitting the side of the jeep with the force of a bullet.

They would see the jeep standing here, not far from the track, couldn't miss it. It was camouflaged, a military or paramilitary vehicle—that was why I'd chosen it—but it didn't carry any kind of insignia. Had the staff car carried insignia? I hadn't been close enough to the rear to see if it had or not. Did *all* the Khmer Rouge vehicles have insignia? It was important, because if they did, the one moving past me now would hit the brakes and slide to a halt across the stones and boots would thud to the ground and the driver would come walking across.

I waited.

Exhaust gas came drifting, and another stone hit the jeep and the nerves jerked because it was so like a shot.

Insignia. Did they carry insignia, the transports of the Khmer Rouge forces?

The vehicle wasn't slowing; no brakes, no boots. It was alongside now and still moving at the same speed, equipment, maybe a spade, rattling in its straps to the vibration. Voices, calling in Khmer above the noise. What were they saying? What's that jeep doing there, it's not one of ours, there's no insignia?

No. They weren't interested, hadn't noticed anything wrong with it, assumed the jeep was out of petrol and that the driver had walked to the camp to fetch some.

Moving on, they were moving on, and I gave them sixty seconds and climbed back into the jeep and started up straightaway, using the other vehicle's engine as sound cover as it rolled into the camp past the guards.

Were there guards? That was important too.

Started up and made a tight turn and drove back along the track, using the manual gear change to shift ratios with as few revs as the engine could take, keeping the noise down.

So you located the camp and came away, with no opposition?

I was lucky. There weren't any guards at the perimeter.

The sun on my right now and a little behind me, stones banging under the wings, the canvas top flexing as the chassis twisted to the uneven surface of the track, nothing in the mirrors until the flash came, the flash of the sun across glass a mile behind me, the glass of a windscreen, the windscreen of a vehicle on the move.

My thoughts on the debriefing had been premature, then, presumptuous, counting chickens, *shit*, we need policy here, and make it quick.

I could gun up and try driving my way out but I didn't know what vehicle they were using—it could be half as powerful as mine, or twice. There would be two men on board: if they were coming to check out the jeep there would be two of them, both armed. Add, then, the weight of one man plus the weight of his assault rifle and ammunition belt, but that wouldn't give me any advantage if they were driving something more powerful.

Policy, then? Because if we're going to make a run for it we'd better start *now.*

The flash came again, brighter. They were closing the distance, coming flat out, the vehicle bouncing, the windscreen flashing like a semaphore, it wasn't just a routine transport leaving the camp.

There had, then, been guards, and they'd seen the jeep when I'd turned, and they'd sounded the alert.

Decision, yes, and this was it, not terribly sophisticated: I couldn't hope to drive clear, because it was daylight and I was stuck on this one narrow track and they could start picking me off at any time now, any time they wanted to.

So relax—fifty kph on the clock and I left it like that, medium speed, out for a Sunday afternoon drive, this was a pleasant route, winding through the rocks, wildflowers here and there, yellow and red, a scenic route, you might say, we must bring Fred and Gertrude here next weekend, they'll really—

Shots, just a short burst, and then fluting overhead, a warning, then, their aim couldn't be that bad at half a mile. I didn't slow, waited for the second burst, got it, took my foot off the throttle, stuck my hand out of the window and waved, yes, I've got the message, hold your bloody fire.

I was stationary at the side of the track when they arrived, two men in military fatigues with red-checked *kramas*, both carrying assault rifles as they jumped down from their Chinese-built jeep while I sat with my hands on the wheel, raising them as they prodded with their guns, shouting Khmer in my face.

"English," I said. "*Anglae*." It was one of the few words I knew.

More shouting while one of them looked around inside the jeep, turning the cushions over, scattering the bottles of Evian water.

"*Qui es toi?*" the other one asked, using the familiar, but of course, the Khmer Rouge can do that, they can do anything they like.

"*Je suis anglais.*" I used one hand, cautiously, to show them my papers, and they took their time to look at them, didn't give them back. My papers, I said indignantly, give me my papers back, not bloody likely, who do you think you are, working out the odds, I was working out the odds while they walked slowly round the jeep, not looking for anything, simply showing me they weren't going to miss anything, I was to take them seriously, even with those red-checked *kramas* round their heads, a dishcloth is a dishcloth, whatever you choose to call it.

Then one of them slapped the bonnet and shouted *"Viens!"* and jerked his head toward their jeep.

"Mais j'ai trompé de chemin," I said indignantly, *"c'est tout!"* Missed the road, that was all, but he wasn't interested, pushed his rifle into my chest. The other one joined in, so I said *"Merde!"* and left it at that, having established my cover story, and climbed out of my jeep and into theirs, one of the bastards going too close to the spine with his gun, prodding my back, no respect for the vertebrae, and *this* is one of the things, the many things, that can tilt the balance and leave you undone, a pinched nerve robbing you of agility just when you need it most—we shall have to start thinking now, my good friend, of things like that, start making preparations in the mind; that's a hornet's nest down there, if you'll forgive the cliché, and my presence has been requested, so that death might not be long in coming unless we are nimble: these are the Khmer Rouge, and they murdered a million souls in the Killing Fields.

You've only got to make one little mistake with Pol Pot, and that's your lot. Tucker, drumming his fingers on the control column of the Siai-Marchetti. *People have disappeared, you know what I'm saying?*

Yes indeed.

Then one of them got behind the wheel and started up while the other dragged my jacket half off and used the sleeves to bind my arms behind me; then he whipped the *krama* off his head and tied it round my eyes and pulled it tight; it smelled of sweat and something else—hair oil? Scents were important now because we were in a red sector and I couldn't see anything—scents, sounds, tactile impressions, whatever information I could pick up, however slight; I might need to recognize this man again, and the hair oil might do it for me if he came close enough.

Bloody gun in my ribs, to remind me not to do anything silly; he hadn't cleaned the barrel for God knew how long, I could smell it, these weren't the Queen's Light Infantry.

Stones pinging from under the tires as we bumped our way down to the camp, the driver shouting something in Khmer and my escort shouting back, *We going to put him against a wall, are we?* But we must use the mind for preparation, yes, not for glum conjecture.

Twilight suddenly, cast by the camouflage net as we rolled to a halt, no more than a lessening of the light at the edges of the *krama* by a few degrees but enough to inform me. A strong smell of canvas—the camouflage net—and diesel oil, rubber, cooking stoves, tobacco smoke, chickens.

The rifle prodding again. "*Bouges-pas!*" Don't move, but of course not, with my arms bound, what would it profit me, you *espèce d'idiot?*

The other man had gone off—to fetch someone in authority?—but my escort stayed close, the muzzle of his gun resting against my chest the whole time. There was a line of light along the top of the blindfold but even when I turned my eyes upward as far as they'd go there was no useful vision taking place: it was just peripheral, capable of detecting movement but no images.

"Look," I said in French, "you're making a mistake."

The man didn't answer.

"And that's okay," I said. "People make mistakes. I do it all the time. But the thing is, my government isn't going to like—"

He told me to shut the fuck up and when the other man came back they hustled me across the camp to a concrete cell and threw me inside and slammed the door and locked it.

11

CHOEN

Bare walls, bare floor, cracks in the concrete, streaks of dried blood near the door, a sandal lying in a corner with the strap broken, human feces, dried, not fresh, they hadn't put anyone else in here recently, the door made of metal, streaks of rust where rain had come in through the gap at the top, the lock massive, the only light coming through a grille in the ceiling.

I'd twisted my arms free of the jacket and then taken the blindfold off as soon as my escorts had gone; that was some time ago, perhaps two hours. I hadn't untied the sleeves or the knot of the *krama*. When I heard them coming back I would restore the image of the helpless captive, because that was what I wanted to show them—a man who didn't even try to free himself when left on his own, who would not, therefore, be expected to make any attempt to escape.

There had been vehicle movement during the time I'd been here, regular, routine, as if base maneuvers were being conducted under cover of the camouflage net. At least one of the vehicles was a half-track or a tank—I heard the links rolling—and once I caught the gear-whine of a gun turret swiveling. But most of it was light stuff, its exhaust gas smelling of petrol engines, not diesel.

In between the bursts of mechanical noise I'd heard chickens clucking, the falsely reassuring sound of a sleepy farmyard: those smooth brown eggs had supplied the fats and proteins to the human muscle that would keep this intruder overpowered, perhaps drag him to the wall and squeeze the trigger.

Getting thirsty.

In the small grille overhead there was no direct sunlight, but by its waning strength I put the time at close to five, on the threshold of evening. They'd taken my watch, of course: the impoverished soldiery always enjoys toys. It's also the first and essential step in the process of disorientation, denying the captive the knowledge of time, but in this case I didn't think they'd be keeping me here long: if they thought I was an intelligence agent they'd do what they'd done to the one in the Piper Seneca at Phnom Penh airport.

Another diesel engine rattled suddenly into the first few hundred revs and stayed there, sending exhaust gas through the gap under the door, and of course I thought of Auschwitz and it didn't improve my day. Not that they'd take the time for that sort of thing if they decided to write me off: they'd use the bullet, their favorite toy of all.

Hot in here, and the thirst was getting worse. I would ask for some water when they came back: they'd expect me to, and that would conform to the first principles: *Never worry your captors, we* tell the neophytes at Norfolk. *Do what they expect you to do, keep them relaxed, get them to trust you, so that when you make your break you'll surprise them. Never underestimate the value of surprise: in any delicate situation it can gain you at least a second, sometimes even more, and that can save your life if you've planned your break with care and the timing is critical.* The "delicate" is classic Holmes: he delights in understatement.

The drumming of the big diesel died away, and now I heard boots nearing, crunching over the stones. For the fifth time I twisted back into my jacket and slipped the *krama* over my eyes and waited, dropping and sitting against the wall with my hands over my knees and my head drooping, even when the door was banged open and the boots came in. Then I raised it, as if I could see.

"*Who are you?*" In French, with an atrocious accent. But it was the bark that got my attention.

"I gave them my papers," I said. Tone weary, resigned.

A rush of Khmer and someone came and whipped the blindfold off, not Choen, one of his men—but on Choen's orders: he wanted to see my eyes, to tell when I lied.

"I not ask about your *papers*. I ask who you *are*."

He wasn't a short man, for an Oriental, but stood with his chest out and his shoulders back as if he sensed he ought to put on a bit of height; or it was simply a caricature of the pigeon-chested parade-ground posture. His face was flat and his mouth pulled down in an expression of arrogance, inflexibility; his eyes were narrowed and unblinking, one of them not perfectly aligned with the other. His red-checked *krama* had some sort of emblem pinned at the side; perhaps it signified his rank.

I struggled onto my feet. "Can I have a drink of water?"

"*Who are you?*"

"David Jones," I said. "And you?"

I didn't expect him to answer that one but he pulled his shoulders back another half inch and said, "I am Colonel Choen of Khmer Rouge army."

"How do you do, Colonel?"

He ignored this, as expected. "What are you doing on private road out there?" he asked me.

"I told your people—I lost my way."

"What was destination when you 'lose way'?"

"I was trying to find the lake."

"In *this* direction?"

"Look, Colonel, I arrived in Cambodia only a—"

"In *Kampuchea*!"

"Oh, right, yes, Kampuchea. I've only been here a few days, so I haven't really got my bearings yet. I thought—"

"Why you want to find Tonle Sap?" The lake.

"I'm with Trans-Kampuchean Air Services. We're thinking of running a Beriev Tchaika amphibian service to the coast, bringing fish into Phnom Penh, pretty well straight out of the nets. The hotels—"

"You alone in jeep?"

"Yes. Look, I'm sorry if I was trespassing, but—"

"Yes. Will be sorry. Yes."

"For God's sake, can't anyone lose their way in this country?"

Choen looked quickly at the private, and as his hand came up and across I turned my head away just late enough to let him feel he'd made an impact; then I went through the business of crashing against the wall and hitting the floor and grunting in pain and so on, which was easy enough to do with my arms still pinned behind me.

"Why you come to Kampuchea?"

I got onto my feet again. "Well, quite a few reasons. For—"

"*Why you come?*"

The private's hand moved and I waited but he didn't do anything this time. "I was with the UN, originally, and then when I—"

"*UN stupid idiots!*" He spat, accurately, at my face, and I would have done a great deal to be able to wipe it off. "This is not their country! This Kampuchea! What this country?" It sounded like a question, and he came forward a step, chest out, one eye staring, brighter than the other. "*What this country?*"

The private lifted his hand in readiness.

"What? Oh. Right. Kampuchea. *Kampuchea.*" It was the name they preferred, these people: when the Khmer Rouge had been in control of the country they'd insisted on it, then it was changed back to Cambodia after their defeat. They hadn't liked that. This man didn't like it. His spittle was drying on my face: think of something else.

"UN stupid!" he barked again. "You English?"

"Yes." I'd told him that already.

"English stupid idiots! Queen of England stupid cow!"

"I rather think otherwise," I said.

"You meet Queen of England?"

"Actually, no."

I could really use a glass of water.

"You fuck Princess Diana?"

"I've yet to enjoy that privilege."

Knew his London tabloids, kept up with high society.

Suddenly he turned at right angles and strutted to the wall and back to the one opposite, boots grating on the concrete, back to the door, turned, looked at me.

"Who know you in jeep?"

"I'm sorry, I don't quite follow."

"Who know you in jeep? Answer!"

"Who knew I was driving the jeep?" Oh, right, this was rather important. "Who knew I was going to the Tonle Sap?"

"Yes."

"My manager," I said, "and the head of the airline, some of the staff, two of my friends, a few other people. I was given the assignment, you understand."

"When they last see you?"

Things didn't sound terribly good. "When I left our office. That was—oh, about one o'clock."

British agent for Trans-Kampuchean Air Services reported missing. Just joking; the only person who'd miss me was Pringle, biding his time in the Hotel Lafayette, ready to pick up on the first ring: I hadn't signaled at noon, so I was technically overdue.

Choen was eyeing me steadily, his mouth pulled down. "Jeep rented, or belong to airline?"

"It belongs to the airline. Look, I happen to be a man who can keep his mouth shut, Colonel. I strayed onto your territory by accident, but there's no need for me to tell anybody I saw anything; it's none of my business—or theirs. All I'm interested in is working out how we can fly fish to the capital from the lake."

He didn't say anything, seemed to be waiting to hear more, stood watching my face, one eye filmy, the other bright, deep now, concentrating. So I took it from there, because maybe there was a chance he'd just leave me here in the cell without water or food for a couple of days, have me roughed up a little to warn me off, and then kick me out, have me dropped back on the main road.

"I agree the UN was wrong," I told him reasonably, "to come busting into your country, and quite frankly I wasn't sorry when they pulled out. But I'd got to know the place by then, and"—with a shrug—"I'd met a Kampuchean woman here, you know? I'm see-ing her again . . . she's very pretty."

The private was staring at me too with his lidless eyes, probably didn't understand what I was saying, was just watching for a wrong move. I didn't have one in mind.

"I was a bit embarrassed, I suppose," I told the colonel, "to give you my real reason at first for coming back to Kampuchea. *Cherchez la femme*, right?"

A diesel rumbled past, one of its tires sending a stone banging against the metal door. The noise was unexpected and hellishly loud in these close confines but the colonel didn't flinch.

I left it at that, didn't want to overdo things. I was interested now in how Choen was going to answer me. A lot depended on it.

But he didn't say anything at all. He turned to the private and barked some Khmer at him and the private swung round and pulled the door open and yelled something and another man came trotting up with his assault rifle and gave the colonel the revolu-tionary salute with his fist, but Choen didn't respond. He just looked at me and then at the two men and raised his elbow to the side and held one finger straight against his temple for an instant and took it away with a little jerk and walked out of the cell.

Let there be a rose, then, for Moira.

12

EXECUTION

Three half-tracks, two personnel carriers, a dozen Chinese-built jeeps, and an armored car. Five or six rows of bamboo huts, a concrete building next to the cell, a big wood-fired stove with a corrugated iron roof over it to protect the camouflage net.

A dozen rebels standing around leaning on their vehicles, laughing and chattering in Khmer when they saw me led out of the cell by the two guards: a round-eye in the camp was an event.

I couldn't see my jeep anywhere; maybe it was still out there on the track through the mountains, and they were going to bring it in later.

My guards hadn't put the blindfold back on; I don't think they'd forgotten to; it was just that they knew it didn't matter now what I saw here, I wasn't going to tell anybody.

They pushed me into the jeep, my arms still tied behind me by the sleeves of my jacket. One of them got behind the wheel and the other sat beside me with the muzzle of his assault rifle dug into my side. I could smell his hair oil: he was the one who'd spoken in French when they'd seized me.

The air came in hot waves against my face as we set off, and when we left the shade of the camouflage net the sun was below the foothills and the sky was deepening toward the west. The infrared had been pouring into the canyon all day long, leaving a flood of heat for us to drive through.

"I told your colonel the truth, you know," I called in French to the man next to me above the rattling of the jeep. "I haven't any interest in politics, or who runs this country."

He didn't answer, dug the gun harder into my side. The driver twisted his head round and called out something in Khmer, asking what I'd said, I suppose. I was glad he was interested: it could make a difference.

"All I want is to increase my employer's business. The airline's doing pretty well already, and this would make me quite a bit of money, as a bonus."

The shadow of the jeep ran ahead of us, twenty or thirty feet long, rippling over the stones and the tufts of scrub in the middle of the track. Farther ahead I saw my jeep, standing where I'd left it, and we began slowing. So it had just been a joke on the part of Colonel Choen when he'd put his finger against his head like that: what he'd barked to the soldier in Khmer was an order for him to take me back to my jeep and let me go, because I'd convinced him I'd lost my way.

Then there's the one about Little Red Riding Hood and the wicked wolf who dressed up as her grandmother and everything.

"So I'm just a businessman," I said to the guard, "that's all, looking for profit. Are you a businessman?"

The gun prodded. He knew perfectly well what I was saying: his French had been fluent, idiomatic, the few times he'd spoken.

"My freedom means a lot to me," I told him. "So what about ten million riels to share between you and your comrade?"

His head turned to look at me as we slowed alongside my jeep and pulled up. They were going, then, to drive it back to the camp when they'd finished with me.

"Ask your comrade," I told the guard, "what he thinks of ten million riels, in cash."

He went on watching me. In Cambodia that amount of money

would set them up in business as travel agents, buy them a brand-new Volga.

He didn't say anything. The engine of the jeep idled.

"With ten million," I told him, "you could buy a brand-new Volga, or set yourselves up in business, or buy enough raw cocaine coming through from Thailand to turn ten million into a thousand. You want to think about that? A thousand million riels?"

The man behind the wheel switched off the engine and looked round at us, jerking his chin up, wanting to know what was going on.

"Tell your comrade," I said, "that you're looking at a thousand million riels."

He went on watching me for a bit and then turned his head and spoke to the driver in Khmer, and the driver laughed and swung his fist to the side of my head and knocked me half out of the jeep and left me dizzy, couldn't see much for a while except a blinding light that went on throbbing as I got my breath back, both of them laughing now, but I swear to you that the one who spoke French had been interested, I'd seen it in his eyes, we could have made a deal and I could have got into my jeep and driven away, just a mental exercise, that's all, it's of no importance.

Then they dragged me out and we began walking across to the ravine not far from the track, maybe fifty yards.

It was quiet here except for the sound of our boots. The sky was turning from saffron to rust-red in the west, and I saw the first star pricking the twilight. Three waterfowl threaded the air above the ridge, homing to the Tonle Sap, and as I looked down I wondered if I would see the leopard again.

The two men weren't talking anymore, and I thought it possible that as Buddhists they were aware that a life was soon to pass, here in this quiet place, and that even though they themselves were going to take it, there should be peace until the thing was done.

"What, then," I asked the man who spoke French, "can I offer you?"

One has to try, however late the hour.

There was no answer. He was walking beside me, his assault rifle at the slope. The other man was behind, the muzzle of his gun pressing against my spine.

"Talk it over," I said, "with your comrade. This is a unique chance for you—there's nobody more generous than a dying man, and I have plenty to give."

He didn't answer. Our boots crunched over the stones in the silence, and I changed the subject.

"I saw a leopard," I said, "earlier," simply to engage his attention as I swung round hard and forced the gun downward with my elbow and smashed my head into his face and drove the nose bone into the brain as the first shot banged before his finger was jerked clear of the trigger. I'd practiced twisting in and out of the jacket five times in the cell but it seemed to take a long time now before I got my hands free and went for the one who spoke French as he started backing off to give himself room, suddenly learning that a gun at close quarters is useless, a dead weight, just something that gets in your way—I wouldn't have stood a chance if they'd kept their distance on the walk here from the jeep, couldn't have tried anything at all.

He got out a short burst but it was wide because he hadn't had time to swing the thing round into the aim and I was there now, forcing the barrel down and bringing his shoulders down with it, his shoulders and his face, then I smashed upward again but missed because he was ready for that, had seen what I'd done to the other man, didn't want it to happen to him, he was worried now, crouched over his gun and trying to find his balance again because when I'd tried the upward smash he'd half-twisted round to avoid it, so I had a half-second to work with but it wasn't enough because I was off-balance too and he recovered first and began swinging the gun into me—he'd forgotten already, forgotten the bloody thing was no good at close quarters, they hadn't taught them that at the school for revolutionaries, all they'd been taught was bang and you're dead, forcing, I was *forcing* the gun *down* again and the muzzle hit the stones and then he was on me, learning fast, remembering he'd got hands with strength in them, had them closing on my throat and I relaxed, went limp and dropped as far as he'd let me before I went for his eyes and felt his hands come away from my throat but they'd been squeezing hard and my breath was sawing in and out as we both went down now and he put a lock on me and trapped one arm, Christ he was strong, strong and lean and athletic and with the spirit in him, the spirit of the die-hard revolutionary, red flags in his eyes, the Khmer Rouge forever and all that jazz, and it wasn't helping me, it was giving him the strength of two men, three, and I wasn't getting in there with the center-knuckle strikes, kept missing him because he wouldn't keep still and I was on my back now with the last of the daylight in the sky and his head and shoulders etched in black against it, the silhouette of the death-bringer bearing down on me as he trapped my other arm with his leg across it and I couldn't find the force I needed because of the breathing thing, couldn't get the oxygen to the muscles and it felt like drowning, not being strong enough to use purchase, leverage, the twilight fluttering now as the man above me raised his hand and in his hand I saw the rock and it looked heavy, black against the sky, and as it came down I jerked my knee and connected with his tailbone and he screamed and his arm went limp and as I twisted round the rock crashed down beside my head and I took it from there, kneeing him again and this time hard enough to paralyze and he screamed again in agony and I rolled clear and lay there listening to him, listening carefully in case he came out of the trauma with any strength left, but he wasn't moving, couldn't move.

I was getting my breath back but it wasn't easy, it was taking time. A lot had been happening and I think I must have hit my head on the ground somewhere along the line because the fading light of the day was still fluttering, vibrating in slow waves, while I tried to get a grip on things mentally—had they heard him scream, down there in the camp? If they had, they would have thought it was me, screaming for mercy, *would* have or *might* have, the difference was very great, potentially lethal, because if they'd heard the scream and hadn't thought it was me, they'd have jumped into a jeep and would be on their way here *now*.

He rolled over suddenly, my bold revolutionary, and started vomiting, which I'd been expecting him to do: the knee strike had been to the coccyx and I'd done it *twice* and the nerve center there would be a conflagration now, giving him so much pain that he couldn't be more than half-conscious, forget the rush of user-friendly endorphins when that area's been hit, you're strictly on your own. I was surprised he hadn't passed out by now and he could do it at any time but I couldn't trust that, daren't rely on it, a man like this would have formidable reserves.

Think: Were they on their way, because of the scream? That would be conclusive, the odds unacceptable, so don't waste thought on it, there were other questions: What had they thought of the shots, the bursts of fire, the *two* bursts, more than an execution required? If they'd thought there was trouble of some kind they would be—once again—in their jeep by now and on their way here. The answer was the same: it would be conclusive, *finis*. So don't waste thought on that one either.

He'd finished vomiting but the air was putrid and I moved away a little, observing him. His face was bloodless under the dirt, his eyes closed; his breathing was steady but faint, his chest hardly moving. The assault rifle was lying near him, but not near enough for him to reach it before I could if I saw him move.

He began moaning now and I hated that: a scream I can handle because it's simply the sound of shock, but a moan is a plea for help and I couldn't help him.

He's one of the people who blows the legs off little children.

Well said, and timely.

Think, keep thinking. How long would it be before they came out here to see why these two hadn't returned, performed the execution and returned?

Not long.

I crawled toward the man and lay close to him, put my mouth to his ear.

"What will happen on the nineteenth?"

He didn't answer.

There would be a case, there would be a case here of inflicting further pain on him, if I thought it would impress him, persuade him to answer me, and it would have been acceptable for me to do that, to further traumatize this blower-of-the-legs-off-little-children; but it wouldn't physically be possible: pain was already roaring in him, and there was nothing I could add that he would feel.

Fear, then, of death? I felt for his throat.

"What will happen on the nineteenth?"

It would be nice to have something to debrief to Pringle, Flockhart, something perhaps conclusive: a Pol Pot attack on the capital, an assassination attempt on the king, something I could call information, which was what I was here for, putting more pressure on this man's windpipe, letting him think of death, using both thumbs and working inward—*and then he moved* and I was fighting off a claw-hand strike to the eyes and going down and rolling over, blocking a fist and forcing a heel-palm to the nose and missing, feeling the slickness of blood as the skin came away, my breath coming short as he struck again and the fear of death was mine, not his, until I found purchase for my left shoulder and drove a half-fist into the larynx and felt the cartilage snap and he reeled sideways and dropped, dropped like a sack, with blood creeping from the corner of his mouth.

I got up and stumbled across the stones, found my way to the nearest jeep, my own, and dragged out two bottles of Evian water and went over to the other jeep and found the key still in the ignition, here was the trick, the point of no return: I hadn't got the strength to make my way out through the mountains on foot— they'd be here soon now, wanting to know why their comrades hadn't returned.

The engine fired at once and I took the thing through the gears as quietly as I could. The Chinese-built vehicle was larger than mine, would be faster—but they'd hear it from the camp, I knew that, would think for a moment that the jeep was on its way back until they heard the sound fading—then they would react. It was simply a question of time, and I shifted into overdrive as soon as the engine could take it, pushing the speed up and switching on the headlights as the track began turning through the hills.

With one hand I tore the cap off a bottle of water and took swigs at it and then washed the dried spittle off my face, flicking my eyes across the three mirrors in turn as the track straightened and ran between boulders for half a mile and then began twisting and rising, the bottle of water empty now and the mirrors still dark, the waxing moon afloat in the southern sky and the rim of the mountains lying in waves below it, touched here and there by its reflection on flat rock.

The jeep lost traction sometimes over the loose shale, skating at an angle and coming back as I shifted gears to get control; there was something like fifteen degrees of play in the steering box and it was tricky to keep this brute from Beijing on course. I was using third gear now, because—

Lights.

In the left-hand mirror, fanning between the hills behind and below me, flashing once as they came directly in line and then fading, blacked out suddenly by a turn in the track. They would belong to a vehicle leaving the camp: all traffic on this route was strictly Khmer Rouge.

The major road to Pouthisat was still some way ahead, two miles, two and a half, and there wasn't a single chance of driving out of this. Their lights were in the right-hand mirror now, flashing again as they lined up, brighter this time. The crew on board had already found my jeep standing there and this one gone; they might have stopped long enough to take a look around and seen the two soldiers lying there among the rocks. They would therefore be driving flat out and with purpose, and even if I got to the major road before they did I'd be within range of their guns, *finito*.

The terrain was steeper here, with rifts and gullies filled with shadow in the peripheral glow of my lights, and I began watching for somewhere to ditch.

There might of course be nowhere—I might simply have to stop this thing and get out and walk, run, while there was time. Question: How long would it take those people behind me to raise the alarm and bring a search party of a hundred men here in packed transports, two hundred, five?

The jeep was skating again and I shifted down and got traction. Light came suddenly and in all three mirrors this time as the track ran straight for a while; then they blacked out through another turn. They'd closed the distance by half, by more than half, and in another two minutes at this speed I'd come into range of their guns.

There was a gully showing up in the headlights, leading away from the track, deeper than a gully, a small ravine, and I wrenched the jeep into a spin with the power still on and sent it toward the slope, dousing the lights and hitting the brakes and jumping clear, with enough momentum left in the thing to take it to the bottom.

I was lying flat among boulders when the Khmer transport came storming past, and as soon as its lights had died away toward the major road I stumbled down to the jeep and got the flashlight off its bracket and found the last bottle of water and took it with me as I moved higher, away from the track.

The moon was down, and in the east a pale flush of light threw the length of a mountain ridge into silhouette. Below and to the west the valley was lost beneath a veil of mist. A bird called, piping thinly in the silence.

I hadn't slept. The Khmer transport that had gone storming past the place where I'd ditched the jeep had driven as far as the major road and turned north toward Pouthisat; then within twenty minutes the lights of a dozen vehicles had come swinging past from the camp, alerted by radio, half of them turning north and the others south to take up the hunt. It was long after midnight when I saw them again, threading their way through the valley back to their base.

I had lain down, then, using the half-empty plastic bottle for a headrest, listening to the silence that had now come down from the hills to rest along the valley floor. But sleep was out of my reach. Bruises from unremembered blows were throbbing now; injuries I had not been aware of were bringing pain, demanding my attention. And there were thoughts running wild in my head, disallowing peace, baying like hounds at the kill. Later I would have to deal with them.

When the flush of light in the east became strong enough to cast shadows I finished the last of the water and left my shelter in the rocks to climb into the eye of the sun toward the road.

13

DEBRIEFING

"And your wife?" I asked the man with no teeth.

He looked down. "She dead," he said in halting French.

So I didn't ask directly about his sons, his other daughters.

"I'm sorry. There's just you and Cham?" It was short for Chamnan.

I had followed her home through the streets this morning, walking slowly. She was perhaps fifteen, though she looked more, hunger and shock and grief having wasted her small sharp-boned face. She was watching me now from the cramped little kitchen, her crutch leaning against the wall. By her eyes I saw she wasn't sure she wanted to share her home with a round-eye and his odd manners. I'd followed her because I needed a safe house, and if she had a father or a mother they wouldn't favor the Khmer Rouge, wouldn't be informers. We'd had to pause several times, Cham and I, on our way here, because this one had gone off not long ago, maybe near her school, and she was still trying to get used to the crutch—it was rubbing under her arm, and the rag she was using to cushion it kept shifting.

"Yes," her father said—there were just himself and Cham here in the house. It was on stilts and made of mud and bamboo, and he told me there were two rooms to spare and I could take either one. His sons, I supposed, or his two other daughters wouldn't be needing them anymore.

"I don't want," I told him, "to be talked about. Do you understand that?"

He looked surprised. All the round-eyes he'd seen hadn't minded in the least being talked about; they'd come into his country with their good new clothes and stout boots and loud voices and treated him and his neighbors rather like children. I thought I'd better spell it out for him.

"I don't want anyone in the Khmer Rouge to know where I am."

He frowned, then nodded quickly, looking across at Cham and saying something in Khmer, his tone emphatic.

"She understands?" I asked him.

"Yes. We not talk about you. She can keep secrets. All my people know how to keep secrets."

"Of course." I offered him two thousand riels per day for my board, and he was pleased, glancing quickly around the room as if he'd never realized its value.

I slept through the heat of the day on the bamboo bed in the room I'd chosen; there was no other furniture in it except for a chest of drawers made from packing cases still with their Oxfam labels on them. This had been another daughter's room; there were long black hairs still caught in the split ends of the bamboo behind the straw-filled pillow, and even though I'd been awake all night, sleep didn't come easily, or soon. In none of the missions I'd so far worked had I felt anything in particular about the opposition: they had simply represented the target, the objective. The Khmer Rouge were different, and when the first wave of sleep came over me it was borne on a dark, tugging undertow of rage.

On a patch of waste-ground near the railway station there was a bombed-out bus with KAMPONG CHHNANG still readable on the side, and I stood in the shadows watching it. The streetlamp on the corner was flickering the whole time as the power station struggled to cope with the load. Voices came from the café down the street, and a Mine Action van turned the corner and came past, its lights throwing the rubble on the waste-ground into sharp relief. Then Pringle arrived, dead on the minute, not looking around him as he skirted the building on foot and got into the bus, experienced enough to rely on me to have screened the area beforehand.

"So we've got something now," he said when I'd finished debriefing, "for London."

"Oh really?"

He didn't answer for a moment, hearing the acid tone. The streetlamp flickered again and this time went out, and we could see nothing now through the filth-covered windows of the bus. That was all right: it worked both ways. It's always a strain when the local director and his executive are holed up at a rendezvous, and tonight I was a distinct risk to Pringle: I'd been seen at the Khmer Rouge camp yesterday and was recognizable, even though my two executioners *manqué* were no longer a threat. I couldn't show myself at the Hotel Lafayette or invite Pringle to my safe house either, and the bus was the best place I could find; it was in deep shadow and didn't interest anybody at night, though in the daytime it was a playground for children: there was a small rubber flip-flop in the gangway, and a broken toy gun—of course, we must train them young—on one of the ripped, stained seats.

"You located the opposition's base," Pringle said in a moment, "and infiltrated it, bringing out valuable information as to personnel and equipment. In addition—" He broke off as three shots sounded in the distance from two different guns, some kind of shoot-out, par for the course in exotic Pouthisat. "In addition," Pringle went on, "you confronted a high-ranking officer of the Khmer Rouge and can recognize him again. I think Mr. Flockhart would certainly wish me to signal him."

An apple for the teacher—he sounded just like that bastard Loman. "I found the camp," I said, "but I'd imagine quite a few people in this town know it's there, other than the Khmer Rouge. They know how to keep secrets in this place."

"Possibly so"—Pringle's voice came from beside me—we were sitting in the pitch dark now— "but despite their ability to keep secrets, *we* know the camp is there now, and that's rather more important."

Had a point but I wasn't in the mood to admit it; he was so bloody reasonable, wouldn't give me a chance to spill my guts—some directors are like that, they don't realize the shadow needs to debrief what's on his mind as well as the information he's picked up.

"Then tell Flockhart," I said, "make his day. You'd also better tell him there are two more down." I hadn't said anything in my debriefing about getting clear of the camp: it wasn't usable information; but we're always expected to report it if we put someone down.

"Very well," Pringle said, and I heard him move, crossing his legs or something. "This was in self-defense?"

"Call it that."

In a moment: "Was it? Or was it not? I'm sorry to—"

"The first one, yes, I couldn't have done anything if I hadn't put him down right away—they both had loaded assault rifles. I could have got away from the second one by knocking him cold, but I'm not sure he would've thanked me—with no surgeons in this place his legs would've been paralyzed for life."

"I see. But during the confrontation, he had been attempting to kill you, is that right?"

"Yes."

"Then London will be perfectly satisfied."

It was no big deal, but the hierarchy upstairs starts worrying if any particular shadow reports too many people down during the course of his mission: for some among us the taste of blood can become addictive, though I've never fancied it myself.

"Well and good," I said.

"And I understand perfectly." He didn't.

"Look, they were soldiers, weren't they? Aren't soldiers expected to give their lives for the cause?" My voice hadn't got louder; it just had an undertone and I couldn't do anything about it.

Pringle shifted slightly on the seat toward me. "Mr. Flock-hart—not to mention the Minister of Defense in London and the Chairman of the Joint Chiefs of Staff in Washington—would be delighted if you were to put down the entire Khmer Rouge army in Cambodia, so I wouldn't fret too much about the two you dealt with yesterday."

So he did understand—he'd looked at my profile in the files in London rather carefully. Even in this most inhuman of all trades I've never taken a man's life without feeling another scar forming on the psyche, and this time I'd been able to sleep only because of the long black hairs caught in the bamboo, guilt relieved by rage.

In a moment I said, "In any case, London won't know, will it?" Pringle had just said that London would be "perfectly satisfied." The streetlamp flickered into life again, and I turned my head to look at him. "Or has that changed?"

"It was a generic term. I meant Control, not London. But since you ask, it may be that the Bureau will be brought into things, somewhere along the line."

Oh *really*. I'd thought we were meant to be a one-man show, with Flockhart pushing a single pawn across the board toward the enemy lines. "Why?" I asked Pringle.

"Let me clear up a few aspects of the debriefing," he said, "be-fore we get to that. Do you mind?"

Kid gloves, and I didn't like it. At a debriefing the director calls the shots.

"No, but I'm not going to forget the question."

"I'm quite sure. But in the meantime, tell me why you think the Khmer Rouge have established a camp in this area, not far from the town?"

"If they're planning some kind of assault on the nineteenth— or at any time—it'd give them a springboard."

"An assault on Pouthisat?"

"On Phnom Penh. This is the nearest airfield from the capital to the west, where the main camp is supposed to be. And by road it's only a couple of hundred kilometers from the camp to Phnom Penh, if they want to transport troops en masse and by night."

Pringle uncrossed his legs again, crossed them the other way. I didn't like it that he was so restless; he hadn't been like this at the airport when we'd first met. But perhaps he was sitting on an exposed seat spring, as I was.

"Do you believe an assault is imminent?" he asked me. "As close as the nineteenth—in five days' time?"

"The men I saw at the camp were active, wearing battle dress, moving vehicles around. But it could've been simply because Colonel Choen was there."

"By 'there,' do you mean paying a visit? Making an inspection? Or do you think he's based there?"

"I couldn't tell."

"Make an educated guess."

"I'd say he's visiting, just as he visited the people in Phnom Penh. Going the rounds, tightening security near the capital."

"And then he'll report back to Pol Pot, in the west?"

"Just a gut feeling."

"You've no actual—"

"Look, you asked me for an educated guess and you've got it."

Not at my best, no, but what do you expect, I'd done nothing useful yesterday, *nothing*, it didn't matter what Pringle said, he was just eager to signal Control with *something*, to show we were in business, but we weren't, not on any effective scale. Listen, what actually happened? I'd located a camp that half this town probably knew about and I'd got spat on by a street urchin in uniform and then been led like a lamb to the bloody slaughter, and if it hadn't been for my training and experience this whole thing, *Salamander*, would have gone straight down the drain, *finito*.

"I'm sorry," Pringle said. "You're perfectly right."

"Next question?"

He uncrossed his legs. "I rather think that's all. Now tell me, have you any—"

"Why is it possible," I asked him carefully, "that the Bureau will be brought into things, somewhere along the line?"

"Ah, yes." As if he'd quite forgotten. He hadn't. The street-lamp flickered and went out again, and I sensed that he was glad of it, didn't want me to see his eyes when he spoke. "Nothing has changed, actually, no. Or not yet. We are still running a totally clandestine operation—not only vis-à-vis the Khmer Rouge but also the Bureau itself. But if you succeed in getting closer still to Pol Pot—to the man himself—your further actions might well in-volve the highest military authority in London and Washington."

"They'd give me the battalion I asked for?"

"It's not quite like that." He hitched himself toward me a little. "Neither the CIA in the States nor DI6 in London is officially in-terested in what happens in Cambodia at the present moment. There are too many other turbulent theaters of unrest engaging their attention both in Europe and Asia. But if it were known with certainty that Pol Pot means to make a final attempt to seize power again, and has the capacity, there might be a decision by—shall we say—the more covert factions of government in Washington, Lon-don, Tokyo, Bonn, and Paris to stop him—with or without refer-ence to the United Nations."

"By military force?"

"I suggest we leave that to them. The point is that when I say, 'if it were known' that Pol Pot has this ambition, I clearly mean *if you can find out*. All we are asking you for, you see, is information, as I told you at the airport in Phnom Penh."

"You don't think it's asking just a little too much," I said, "for one solitary spook to stand in for the CIA and DI6 because they're busy?"

"I also suggest we leave that to Mr. Flockhart."

"What you want first," I said as the streetlamp flickered into life again, "is the precise position of the main Khmer Rouge camp in the jungle, somewhere west." Because if this man was talking about "highest military authority" and "covert factions of government" he was talking about an air strike, and just because the U.S. had brought coals on their head for doing it before, it didn't mean they wouldn't do it again if they thought it was necessary, history being repetitive.

"We would very much like to know, yes," Pringle said, "the precise position of the main KR forces. And we might assume that this would also give us the precise whereabouts of Pol Pot."

"He's still the target."

"Specifically. And you should bear that in mind."

"Noted."

"What the major democratic powers want to avoid, in fine, is the potential destruction of a further million Cambodians in new and improved killing fields, and the potential risk of Pol Pot's subsequent invasion of North Vietnam, which is at present militarily vulnerable, with the blessing and support—in terms of bargain-price matériel—of China, creating a Communist bloc."

I gave it some thought for a moment and Pringle left me to it, shifting slightly away in a symbolic gesture of withdrawal. Through the filthy window I watched a dog crossing the waste-ground, dragging something heavy, some kind of food it had seized from somewhere, perhaps, and wanted to hide, its ribs showing and its legs buckling sometimes, forcing it to rest, its jaws still locked on the trophy, the means of maintaining life for a few more days. I couldn't see exactly what it was but it was angled like a human foot, deep crimson, almost black in the acid light of the streetlamp as the dog got up and went on again, dragging its spoils through the rubble.

"Is the Prime Minister," I asked Pringle when I was ready, "being kept informed?" The Bureau is directly and exclusively responsible to the PM in all its activities. Hence its ability not, virtually, to exist.

"I'm not sure," Pringle said.

"You mean you don't know? Or you think so, but you're not sure?" It was important. If the PM was already aware of *Salamander* then we were operating close to the "highest military authority" Pringle had mentioned.

"Frankly," he said, "I don't know. But let me put it this way: the moment you achieve any kind of breakthrough, the Prime Minister will indeed be informed that we have a mission running, and told the nature of the objective."

"And will you let me know when that happens?"

"You have my word."

"I want assurance," I told him, "that I can eventually get support on an effective scale if I need it, since I'm taking on an army."

"And with the Prime Minister in the picture, that would of course be guaranteed. I understand."

He was very understanding, was our Mr. Pringle, and he wore kid gloves and was stroking me with them. Why in God's name couldn't Flockhart have given me Ferris? Ferris or Pepperidge or even that bastard Loman, who at least has the grace to return my disregard. I don't like people who help me gently up the steps to the guillotine.

Pringle uncrossed his legs. "Questions?"

"No. But you can get a couple of things for me. A Mine Action van and some field glasses, 10 X 50's if possible, nothing less than 7." He had a connection with Mine Action: they'd flown me out here from Phnom Penh.

"When do you need them by?"

"First light tomorrow." I got off the seat and started down the aisle, and Pringle followed.

"May I ask what you have in mind?"

"I want to get close to Colonel Choen again—at the moment he's the only lead I've got. But this one's a long shot." Pringle was waiting for me to tell him more, but I wasn't in the mood, didn't trust him yet.

As we dropped from the twisted step of the bus and kept to the shadow along the wall I heard him saying, "Gabrielle Bouchard is in Pouthisat, did you know?"

I told him I didn't, and kept on walking.

"She's at the French Catholic mission."

"How is she?"

"Pretty well."

I stopped just before the shadow of the wall came to an end. "We break off here."

"All right. So when do I expect a signal?"

"God knows," I told him. "As soon as I've got anything for you, that's all I can say." Then I gave him the Church of Christ pamphlet the Caucasian woman had slipped through the open window of the Mazda. "Get it to London for me. Wherever it can do the most good."

Pringle looked at it briefly in the poor light. "Oh, yes, we've all seen these. Unfortunately, it takes a political dissident's arrest to outrage the human rights groups. Driving children into brothels by the thousand doesn't worry them. But"—he shrugged, putting the pamphlet away—"I'll see it reaches London, of course." He melted into the night.

I would pass close to the French Catholic mission on my way back to the safe house, so I made a detour by a couple of turnings and found the place and knocked at the door and asked if Gabrielle was there, but the nun said no, she'd been shot in the street half an hour ago.

14

SNAKESKIN

"It could have been worse," the black American nurse said. "The bullet passed within a couple of inches of the liver, and this place ain't Bellevue, honey, there would have been nothing we could've done. C'mon in, this is what we call the intensive care unit, mostly for gunshot wounds and crashes and stuff, excuse the packing cases, we have to have something to sit on when our feet ache."

An electric fan turned slowly overhead, fly-encrusted, wobbling, stirring the smells of blood, antiseptic, and tobacco smoke. A young Vietnamese lay propped up on a dirty straw pillow, smoking—he was dying of tuberculosis, the nurse told me, so he was allowed two cigarettes a day to keep him from going crazy, and it smelled better anyway than most of the other things in this place. Her name was Leonora, she said, and she was from the Bronx.

"Fancy meeting you here," I heard Gabrielle saying. She was in the end bed, half in shadow, her dark eyes luminous in her pale face, reflecting the kerosene lamp. She didn't smile, maybe couldn't.

"Don't *do* that!" Leonora told her as she tried to sit up. "You can shake hands just the way you are, or kiss or whatever you have in mind."

So I leaned down and kissed Gabrielle; her mouth was hot, moist, feverish. The nurse pushed a packing case across for me—"I don't want you sitting on the bed, which is what you're dying to do. She has to keep *still*, you with me, honey?"

"Got it. How much blood did she lose?"

"Maybe a pint; we didn't have to give her any—not that we could have, none she would've wanted in her."

"Did it go through?"

"How's that again?"

"The bullet."

"Oh, right, yeah, clean through, which made it a whole lot simpler for me."

"You're the surgeon?"

"R.N. The only doc we got here is out on a mine accident. Jesus, did I say accident? But I sew real good, don't I, honey?"

"Real good," Gabrielle said. She still didn't smile.

"Are you in pain?" I asked her.

"No."

"You bet your sweet ass she's in pain," Leonora said, "but she refused anything, don't go for drugs, well okay, that's pretty smart so long as you can take it. Thing is, it keeps the fever going longer than I'd like." She put a hand on Gabrielle's forehead, then looked at me again. "I'm going to give you five minutes, honey, then she has to sleep if she can, you wanna cuss me out, I ain't listening." She went down the aisle to talk to the dying Vietnamese.

"Was it the KR?" I asked Gabrielle.

"Yes." She didn't sound angry. I would have expected her to.

"D'you want to talk about it?"

"I'd rather hear what you've been doing."

"Nothing terribly interesting. Pringle told me you were in Pouthisat."

"When?"

"Half an hour ago."

"You went to the mission?"

"Yes."

"That was nice." She reached for my hand. "You remembered where I said I'd be."

"Of course."

"We could have had dinner somewhere." She watched me steadily, her eyes deep in the faint light. "I'll be out of here in the morning."

"Not if it's up to Leonora."

"It's up to me. There's so much infection here—tuberculosis, diphtheria, dengue fever; I don't want to take anything back to the mission. And anyway it's only a flesh wound."

"I can't be here in the morning. Do you want me to ask one of the nuns to come and fetch you?"

"They know," she said. "I've already asked them." She tilted her head. "How did you bruise your face?"

"I can't remember."

She watched me in silence, then left it. "I don't know where I can find you, and you wouldn't want me to."

"I'll make contact when I can. I can't say when."

"As long as it's sometime."

"It will be." I pressed her hand. "I'm going now, so that you can sleep."

"All right."

I rested my mouth on hers again, this time for longer, and we didn't close our eyes, so that all I could see was the deep indigo blue, with her soul floating somewhere in its shadows, and I found myself wanting, very much, not to leave her.

"Until soon," I said.

"Yes. Until soon."

Then as I pushed the packing case back against the wall I remembered the sounds we'd heard, Pringle and I, from the bus not long ago, the sudden exchange of fire in the night.

"The man who shot you," I asked Gabrielle, "did you see him?"

"Yes."

"Well enough to recognize?"

"I won't be seeing him again," she said. "He's dead."

•   •   •

The sun was behind me when it lifted from the earth's rim, and I watched my shadow growing across the stones.

The Mine Action van was standing on the east side of a rock, concealed from the track that led at right angles from the major north-south road. This was the turning I'd missed when I'd been tracking Colonel Choen to the camp. Any traffic from there would have to come past where I was lying facedown among the smaller rocks; I'd chosen a gap I could sight through, and when I had to lift the field glasses their lenses would be in shadow.

It was a long shot, as I'd told Pringle, because I was relying simply on the feeling I had that Choen wasn't quartered at the camp, had only been paying a visit, just as he'd paid a visit to the villa in Phnom Penh. But even so, he could have left the camp yesterday, for Pouthisat and the airfield.

By 10:00 hours the sun was too hot on my back and I had to shift to the next position I'd worked out; it was less satisfactory because this gap was narrower and the rocks blurred the sides of the vision field through the lenses, but I was in shade now as the sun began reaching toward noon.

Three vehicles had left the camp since I'd arrived: a battered Landcruiser and two jeeps, all camouflaged and all turning north for the town. I didn't think Choen was in any of them, but couldn't be certain, didn't expect to be certain: a long shot is uncertain by nature. A man in faded battle dress and checked *krama* had come south on a motorbike and turned toward the camp, an AK-47 slung from his shoulder.

I had seen the leopard again: that was his territory down there where I'd seen him before. And ten minutes ago I'd watched two cobras weaving slowly out of a cleft in the rocks a few feet away, presumably a mated pair, one larger than the other, their scales shimmering in the sunlight. They had sensed me, and for a while had become still, their tongues flicking to analyze my odors and my body heat; had I been a vole or a musk rat I wouldn't have lived.

At noon I drank some of the water I'd bought in the market on my way from the safe house; it was warm and unrefreshing but I took in half a liter to prevent dehydration.

Three shots . . . There'd been a lot of time for thinking today, though none of it, in this heat, had been very structured. But the three shots had interested me because they'd been from two different guns, and Gabrielle had told me the KR was dead. I hadn't asked her any more about it when I was leaving the hospital because she'd been in pain and needed sleep, so all I had was a handful of scenarios: Gabrielle had got in the way of a stray bullet when a KR and someone else had exchanged shots, and she'd seen the KR killed; a KR had seen her with her camera and decided to shoot her as an undesirable foreign journalist, and someone else had killed him in her defense; for some reason she herself had been carrying a gun and had used it when she'd been fired on.

The shots had been exchanged in a definite sequence: replaying the sound of them in my mind I remembered that Gun A had fired twice and Gun B only once, in the sequence A-B-A, which would match two of those scenarios. But anyway she would tell me what had happened, the next time we met. Or perhaps she wouldn't . . . I knew so little about Gabrielle Bouchard, except that in her face I had come to recognize, even with those blue Caucasian eyes, the face of Cambodia, of courage, endurance, and suffering. I would have been attracted to her by her looks and her nature alone, but there was this extra dimension: seeing the bullet-scarred walls and the riven palm trees and the legless children in the streets I had begun to ache for this small, tormented country, and also for Gabrielle.

High noon and the heat poured from the molten heights of the sky and my bush shirt was dark with sweat, the second water bottle empty and the field glasses hot to the touch, and then movement came again and I shifted onto my elbows and got into focus and watched the camouflaged staff car as it climbed the mountain track from the camp through the shimmering heat waves, the glass of its headlamps flashing as it bounced over rough ground, stones flying from under the tires. It looked like the one I'd tracked here from the town.

Two men, both sitting in the front, their faces blurring as the vehicle neared and I overcorrected the focus and then got the sharpness back, the driver's face unfamiliar, the other man's recognizable, I thought, as Colonel Choen's, the eyes not quite balanced, the mouth drawn down, censuring all mankind. Then as the staff car turned off the track onto the major road I saw the emblem pinned to the side of his red-checked *krama*; from this distance I couldn't make out if it was the one I'd seen before in the detention cell, but I decided the odds were good enough, and within a kilometer I was keeping station in the Mine Action van, half that distance behind.

The target drove straight through Pouthisat, crossing the railway and turning east, passing the Hotel Lafayette, not stopping at the building where Choen had stopped before, and when the airfield sign came up I knew there wasn't going to be any information for Pringle, other than that I was right: Colonel Choen had been visiting the KR camp and was now flying out again. There might have been a chance for me to get close to him again if I could have caught him somewhere distanced from his escort, and that was why I'd spent half the *bloody* day lying on my stomach watching the local fauna: we'd got *nothing* for London so far, in spite of what Pringle said, and I was looking for a breakthrough, just one *small* bloody breakthrough was all I asked, for God's sake, chopper in the sky, there was a chopper lifting above the sugar palms in the east, and as the staff car turned into the freight area the Kamov KA-26 made its descent, the same aircraft that had brought Choen here two days ago, standard military camouflage, the Khmer Rouge shuttle from Phnom Penh.

I rolled the Mine Action van between two hangars facing away from the apron and pulled up and switched off and watched the outside mirrors, waiting for the final scrap of information that would soon become available: Would Colonel Choen be flying southeast toward the capital or west toward the main guerrilla base across the mountains?

He was out of the staff car now, standing with his escort and waiting for the chopper to land, dust and heat waves blowing across the apron in the draft from the rotors, a foam cup bowling along the ground as the undercarriage took the shock and the pilot cut the engine and Choen went on standing there, not going toward the chopper even when the door swung open.

A man showed there, looking around him for a moment and then dropping to the apron, seeing Colonel Choen and going across to him in a crouching walk through the draft from the rotors, smoothing his hair back and hitching his briefcase higher under his arm, fairly tall, a light gray European suit with an inch of white cuff showing and a pocket handkerchief displayed, a pair of handsome tan-colored brogues—and now a smile for Choen as the colonel came forward to meet him, both men giving a perfunctory bow as they shook hands, the pilot coming across to the staff car with a suitcase, presumably the visitor's.

Flying, then, neither southeast to the capital nor west to the guerrilla camp across the mountains, no information on that. Information, instead, on this.

I waited until the staff car was through the gates to the perimeter track before I started up, the chopping of the Kamov's rotors echoing from the hangars as it took off again and I moved the van to within a hundred yards of the target vehicle on the curving track and then dropped back to keep station.

The town was dead now as we drove through it; the heat at this hour filled the streets. Bicycles leaned at doorways; a dog sprawled asleep in a patch of damp earth below a water pump; the remains of a chicken colored the ground, its blood marking the track of the wheel that had crushed it.

They were both sitting in the back of the staff car, Choen and his visitor: I could see their heads through the rear window, leaning together in conversation until they reached the Hôtel du Lac, where the car pulled in.

I was in the lobby by the time the colonel's escort was bringing in the visitor's baggage. There was good cover here: the balustrade of the staircase, three potted palms, and a fluted column, and I was within earshot of the two men as they took the stairs to the next floor, the visitor with the briefcase still under his arm and Choen carrying a worn leather attaché case. Both were talking in French, the colonel haltingly, the visitor more easily but with a Russian accent, so that I knew that in waiting out the hot, jading, and seemingly unprofitable hours of this day we had arrived at a breakthrough.

15

FOOTSTEPS

It was just after six in the evening when the Russian came down the stairs and looked around him and walked across the lobby to the bar.

I got up from the table in the corner and went over to him.

"Boris Slavsky!" I said. He turned to look at me. I was holding my drink, to let him know he wasn't expected to shake hands. "Voss," I told him, "Andrei Voss." In Russian I said, "You don't know me, but I've heard of you, of course." He watched me with great attention, a touch of suspicion in his pale clear eyes, which didn't surprise me. He wasn't a man who liked to be heard of by strangers. He smelled strongly of a mediocre cologne; I'd caught it when he and Colonel Choen had gone up the staircase earlier in the day, and that was why I hadn't come here alone this evening.

"Would you care to join us?" I half-turned to look across the room. "We're at the table in the corner."

Slavsky looked in that direction, then back at me, a token smile touching his mouth. "Why not?"

"You want to order your drink here, or at the table?"

"I'm in no hurry."

I led him across the room. "Gabrielle, this is Boris Slavsky, from Moscow." He looked down at her, the smile more relaxed. "Gabrielle Bouchard," I told him, "from Paris."

She held out a hand and he leaned over and kissed it; he was a big man, would be broad-shouldered even without the padding in the flashy tropical suit, made, I would think, in the Czech Republic. Forty, forty-five, starting to brush his hair carefully across the scalp, his face also broad, Slav, the cheekbones prominent, the mouth full, predatory in Gabrielle's presence, but would become hard if he were challenged, would sneer, watching the death of an opponent. I didn't know Boris Slavsky but I knew his type, had worked with people like this, had worked sometimes as one of them. I knew his name because it had been in the hotel register when I'd booked a room here just after he had gone upstairs with Colonel Choen.

"Is she for rent?" he asked me as he sat down. He was still looking attentively at Gabrielle.

"I don't know," I told him, "I only met her this morning. But I doubt it—she works for a top French magazine." He hadn't noticed her camera, slung from the back of her chair, but in any case he didn't really think she was a prostitute: she didn't look like one, and this wasn't the kind of hotel where they would sit with their clients. He just wanted to know if she understood Russian, had been watching her eyes for any reaction to his question, had been prepared, even, to get his face slapped. "Boris says he's delighted to meet you," I told Gabrielle in French, and she smiled nicely to him.

Having seen this man's flashy suit when he'd come out of the helicopter, and having smelled his *eau de Red Square* in the hotel lobby, I thought of visiting Gabrielle at the Catholic mission, partly to know how she was and partly to tell her about the Russian visitor to Pouthisat. I told her I needed to meet him, and she agreed to help.

"I was afraid you might see it," I said, "as being asked to use yourself as bait."

"How do you see it, then?"

"As using yourself as a weapon against Pol Pot."

"Exactly. That's why I'll do it."

So when Boris Slavsky had looked across the room at the table in the corner he'd seen Gabrielle sitting there in a raw silk sarong, one slender arm across the back of her chair, her head tilted as she watched him with her deep aquamarine eyes.

"What'll you drink?" I asked Slavsky now.

"Smirnov."

"How?"

"Straight up."

Gabrielle's Pernod was low in the glass, so I ordered another one and two vodkas. "Boris has just arrived," I told her in French with a Russian accent, "from Phnom Penh." I glanced at Slavsky. "How was the flight from Moscow?" I'd said that in French too, and he was looking blank, so I switched to Russian again. "I'm sorry, I just thought we might talk in French as a courtesy to Gabrielle. I was asking how your flight was from Moscow."

"How is any flight from Moscow, in a TU-154?"

Cagey as hell, didn't even admit he'd come from Moscow. I wasn't going to be wasting my time. He'd tested Gabrielle to see if he could speak Russian freely in front of her, and didn't admit to any French, so that I would feel free to say anything I liked to her, anything I didn't want him to understand. He was in the top eche-lon, I knew that—I'd been in signals with Pringle today. All the top arms dealers make it their business to swat up a bit of French, En-glish, German, Spanish if it's not their native tongue; their trade is international and they don't want interpreters listening in.

Pringle had done well. I'd telephoned him from the post office, gone straight there after I'd booked in at the hotel.

"How soon can you contact Moscow?"

He couldn't have been ready for that but he didn't react, got straight on with it.

"I can go through the Russian telecommunications satellite di-rect, but it'll depend on the traffic."

"I need an updated coverage of the top Russian arms dealers and their networks, particularly those who might be supplying or intending to supply our target."

"Understood. This is interesting."

"Yes." A couple of Khmer Rouge rebels came in from the street cuddling their AK-47's and I turned to face the wall. "A Russian flew in half an hour ago and he was met at the airfield by Colonel C. He's now booked in at the Hôtel du Lac." This amounted to an interim debriefing, and yes, this time Pringle had something for London. "Colonel C.," I told him, "was carrying an attaché case, something like half a million U.S. dollars in size. He left the hotel twenty minutes later, without the case."

"What is the visitor's name?"

"He booked in as Boris Slavsky, and I've no reason to think it's a *nom de guerre.*" Arms dealers, especially those who wear flashy suits and *eau de Red Square,* are proud of their names and their reputations for selling megadeath in the marketplace."

"So you need information specifically on him."

"Yes. By this evening if you can."

"I shall make every endeavor."

Pringlese for try like hell and we shut down the signal.

It took him less than two hours to contact our chief agent-in-place, Moscow, and when I phoned Pringle at six o'clock he had what I wanted, even down to a recent bit of scandal concerning Slavsky's involvement with one Fifi Dufoix, the daughter of the French ambassador to Spain: Slavsky had jumped, of necessity, from a third-floor balcony right into a garbage truck to avoid the attentions of her fiancé, a national hero of the bullring at that moment murderously enraged. This I would use, but the main briefing concerned the Dmitrovich organization.

"I heard on the grapevine," I told Slavsky now, "that you'd be coming to town."

He swung his head away from watching Gabrielle, and his eyes changed, blanked off. "Which grapevine?" I knew he'd have to ask: there could have been a leak, and leaks are unwelcome in any extensive enterprise, can wreck a deal, cost money.

"There are so many grapevines," I said, "aren't there?" I turned to Gabrielle and said in French, "Would you excuse us? This is business, and Boris doesn't have any French."

"But of course."

She was sitting stiffly in her chair, and Slavsky noticed. "She's had an injury?" he asked me.

"Apparently she was getting a heavy video camera off a shelf, and it swung down and bruised a rib."

"She's a beautiful woman."

"Isn't she? I wish I could see more of her, but I'm flying out tomorrow, and I don't want to spend tonight—you know—getting involved." I spread my hands flat on the table. "So many grape-vines, we were saying, weren't we? Look, I'm with Dmitrovich." I waited, watching him.

His eyes didn't change. "Who is he?"

I sat back, leaving my hands on the table, ignoring his question. He knew the Dmitrovich group perfectly well—they controlled almost half the underground arms trade in Russia. "The thing is," I said, "your client approached us first for what he needed, but our price was too rich for his blood. As you know, we choose not to be competitive, since we can always guarantee the supply and can often obtain merchandise difficult for others to acquire. Also, your client gets his pocket money from Beijing, but that's about all it is. So, frankly, when we heard you were meeting his proposals, Dmitrovich was quite pleased." I leaned forward again. "It's in our interests that this particular client succeeds in reversing the status quo in Cambodia—or should I say Kampuchea?—and we're quite confident that you'll be able to help him."

I let him think about that, and turned to Gabrielle, saying in French, "Even if you could understand us you'd be just as bored, business being business in any language."

"I'm not bored," she said with a smile. "I'm playing a game, picking out the *da*'s and the *nyet*'s, which are the only words I know. He seems a very nice man," she added.

I'd briefed her at the mission that Slavsky spoke French but might pretend otherwise. She knew he understood what she'd just said, and that was why she'd said it.

"He's interesting"— I nodded— "yes. Women find him attractive. Excuse us again." I looked at Slavsky and switched to Russian. "She's quite taken with you, I think. And by the way, you know who I ran into last week in Madrid? Little Fifi Dufoix! She married that awful matador fellow, did you hear?"

His eyes changed now. He could have killed me. Some men might have laughed it off, seen the funny side of it by this time, but not this one, not Boris Slavsky; he didn't like to have people picture him wallowing among the ripe and reeking contents of a Spanish garbage truck. But the mention of little Fifi had done its job, as I knew by the next thing he said.

"If you people turned down my client's offer in the first place, why has Dmitrovich sent you to Cambodia?"

Gloves off now.

"I wasn't actually sent. It was my own idea to come here." Leaning forward again: "As I say, we have every confidence in you, but as you know as well as I do, accidents happen—the source suddenly dries up, or official suspicion is aroused, supply lines are compromised, even the weather can be a problem: remember when our group was trying to deliver some goods to Serbia a couple of years ago and the transports ran into mud slides because of the rain?"

"That was Plechikov?"

I looked at him steadily, frowning. "Plechikov?"

"Running that assignment."

I shook my head. "We haven't got any Plechikov with us."

We watched each other. He'd left it late, and I'd started waiting for it, listening for it—a word or a name thrown in to check me out. I was onto it at once because it was a stock trick: he knew there was no one working with Dmitrovich called Plechikov, and so did I.

"Someone else," he said at last.

"Actually," I said, "it was me. Mud up to our ears, I can tell you—and you know what those fucking Serbs tried to do to us? They gave us counterfeit German marks!"

He lifted his head an inch, leveling his eyes. "So somebody got shot?"

"How well you know us," I said softly. "Two of them, in fact, the minister and his aide. Dmitrovich offered me the pleasure of taking care of it personally." In a moment he looked down, having seen enough of what I'd put into my eyes for his attention. "But anyway," I said, "you get my point, I'm sure: in any enterprise, however well managed—as I know yours always are—there can be problems. And I am here, with Dmitrovich's approval, to offer you our full support should you need it at any time."

In a moment: "Why?" He didn't like this. The door-to-door megadeath salesmen don't support one another, they cut one another's throats, and everybody knows where they are.

I shrugged. "If you fall down on it, we'll pick it up and deliver. At your price."

"Why at my price?"

"Because we want this man to succeed, so we don't mind losing a little on the deal. If he succeeds, he won't stop there. With Beijing's encouragement he'll catch North Vietnam vacillating between sucking up to the Americans for favored-nation status, with all it implies, and going ahead in the caves and cellars concocting their very first little nuclear bomb. Then there'll be *South* Vietnam in your client's sights." Hands flat on the table again, my voice down almost to a whisper: "Can you imagine how much joy it would give that man to destroy the very nation that drove him out of Cambodia?" I sat back. "But you know all this, Slavsky. As a lackey of Beijing this client of yours could create a Communist bloc in Southeast Asia at a time when the West is desperate to establish democracy here on China's doorstep. We don't see this man as just another sadistic terrorist still ambitious to kill off another million peasants; once he's got *real* power in his hands he'll rise to the occasion politically and of course ideologically—and he'll need *real* toys to protect his new territories, not just the bundle of surface-to-surface missiles you're selling him now. And with the huge treasure chest of merchandise still stockpiled in Russia and Ukraine—conventional and nuclear—we're looking at a brandnew and rapidly developing market, and *that* is what interests Dmitrovich."

Above us the ceiling fans stirred the tobacco smoke, and moths began tracing the air with gold under the flickering lights; through the windows the sky was blood-red as the long day neared its end. I hadn't taken much of a risk when I'd talked about a bundle of surface-to-surface missiles: if Pol Pot wanted to take over this country again he could only do it by threatening the capital, and since he'd failed to do it politically he had to do it by a show of force and from a distance, and a cluster of short-range missiles was the perfect tool.

Slavsky drained his vodka and I signaled the boy. Gabrielle's glass was still full, and so was mine—something that Slavsky hadn't noticed yet, but if he did, he'd comment: for a Russian to sit in front of a glass of vodka for more than five minutes was almost an outrage. I would tell him, if necessary, that I'd eaten some uncooked vegetables here and my stomach was queasy. Tonight I had work to do.

"Will your friend," Gabrielle asked me, "be staying overnight?"

"I'm not sure, but I should think so. He can't get a plane to Phnom Penh at this hour in any case, otherwise I'd be on it myself—regrettably." I gave her a rueful smile. "He might speak a bit of English, by the way—would you like me to ask him?"

"Perhaps."

The boy was coming up in his rubber flip-flops, and I ordered a single vodka. Slavsky was staring into his empty glass, his strong thick fingers turning it slowly round. I didn't interrupt him, and in a moment he looked up.

"It sounds like a threat," he said.

"What does?"

"Your offer to 'pick things up and make a delivery' if I can't manage it."

I leaned back, raising my hands to shoulder level, palms toward him and fingers spread. "My dear Boris, if we'd wanted to move in on your deal we would have done so before now. Be logical."

He turned his large head away to watch the sunset in the windows, turned it back to watch the innocence in my eyes. "How soon could you deliver the merchandise," he asked, "if something went wrong with my own plans?"

I shrugged. "Almost immediately. We've got underground stockpiles of stuff like that all over the place, as I'm sure you know. But you don't need to worry yourself over—"

"And what kind of accident would you think I might have, that would prevent delivery?" He was forgetting to leave his eyes blank now, was concerned, defensive.

I leaned forward. "Look, all you need consider is how much my group stands to profit in the long run from your client's success, and you'll understand—I very much hope—that Dmitrovich is more than happy to see you deliver on time by the nineteenth, without impediment. Tell me, have you ever met him?"

"Dmitrovich?"

"Yes."

"I've not had that pleasure." His sense of humor was surfacing, and I noted it.

"He's tough," I said. "Dmitrovich is very tough. You know that. But he's prone to indulge himself, and for him to watch over your successful enterprise out here as a kind of benevolent patron is rather attractive to him. The bear that refrains from cuffing the badger is simply demonstrating his greater strength—if you'll forgive the analogy."

"Well, yes, that I can believe. He's an arrogant bastard—if you'll forgive the description."

I laughed generously, and it wasn't difficult. The breakthrough I'd made was holding up, and if this man wasn't yet convinced I was a potential ally he seemed to be getting close. But we'd reached the point where it could be dangerous to push things, and as the boy brought Slavsky's drink I looked at my watch and then at Gabrielle. "As you can tell, we've finished our business."

"Did it go well?"

"We needed to reach an understanding, and I think we've done that. He's a good man to negotiate with. But I'm feeling a bit under the weather—I ate some raw vegetables at lunchtime, which was pretty stupid, and I'm ready for an early night. Would you like me to leave you in Boris's good care, or shall I see you to your hotel?"

She turned away to look across the table for a moment, a mischievous smile on her mouth. "Perhaps he might ask me to dinner," she said, "who knows?"

"I'm damned if I like sitting this one out, but I wouldn't be much company, the way I'm feeling. How long will you be in Pouthisat?"

"For quite a while. I'm here on a photographic assignment."

"Then maybe I can see you again."

"I'd like that," she said.

I looked at Slavsky and switched back to Russian. "So let's leave it like that, Boris. If you come up against any problem with delivery, I'll be there to help."

"How will you know?"

I smiled. "I shall know because I'm here on what we might call a watching brief."

"You've got your spies out."

"Oh, my dear fellow, that sounds so uncharitable. Do you speak English, by the way?"

"When necessary."

"That's a good answer, because the lady was asking just now if you're in town overnight."

"And what did you say, since you know so much?"

I laughed again. "I told her there are no more planes in any

case. She also suggested you might be in the mood to ask her to dinner. I'm out of the running, as I mentioned." He swung his heavy
gaze to Gabrielle. "But you'll have to do better," I told him, "than
'the cat sat on the mat,' or there won't be much conversation."

Leaning toward Gabrielle he said in careful English, "It would
give me greatest pleasure if you may have dinner with me tonight."

I got up, leaving some money for the drinks on the table as
Gabrielle said in pleased surprise, "I'd be delighted."

"You're a dark horse, Boris," I said, "your English is better than
mine. The best restaurant in this dump is Les Deux Magots, by the
way, and I recommend the *escargots* and the *coq au vin*—but for
God's sake don't eat any salad or anything else uncooked. Have a
nice evening, and don't worry about a single thing." I kissed
Gabrielle's hand and said in English, not to be outdone, "It is nice
for me when I may see you again."

"*Au plaisir, m'sieur.*"

The clock over the bar was at twenty past six when I left, and I
was stationed in cover not far from the hotel entrance an hour
later when Slavsky and Gabrielle came out and climbed into a
cyclo, sitting side by side as it started off in the direction of Les
Deux Magots.

It was a simple tumbler lock on the door of Room 27 and I went inside and left it half-open to give me acoustic access to the passage;
then I went across to the window and opened that too, looking
down. There was a drop of eight or nine feet onto a pile of what
looked like empty crates outside the back entrance, be a noisy exit
and I'd have to watch I didn't get a foot stuck between the broken
slats when I landed, cost precious time, but there was no yard wall
or anything to stop a clear run if I needed one.

From the distance a bell tolled in one of the temples, like the
incessant chiming of a clock; the relative cool of the evening crept
into the stifling warmth of the room; through the plaster-and-
lattice wall came the faint sound of voices, Asian by their tone.

There was a flashlight on the bedside table and I used that instead of putting the lights on, found Slavsky's midnight-blue silk dressing gown and hung it from the top hinge of the door to cover the narrow gap. Then the bathroom: Slavsky wasn't an espion, wouldn't have had any training in clandestine operations, hadn't shown himself to be terribly bright this evening in the bar, was simply a man who shipped munitions out and took the money home, but he might have learned that the underneath of the toilet cistern cover and the space between the bathtub and the wall are the only places you can hope to find if you want to hide anything.

Nothing there.

I didn't know how long I had. I'd briefed Gabrielle to avoid putting any questions to Slavsky as to what he did for a living, simply to accept the standard cover I knew he'd give her—that of an import-export agent. But at some stage he might think she'd been set up to coax information out of him, and that would put an end to their cozy little evening and he'd be back in this hotel in a panic trying to find a vacant line to his base in Moscow—*Have you heard of a man called Voss who's meant to be working with the Dmitrovich group?* He would also be through that doorway over there at a run to make sure the attaché case was still where he'd left it.

I checked for hairs drawn taut across the gaps between the tops of the drawers in the dressing table, found none; the telephone directory wasn't lined up in any particular way on the bedside table, didn't have one corner exactly at the edge or anything; there were no match-ends anywhere, balanced on movable surfaces, no little traps of any kind. I hadn't expected them—again, Slavsky wasn't an espion, didn't imagine anyone in Pouthisat would search his room; but I had to take the most extreme care while I was here, because if I left any sign of intrusion he'd telephone Moscow and change his plans for delivery and we wouldn't know what they were.

We wouldn't necessarily know what they were now: I could come away with nothing, draw a blank.

A great deal would depend on Gabrielle Bouchard. I wouldn't have stood a chance of getting Slavsky to open up in the bar this evening without the distraction she had offered to dull his thinking; I wasn't sure I would even have approached him, despite the in-depth briefing I'd had from Moscow via Pringle. But with Gabrielle there it had gone off well enough—I'd got Slavsky at least to admit, however tacitly, that he was running arms to the Khmer Rouge. And at this moment Gabrielle was still working for the cause, keeping the Russian amused while I checked the drawers, the cupboards, the hidden spaces in the room, coming up with only toys so far: *Madonna's Greatest Hits* on cassette, a plastic sachet of hard-porn photographs, a packet of exotic condoms with stars and stripes, an American DP51 high-capacity 9mm pistol, a half-empty flask of Smirnov.

The attaché case was under the chest of drawers, pushed right back so that it didn't show: Slavsky hadn't trusted the hotel safe and didn't want to attract attention by carrying the thing around in a town where a kid's piggy bank would be an instant target.

Bundles of bank notes, denomination 500 Swiss francs, nothing underneath them. I shut the case and slid it back against the wall. If Slavsky had—

Footsteps and I froze.

They were on the stairs, climbing. Not, I thought, hurrying, but then a man as big as Slavsky might have been told not to hurry up any stairs, not to surprise the heart: cardiac arrest was the leading cause of death among the top international arms dealers.

Climbing the stairs and reaching the passage now.

The window exit was an option only if I'd finished here, and I hadn't. The other option was to stay in the room and take Slavsky and give him to Pringle, have one of his agents-in-place grill the Russian to the point of death, suck him dry if he'd talk at all.

So I moved across the floorboards, placing my feet in time with the footsteps of the man out there to give them sound cover, and stood behind the door.

He sounded heavy, a heavy man. If he was Boris Slavsky his footsteps would slow as he saw the door was halfway open. The 9mm in the drawer might not be his only weapon; if he had something on him he would draw it, seeing the door like this. I hoped it wasn't Slavsky out there: to take him would simply be an alternative to letting him take me, and it would undo everything I was here to do, even if I had him grilled, even if he talked. We needed him to go ahead with his plans for delivery: it was the only way we could hope to stop them.

A cricket was singing somewhere outside the building, and as I waited, listening to the footsteps, I saw a flickering against the wall over there in the gloom as a salamander came in through the open window, tracing a shadow across the plaster.

There was no mirror in the room. The man out there wouldn't know where I was—wouldn't know there was anyone here at all—until he came right through the doorway, and by that time I would see his hand with the gun in it, if he had one with him, and that was all I would need, this close, say three feet from my sword hand to his wrist.

The footsteps weren't slowing, but he wasn't yet within five or six doors of this one, wouldn't have noticed from that distance and in the wan, flickering light out there that this one was open.

He might of course make a dramatic Drug Enforcement Agency entrance, hitting the door wide open and going into the shooting stance and yelling *freeze*. If he did that I'd have to move, and very fast; it could even be a little dangerous if he began sweeping the gun from this angle, be a matter of half a second to work in, all I'd get.

Hadn't slowed, they hadn't slowed, the footsteps. And it's sometimes like this in the course of a given mission, where the whole outcome, success or failure, the executive's life or death, depends on something quite trivial: whether the opposition's vehicle is closing in at three kph or four at a max of ninety, whether the drop from a roof is too high to use without critical injury, whether the footsteps along a corridor in the heat of the night are slowing, or simply coming on at a steady pace.

Signal: *The night hasn't gone well, but for what it's worth I've taken a prisoner.* There'd be one of his bloody silences on the line. They think you don't feel anything, the directors in the field, when things go wrong.

If this was Slavsky coming it wouldn't be Gabrielle's fault; she had what the recruiting desk at the Bureau calls "espion-like qualities," an eye for shadows, reflections, artifice in a man's walk; an ear for echoes, footsteps, deception in a man's tone. Nothing of this was manifest in her; I simply recognized it as a mirror image— or I could never have asked her to help me with Slavsky.

Now they were slowing, the footsteps, as the man out there reached the door of his room, or noticed the door of this one, half-open.

Slowing.

I relaxed my legs, let my right arm hang loose, shook the tension out of the fingers like shaking water off, watched the floor where his shadow would come when he reached the doorway, breathed deeply, slowly, let the nerves receive the automatic signals from the brain—that in a little while, perhaps in fifteen seconds, ten, the organism might be required to undertake action at maximum speed and with maximum force—let the understanding build in the autonomic nervous system that copious quantities of adrenaline might be needed at an instant's notice to fire the muscles, waiting, I was waiting now through the final countdown until suddenly the man was standing in the doorway, his shadow reaching across the floor.

I listened to his breathing.

"Tae mien nehnah tii non te?"

Then the shadow of his arm moved, lifting, and I felt the rush of adrenaline come surging through the system as the mind took a millisecond to rehearse the action of the sword hand swinging up, power-driven from the heel through the hip, the shoulder, the en-

tire organism now taut as a drawn bow as the hand of the man
moved to the door and he closed it and went on his way along the
passage, a janitor, security guard, someone like that, finding a door
open and closing it, a trivial function of his duties done.

It took me less than ten minutes more to find what I hoped I
would find, and as I stood looking at it in the beam of the flashlight
with the unused adrenaline still shaking the muscles and souring
the mouth, I saw that here, yes, I had the specific information
Pringle had asked me for at our first meeting at the airport in
Phnom Penh: the objective for *Salamander.*

16

SHADOW

There was a smell of pigs in here.

"I was able," Pringle said, "to get through to London almost immediately after you telephoned."

Presumably because traffic through the Australian satellite was less heavy at night. I'd phoned him from the hotel with the information as soon as I'd left Room 27, according to the book: the executive is to debrief anything of importance as soon as he can in case he's got at, and can't. I'd simply given him the position marked on the map I found in Slavsky's room: 12°3′N, 103°10′E. The rest wasn't major.

"What did Flockhart say?" I asked Pringle.

"That he would take immediate action."

"What action?"

Pringle gave a slight shrug. "I really can't say."

"But do you *know*?"

I was feeling sour, which is typical in this bloody trade when you've brought home the product and dropped it proudly on the doormat like a freshly killed rat; there's a sense of letdown, especially when things have been easy, and tonight's work had been so easy it worried me. You wonder if you've missed something, some little thing that's going to come back at you like a whiplash. Paranoia, yes, but tonight the adrenaline was still in the bloodstream and there was no kind of physical action I could take to disperse it—you try jogging athletically through the streets of Pouthisat, Cambodia, at ten o'clock at night and you'll be shot on sight by some zealous lad in the police or the army on the safe assumption that you've either stolen a watch or set a land mine somewhere.

"No," Pringle said evenly, "I don't actually know what kind of action Control is going to take. He keeps me less informed than some might suppose, as a matter of principle."

What he was telling me was that I was forgetting that the director in the field is also at risk during a given operation, and that the less information he has in his head, the less the opposition can get out of it when they start work with the burning bamboo sticks under the nails and so on. I hadn't forgotten; I just thought our smooth Mr. Pringle knew more than he was ready to tell me. That was all right, provided he'd got good reason, but I didn't know what it was.

I let it go. "What's that awful smell of pigs in here?"

"I really can't say."

His favorite answer to whatever you asked him, you put the penny in and out it came. It was stifling in this place; the power station was on overload again, so the ceiling fan wasn't working, and all we had for light was a kerosene lamp. Pringle had told me the building belonged to a volunteer mine-clearing unit; he knew them and had asked for the key, and this was also from the book— the executive and his director in the field never use the same rendezvous location twice unless it's considered secure. This place wasn't much more than a big shed, with mine detectors stacked against the wall and pairs of huge padded protective boots as big as snowshoes lined up on the concrete floor. Someone had started everything off with a flair for record keeping when they'd set up shop: there was a map of the town on the wall with big red blotches on it and a sprinkling of little green dots; it looked as if they'd made a red dot every time a mine had exploded, and there'd been so many that the dots had become blotches, mostly around schools, bus depots, temples, where the most feet could be expected to pass. The green dots presumably marked the places where mines had been detected and brought here for defusing, but there weren't enough to become blotches yet.

Pictures on the wall, one of the queen, two of Charles playing polo, no Di anywhere. Photograph of three men and a woman, all smiling happily, black crosses above their heads, one of the men holding a small pig—*that* explained it—some words scrawled underneath the photograph with ornate serifs and curlicues to give them solemnity, *They Did Their Job*. A picture of the pig on its own with a red ribbon round its neck, caption, *Little Stinker*. A picture of a Cambodian girl, eleven or twelve, crutches, radiant smile, two men holding her in a bear hug, huge fatherly grins. On the wall opposite the cluttered desk was a dartboard with Pol Pot's face crudely painted on it.

"How do we know for certain," I heard Pringle's cautious tones, "that the position on the map in Slavsky's room indicates the main guerrilla base of the Khmer Rouge?" He was looking at the topographical map he'd brought with him.

"We don't."

Bastard didn't like the look of my freshly killed rat.

"How certain," he asked, "are *you*?"

"Put it this way. We think Pol Pot is ready to launch a new offensive, possibly on the nineteenth of this month. The only way he can do it is by remote control, because the Cambodian army is virtually on stand-by to counter any land operation. So we're talking about missiles." The ceiling fan began turning again but the lights didn't come on: Pringle hadn't thrown the switch when we'd come in because the lamp was all we needed. "Then I see Boris Slavsky, a known arms dealer—according to your briefing—land in a Khmer Rouge aircraft and Colonel Choen leaving him with an attaché case full of Swiss francs, and we assume it's in payment for the missiles—or if you like it better, *I* assume. I assume also that the map was left with Slavsky to indicate the exact location where delivery is to be made. That location is buried in deep jungle, according to your topo, and even though it's not far from the coast there's a mountain range in the way with absolutely no roads—not even tracks—where any kind of transport can be used. If—"

"You studied the map thoroughly?"

Best left ignored. "The nearest airfield," I said, "is at Phumi Tuol Koki on the coast, and the only access by sea is through a fishing village." Pringle was leaning over his topo, following me. I didn't look at it, kept my eyes on the fly-encrusted ceiling fan, wanting him to know just how thoroughly I can look at a map when I'm searching someone's room for information. "There's a minor road fifteen kilometers from the marked position, but fifteen kilometers of jungle is like fifty kilometers of open terrain, in terms of accessibility. So if the mark on Slavsky's map doesn't show the exact location of the main Khmer Rouge base, I can't think what else it could mean."

I waited.

Pringle let a few seconds go by, possibly to show he'd noticed I'd ignored his question about my having studied the map, and was not pleased. That was a shame, because if he asked me another stupid question I was going to walk out of here—what *precisely* did he mean, had I studied the map? Did he think I was—steady now, yes, it's just the adrenaline talking, no need to go overboard.

"I think I agree with your assumption," Pringle said, "that we now know the exact whereabouts of Pol Pot. I'm just not sure that London will be convinced."

Something tried to alert me when he said that, but I couldn't pin it down. He'd said Pol Pot, not the Khmer Rouge base. Was there a difference? I let it go.

"It's up to London," I said.

"Of course. It's up to Mr. Flockhart." He went on staring at the map, then after a while folded it and turned his cool gray eyes on me, and I thought again how young he looked for this job, for running an executive through a field where the opposition was an army twelve thousand strong.

Was Pringle the only man Flockhart had been able to find for this one? The only DIF prepared to run the executive through the mission unknown to the signals room, unknown even to the Bureau itself? Or had Pringle been like me a week ago, prowling the corridors of that bloody building in Whitehall desperate for a job?

"You've no idea," I heard him saying, "how the assumed missiles will be delivered?"

"By air."

"You discovered this?"

"I didn't have to. The only—"

"By the way," he cut in, leaning forward slightly, his face earnest in the lamplight, "I meant, of course, had you had *time* to study the map thoroughly."

It took a second for me to realize what he was talking about. "Oh," I said, "of course." But Christ, had it been simmering in his mind all this time, until he'd had to blurt it out so that I'd know he hadn't wanted to give offense? Had Flockhart briefed him to be *this* careful with me? *Make quite sure you don't offend the executive—he's touchy and we can't afford to lose him.* So what made them think I might drop this one cold at any given minute and take the next flight home?

I could smell subterfuge again, acrid as brimstone, and when I got to the truth I would take, yes, the next plane to London.

"The only way they can deliver the missiles," I said, "is by air. There's no need for them to risk interception at sea or on the ground, if somebody finds out what they're doing, as in point of face we have. Slavsky's going to move a helicopter in to mow the trees at nought feet and leave the radar screens totally blank. Given something like an SA-321L with an eight-thousand-kilo payload he can ship in fifty or sixty high-explosive and incendiary short-range ground-to-ground missiles, more than the KR would need to blast Phnom Penh into a fireball."

Pringle leaned back, tilting his head and watching me along his nose. There was a shot from somewhere outside in the streets, and

I saw his pupils expand a degree and contract again. "You mean there's no way anyone can stop the delivery of missiles to Pol Pot?"

"Only at the source, and even if you found it and blew it up, the KR would simply go to any one of a hundred other sources and start again."

In a moment Pringle tilted his head down again and said, "We don't seem to have many options, do we?"

"I told you, we'd need a battalion."

"Do you believe Pol Pot would actually turn Phnom Penh into a fireball?"

"He likes to kill, and by the million. So I think that's what he'll do, yes, if the king ignores his ultimatum."

Shots came, a burst this time and more distantly, no return fire. I thought of Gabrielle.

Pringle folded his topographic map, his pale hands deft with the creases. "I need to know where you are," he said without looking up.

I told him. I didn't trust either him or Flockhart, but they wouldn't blow me to the opposition: I was working for them.

"I'll signal Control again," he said, "on the debriefing. After he's taken whatever action seems indicated, he'll get back to me. At that time it's possible he'll want to speak to you personally, and I'll send a contact to fetch you. But it won't be at least until morning. Suppose, then"—looking up now—"you make yourself available at your safe house from nine o'clock onward?"

"Will do."

"I'll be taking the call here in this office." He stood up, tucking the map into his pocket.

"Code designation for the contact?"

He suggested one, and at the door I said, "Perhaps you ought to put a peep on Slavsky, see if he goes anywhere interesting. But it'd have to be someone very good. If he sniffs any smoke he'll go to ground."

"There are two people in Phnom Penh I could use, if—"

"No one local; we need a real pro."

"Symes is in Bangkok."

"If you want to fly him over, yes, he's first-class."

"I'll do that." He opened the door and waited for me to go out first, but I held back.

"I need to make sure you're clear."

"Oh yes, of course." As if he'd forgotten. He hadn't. It had just been another subtle gesture of deference to the executive they couldn't afford to lose, and I noted it, I noted it well.

Someone was screaming in the distance, the sound shrilling in the heat of the night; perhaps there'd be another little red dot for the map tomorrow. I stood watching Pringle's thin figure receding as he walked away, his shadow trailing him and then moving ahead as he passed under a lamp, and the unnerving thought flashed into my mind that if he were suddenly attacked I might not feel inclined to save him.

"I shot first, you see," Gabrielle said.

She watched me from the low bamboo couch, perched on her haunches, naked, her arms across her knees, her body lit and shadowed by the lamp, the wide bandage around her like a sash. I wondered if she always made love like that, so desperately, despite her wound, or whether it had been because she'd thought it might be for the last time, life in this place being so cheap. I'd come to the mission to thank her for helping me with Slavsky, that was all, but she'd asked me to stay.

I pressed the plunger of the big plastic water dispenser and poured her a glass of Kristal Kleer from Chicago, Illinois.

"Then he shot back?" I asked her.

"Yes. Then it was my turn again." She took the water and drank, her face silvered with moisture, her lashes casting shadows on her ivory cheekbones, the surface of the water sending reflections flashing softly across her forehead and the wall behind. She lowered the foam cup at last and I took it from her.

"And you made a hit?"

She nodded. "Yes."

So those were the three shots I'd heard when I'd been debriefing to Pringle in the burned-out bus. "How long have you been doing this?"

She turned her head, watching the stars through the open window, faint in the heat haze. The moon had swung down toward the west by now; it had bathed us in its light as we'd made love, less gently than I'd wanted to because of her wound, but I'd been unable to calm her.

"Oh," she said, "for quite a while. He was the seventh."

I drank some water and went back to the couch to be with her, and the bamboo creaked. God knew what Sister Hortense must have thought, earlier; she'd been the nun who'd let me into the mission, as Gabrielle had asked her to if I came by at whatever time.

"Seven," I said, "isn't a bad score." I realized now why she hadn't shown any particular emotion when she'd told me at the hospital that the man who had wounded her was dead.

"That's a man's way of killing, isn't it? Keeping score, treating it like a game; I never thought I'd understand that. The thing is, I'm going to go on doing it until there aren't any left, or they kill me."

"How did it start?"

"Oh, I happened to see one of them actually setting a mine, under the arched gate of a school—this was in Phnom Penh. I reported it to the nearest Mine Action unit, and started thinking. I knew where most of the mines were being set, so I bought a rifle in the black market and started hanging out at night near the schools and the temples and the other target points, anywhere with just enough light to see by. I called out quietly to the first one, and I think the second, I don't remember, so that he'd turn in my direction and see the gun and know he was going to die; then I stopped doing that—I wasn't killing these people out of vengeance, I didn't want to play God, I just wanted them dead, so they couldn't hurt any more children." I watched a tear creeping on her cheek, jeweled in the light; she didn't lift a hand to wipe it away. "When I was quite small," she said softly, "I started learning flower painting from a Japanese in my father's consulate, and it quite consumed me—I knew I'd never want to do anything else but paint flowers, all my life long." She turned her head to look at me, smiling now. "I'm thirsty again."

I fetched more water for her, and didn't ask her any more about the Khmer Rouge she was killing off by night, didn't need to tell her how dangerous it was: she knew that, and must have found solace in it. Taking pictures of crippled children for her editors in Paris hadn't been enough, in the end, and she'd needed to get involved.

"I don't want to talk about it anymore," she said.

"Then we won't."

"I want to make love again, while there's still time."

We slept, afterward, with her head buried against me and her knees drawn up, and sometimes a nightmare jerked her awake and she had to get her breath before she pulled me tightly and fiercely against her and slept again, sighing like a child.

Soon after dawn there was thunder in the hills, and by eight o'clock, rain. I was soaked by the time I'd walked to the safe house, and so was the contact who came for me soon afterward, telling me I was needed at the place of the pig, the code designation Pringle and I had agreed on.

17

ZERO

"You did rather well."

"Apparently not," I said.

Flockhart favored me with one of his pauses. The line was full of squelch: this was coming through Moscow's Intersputnik—Pringle had told me the Australian satellite was on overload.

"How so?"

"My friend here," I told him, "feels you might not agree I've produced anything all that conclusive"—12°3′N, 103°10′E.

Pringle was watching me attentively, silhouetted against the rain-slashed window.

"That is to be seen," Flockhart said. "But I'd prefer not to pass it on to our people or Washington at this stage, or for that matter the crowned head."

"Our people" presumably being the U.K. Ministry of Defense, who would brief the Prime Minister; "Washington" presumably being the Chairman of the Joint Chiefs of Staff, who would brief the President; and the "crowned head" being King Sihanouk. Because this was the only possible action anyone could be expected to take if they were ready to rely on Boris Slavsky's map: an air strike.

"However," I heard Flockhart saying, "you've certainly made a good start."

I left that.

"We simply require to take things a little further."

I realized he had to watch what he said on a satellite line, but Flockhart also had a penchant for the cryptic, as I'd learned when he'd first talked to me at the Cellar Steps. They get like that, the controls, after years of pushing the pawns across the board in the signals room: they end up talking like a cipher grid.

I waited again. He'd go on when he was ready.

"We can't see the wood at the moment, you understand, even by satellite. What we need is to confirm the evidence, physically."

I didn't answer. He was out of his bloody mind.

"Then everyone would know that action could be taken on a sound premise, and would therefore succeed."

"Yes, but there isn't time. Not if that deadline is real." The nineteenth.

"You would require, what? Twelve hours?"

Or less, but he was talking about a suicide run, a low-level chopper survey with telescopic cameras. "We can't see the wood" translated as "We can't see the Khmer Rouge camp for the trees," even with Landsat, since it was in deep jungle. I understood that, and I understood that neither the UN nor the U.S. would order a strike based solely on a map position. The problem was more local: I didn't see how *Salamander* could keep on running with a dead executive.

I asked Flockhart, "Have you ever put your hand into a beehive?"

A squeal came from the room next door—I suppose someone had picked up Little Stinker and he wanted to be put down again.

"What was that?" Flockhart asked.

"A pig." Over the line it must have sounded like an interrogation cell near closing time.

"Given adequate magnification," Flockhart said in a moment, "you wouldn't have to go in as close as that."

"You can hear a fan at five miles, for Christ's sake." Too late to edit that: I'd slipped, showing the nerves, and he would have noticed. It was this that should have warned me.

"Speed," Flockhart's voice came persuasively, "would be of the essence, of course. Speed and surprise."

A night sortie with infrared cameras—he'd got it all worked out. But he wouldn't be sitting in the chopper when it got blown out of the sky.

The pig squealed again and it plucked at the nerves. That should have warned me too. "You'd never find anyone to do it," I said.

"We're thinking of you, of course."

"Look, I haven't got more than fifty hours behind me in one of those things." The only training we get at Norfolk is just enough to give us a chance if the pilot suffers a heart attack.

"But you've used them before, and most effectively."

The rain drummed on the roof of the building, and a trickle had started below the door, dark on the scarred concrete. Pringle had moved his foot out of its way, was watching me again with his cool gray eyes. I didn't think he could hear what Flockhart was saying, but he could hear me all right and he'd know what was on. Flockhart would have briefed him on it in any case while the contact was on his way to fetch me. *We need him to agree to this, and I want you to do all you can at your end to persuade him.*

But there wasn't anything Pringle could do: I didn't trust him, didn't respect him. Flockhart I would listen to; he was a major player, was seasoned, had authority. I didn't trust him either, but yes, I would listen.

"For this job," I said, "you'd need an ace." We were working with a deadline and there was another rainstorm in and we couldn't wait for it to clear, would have to fly half-blind to the target, and if the rain was still coming down when we reached it there wouldn't be any point in even turning the cameras on.

"We have one," I heard Flockhart saying.

"An ace?"

"Yes."

Covered himself, in case I said no.

"He's tired of life?"

"He is not unsanguine."

"I know him?"

"It's unlikely. But he's world-class."

And a Cambodian, he must be, burning with the holy fire of love for his country, ready to do or die. No one else would touch this one.

"What's the state of preparedness?" I asked Flockhart.

"Launch zero."

Oh, Jesus, he'd been working through the night, he and Pringle, finding a pilot and a machine and putting them on stand-by at the airfield over there, locating the cameras, setting them up. *Or had they done it days ago?* The first time I'd met Pringle at the airport in Phnom Penh he'd told me that the first objective for *Salamander* was to get information on Pol Pot. I was close to doing that, had found him on the map, would have to follow up, make certain, get close to him with the cameras, take his bloody picture and send it to London, wish you were here, the weather's marvelous.

The weather was ten-tenths *shit* and I was standing here with the phone slippery with sweat because of the heat in this stinking hole and because I should have been warned when the pig had squealed and my nerves had jumped, should have been warned even *then* that I was going to do what he said, what Flockhart said, because I was already committed to putting my neck on the block in the name of the salamander, whatever the chances were of coming out of it with anything to show, of coming out of it alive, *chances?* surely you must be joking, they'll have weapons out there, never mind about the leaves overhead blocking their view, they can send up a square mile of firepower in a single blast the moment they hear the rotors, I wish to God they wouldn't keep that stinking *pig* in here.

"Do you have any questions?" Flockhart.

"Yes. Who's going to replace me if I come unstuck?"

Another of his *bloody* pauses. I suppose he was a bit surprised, the brave little ferret in the field had actually agreed to getting himself blown into Christendom without too much persuasion.

"No one would replace you."

Bloody liar. The control *always* lines up a replacement when he sends his executive on a suicide run; I'd been one of them myself on half the missions I'd worked, walking in a dead man's shoes.

"There's no *replacement?*"

"You must take it how you will," Flockhart said, "but for this undertaking you are irreplaceable."

Pringle was watching me, probably saw the reaction in my eyes: you don't blank everything off when you're with your director in the field, you're supposed to trust him.

"You mean this is a one-shot thing?"

Silence, then: "Yes. You are our only chance. Surely you realized that."

"Why should I?" Then I understood. "Where is the Sacred Bull?"

It's what we call the Bureau, we the beleaguered minions in the field.

"Nowhere," Flockhart said.

So he was still running *Salamander* solo, without a signals board, without support in the field, even without a replacement for the executive, going over the heads of Administration and reporting directly to the Prime Minister. Only four people, then, were privy at this stage to the mission: the PM, Flockhart, Pringle, and I. Until they brought in Washington, until they had to, if an air strike was to be ordered.

"When will that change?" I asked Flockhart carefully. The stakes seemed suddenly rather high with only four players in the game.

"At some time in the future."

Shouldn't have asked.

Pringle watched me as the trickle of water spread across the concrete, as the pig in there squealed again and the rain hit the window aslant in the wind and the leaves of the sugar palms out there shone steel-bright under the storm as I stood there looking for more questions to ask, for more information, some kind of reassurance that I wasn't expected to go into this phase of the mission with too much left to chance. But there weren't any questions left; Flockhart had briefed me as far as he needed to, had already set the whole thing up, pilot, chopper, cameras, and had given me the score: launch zero.

"We've got a rainstorm going on here," I told him. "We'll have to wait till it stops."

"Of course." His voice was almost gentle. "Whenever you're ready."

18

<svg decorative separator>

FLAK

"My two sons were killed," the man perched on the oil drum said in local French, and lit another Gauloise from the stub of the last. "They were in the Fields."

He was Captain Khay of the Cambodian Air Force, and he'd been seconded by his squadron to fly me to 12°3'N, 103°10'E. The Sikorsky S-67 was standing behind us in the hangar, squat, matt black, ugly as sin.

Khay stared out at the rain as it came slanting across the open doors of the hangar, stirring the bright gray puddles into boiling steel. The sun was still in the sky somewhere, but low now and drowned in the haze; the light across the airfield was bleak, electric, looking as if someone had forgotten to switch it off.

"So I am doing this," the captain said, "for my sons, for the king, and for my people."

"Doing this?"

Khay looked at me with a jerk of his head. "This sortie."

"You wouldn't fancy it," I said, "otherwise." And listened carefully.

"How do the Americans say?" He tried out his English, "You must do a thing"—then shook his head.

"You gotta do whatcha gotta do."

"That is right, yes!" The smile didn't reach his eyes; they

simply narrowed. His eyes had never lit, I would have thought, since his sons had died. "That is why I do it."

"Did you volunteer?" I asked him.

"No. I am chosen because I am the most experienced pilot in the service, with the helicopters." He flicked ash off his Gauloise.

"What happened to your hand?"

"Oh"—he looked at it—"it is snake bite, long time ago. Cobra."

"You must be pretty fit."

He shrugged. "One simply has to relax. Western people drink whole bottle of whiskey, sometimes works. Meditation best. So why do you do this?"

"Why am I making this sortie?"

"Yes."

"You gotta do whatcha gotta do."

The grimace. "I think that is what you will say."

He got off the oil drum and walked toward the curtain of rain at the entrance to the hangar, looking at the sky. At the mine-clearing unit they'd said the storm was going to last another twelve hours, but Pringle had ordered me down here to meet Khay, who said it could clear by midnight. The sun must be down by now; the sugar palms were lost in the haze and the terminal building was marked only by its lights.

In a moment Khay turned and came back, pulling a map from his jumpsuit and spreading it across the oil drum. "We will go soon," he said. "Maybe another hour—the wind is shifting. But if we run into any more rain we will simply fly around it. If that is not possible, then we will put her down and wait it out, maybe here, or here, somewhere between the mountains. We have rations and water for three days, and enough fuel for four hundred kilometers. We can sleep in the machine if we need to. Have you any questions?"

"What's your ideal schedule?"

"My ideal schedule is that we go in and take the photographs within an hour, maybe ninety minutes, and get out again"—he glanced up at me—"if they let us." He folded the map. "I do not want to have to fly this thing in the daylight. The identification numbers are false and we could be challenged by radio; there are so many factions, you see, suspicious of each other, quite apart from the Khmer Rouge. This is not an Air Force machine, with that identification, but it is obviously assigned to night flying, and that could raise questions." He lit another Gauloise, his hand not quite steady—not, I thought, because he was worried about the flight but because his nerves had been under strain ever since Pol Pot had taken over the country. I'd noticed it in others; the people here lived in the constant fear that it could happen again.

"Is this aircraft armed?" I asked him.

Khay shrugged. "Normally we carry 30mm barbette-mounted cannon, but it was taken off before I assumed command." He dropped his cigarette and flattened it against the concrete with his flying boot. "In any case we are not going to hang around the target area long enough for them to send up a helicopter. We go in, we come out, and if the camera does not jam we get some pictures."

This was at 19:00 hours, and by 20:00 we saw a drenched moon floating in the night sky as the wind shifted again and then died, leaving the airfield steaming. There was still a light rain coming down at 21:15 but Khay said it didn't worry him, and climbed onto the seat of the workhorse and pulled the Sikorsky out to the tarmac.

We took off twenty minutes later into dead air, with the rotor blades churning the puddles into mist as we became airborne and headed southwest toward the sea.

He'd had this helicopter standing by for days, Pringle, on instructions from London; for a week, ever since I'd made contact with him for the first time at the airport in Phnom Penh. He must have.

Because Flockhart was smart.

"ETA ten minutes," I heard Khay calling above the crackling of the rotors.

"Roger."

Flockhart was smart enough to know that if I took *Salamander* on at all I would hit the first objective before long: information on Pol Pot. And he'd known it might have to be confirmed by air reconnaissance, and so had made overtures through Sihanouk's intelligence arm to secure an aircraft and have it put on readiness. Flockhart, I was beginning to understand, left nothing to chance, providing he had control. But he was in London now, with the buds of the daffodils just beginning to show in the pale March sunshine at three in the afternoon as the buses rumbled past the black iron railings, and here it was different, as we skated across the crests of the mountains below a reef of cloud, the land dark below us and the clock on the instrument panel flicking the minutes away to zero; here Flockhart hadn't the slightest control, and could only wait by the telephone for whatever Pringle might signal. My evaluation of this sortie hadn't changed: this was a suicide run.

"Nine minutes," Khay told me, and took us down to three thousand feet as the mountains gave way to jungle. "If there is any wind still blowing down there it will be from the west, and so I am going to turn now a little and approach the target from the east, so they will not hear us so soon." With a shrug: "It will make only a very slight difference, but we need all the advantage we can get." His eyes studied my face. "And how are you feeling, *mon ami?*"

"Everything's set up."

I'd checked the camera three times on our way here, for something to do. It was a one-thousand-frame Hartmann-Zeiss with a twenty-five-degree omnidirectional sweeping capacity, and I'd set it at base maximum, which was where we'd start taking pictures.

"It is not what I mean," Khay said, still with his eyes on me. "I ask you how you are feeling."

"Oh. Quite confident."

That wasn't what he meant either but it was all he was going to get. The guards down there in the camp would start picking us up acoustically very soon now, and we'd be on a collision course governed by our airspeed and the time it took the Khmer Rouge to man their guns. So how would you feel, for God's sake?

Khay looked away and checked his instruments.

"Seven minutes."

The moon was behind us now, and I thought I could see our shadow crossing the jungle below, but it must have been an illusion: at this altitude it would be too far ahead of us, nearing the camp, a ghostly harbinger.

"You have other children?" I asked Khay. "Daughters?"

He turned his head. "No."

"Still have a wife?"

He looked away. "She is missing. She is missing since fifteen years."

I shifted in my seat, getting more control of the camera, pressing the button, shooting a few frames, watching the counter running, shutting down again.

"You have children?" I heard Khay asking.

"No."

"Wife?"

"No."

His eyes were on me again. "You are lone wolf."

"Not quite. Stray cat."

He looked at his instruments again. "Five minutes. Do you mind if I smoke?"

"Go ahead." I hadn't expected him to have held out this long.

He lit up, using his blue Bic lighter.

Below us the jungle flowed in the night; we could tell it was there only by the faint sheen on the leaves cast by the moon. Occasionally there was a clearing, and I saw one with a dark line crossing it, some kind of track.

"Four minutes," Khay said, and drew on his cigarette, narrowing his eyes in the smoke as he let it curl from his mouth; then he dropped the stub and put his boot on it. "We will make our turn now, and go in from the east."

The ocean of leaves swung beneath us, the horizon tilting, flattening out again as the compass spun and settled.

At three minutes to zero Khay turned his head again. "We will be moving into earshot quite soon now."

I gave him a nod and shot another dozen frames, watched the counter, released the button.

"It is okay?"

"Perfect."

"Two minutes." He checked his bearings again and changed course by a degree, brought the Sikorsky back, dropped it a hundred feet, two hundred, until the heads of the palms showed up in clusters with a gap here and there where some of them had died off, their trunks leaning.

"We have one minute to go," Khay said, raising his voice now, wanting to make sure I heard and understood.

"Roger." I watched the jungle ahead. "Give me thirty seconds, will you?"

He nodded, and I was aware of the environment suddenly, sharply aware as the senses became fine-tuned, aware of the vibration of the seat under me, of the floor under my feet, of the steady beat of the rotor and its deep and incessant throbbing, aware of the dry mouth and the adrenaline flush and the need to breathe slowly, keep still, keep patient as we settled again by fifty feet, settled again until the leaves were streaming below us, dark, rushing—

"*Thirty seconds.*"

I hit the button and swung the camera down a degree at a time as we moved into the target area, seeing gaps in the trees, a small lake, but nothing that looked like—

"*Zero.*"

Felt the slight vibration in the body of the Hartmann-Zeiss, swung it lower, lower again by another degree, keeping my eyes on the leaves below in case there was anything I could pick out, a truck, a half-track, huts, whatever was there, moving the camera to the base end of its travel and then up again as Khay banked the Sikorsky and brought it round in a tight turn and dropped and leveled out and began a second run in and a faint rattling began and I hunched into myself and concentrated on the camera as something hit the Sikorsky, nothing big yet, they needed time to roll out of their sleeping bags and lurch to the guns and swing them into the aim and fire, the Sikorsky lifting now, my knees pressing into the floor as a longer burst came this time, heavier, the flash of its detonation flickering among the leaves.

Khay jerked a look at my face. "We go in again?"

"Yes."

There wasn't any choice: with only a twenty-five-degree angle on the camera there was no point in circling the target; all we'd get on film would be the camp's perimeter.

Medium turn this time at the end of the lift, then we dropped again and Khay brought the speed up and I tilted the Hartmann-Zeiss to maximum high and pressed the button and started bringing it down by degrees as we ran in and fetched a barrage and the cabin roof took on a glare and the fuselage felt the shock and Khay half-turned his head to listen and then dismissed it, concentrating on the controls as another barrage crackled from the trees and I released the button and looked at him.

"We cannot go in again," he called above the noise. "But I will turn and stand off for a moment in maybe a mile, for you to take more pictures. Do you agree?"

"Sure, let's do that."

The jungle was booming behind us as they brought their tank guns into the barrage and I saw tracers reflected in the Perspex panel, then the horizon swung again with the moon curving across the darkness as Khay made his turn and vibration came in under the g-load and I started the camera running, the sky threaded with tracers now and the sound of the guns slapping at the cabin and the surface of the jungle down there boiling as the shells ripped through the leaves.

"We go now," Khay called, then there was something else I couldn't catch because a shell hit the tail of the Sikorsky with a lot of noise and he was nursing the controls as we went into a slow horizontal spin and the horizon began tilting and vibration came in very badly now, shaking the whole cabin as Khay shifted the controls and shouted something in Khmer and I hit the flap on the camera and started taking out the cassette, but the cabin was shuddering now and we were losing height, the Sikorsky spinning faster all the time until the centrifugal force dragged me against the instrument panel and Khay's hands were wrenched away from the controls and his eyes made contact with mine just once as he was flung against the bulkhead with his boots flying up and we went into the trees with the rotor whipping and slashing, the sound volume exploding into a roar as the deceleration forces hurled me away from the instrument panel and across the cabin, saw Khay's face again for an instant as he was flung headfirst between the seats toward the storage section, saw just his feet now, his boots, as the roaring blocked out all other sounds and I was aware of the final impact but couldn't analyze it, see or feel details, only knew that we'd crashed and that I was going under.

19

SMOKE

I looked at Khay's boots.

They didn't move. The feet in them didn't move.

We hadn't been here long: I could hear the gyro still winding down behind the instrument panel.

They would look for us.

On this thought I moved, though carefully. It had been a head blow, knocked me out for a minute. Moonlight was in the cabin, but I couldn't see any blood blackening the bulkhead where I was lying. The Sikorsky was on its side, and I could smell fuel, but there was no flame light anywhere that I could see.

I went on moving, because they would look for us, be here soon; we were within a mile, two miles of the camp.

"Khay?"

Bruise on my shoulder, felt it when I got up, just as far as a crouch, testing for anything broken that might be still blacked out under the endorphins. Everything articulated well enough, hands, feet, hips, neck.

"Khay?"

The boots didn't move. The feet in the boots didn't move.

There wasn't enough space between the two rear seats to let me through, because the Hartmann-Zeiss had come unshipped and was wedged there. I had to climb over it to talk to Khay, find out if he was all right.

"Khay?"

The loading flap at the side of the camera was still hanging open, just as I'd left it. The cassette would have to be salvaged but that didn't have priority.

"Khay?"

I could see his shoulders now, and his head. He was facedown, and his head was at a bad angle from his shoulders, a very bad angle; there wasn't, for instance, any point in calling his name again. I felt for the pulse in his throat and found it still there, but weak, rapid but weak. Blood was caking his skull in the occipital area: that was where his head had smashed into the storage door and broken his neck.

A night bird called, disturbed by the noise the Sikorsky had made coming down through the leaves, its rotor threshing among them; I could hear monkeys, also awakened and alarmed. There were no more shots from the Khmer Rouge camp; they would have seen us going down, heard the impact, would have sent out a search party immediately. It was on its way here now.

There was a holstered gun at Khay's belt but I couldn't use that: they would hear the shot. I used my hands instead, talking to him in my mind, wishing him well, speeding him on his journey, asking Buddha to receive his spirit and be mindful of the honor this man had brought upon himself in giving his life for his people. Then, when there was no pulse anymore, I went to pull the cassette out of the Hartmann-Zeiss, but found it was jammed: the camera had been wrenched away from its bracket on impact and the shock had buckled the panels.

I could take the whole thing with me, but it was cumbersome, would slow me down a great deal, critically: if I was going to get clear of this mess I would need to be light on my feet. They should be within gunshot range by now, the people in the search party; all they would need to do was catch sight of me through the trunks of the palm trees when I left the Sikorsky and began trekking.

A thought came: they might have orders to take any survivors alive, and I didn't want to confront the barking man again, Colonel Choen. This time he would put me through interrogation to the point of attrition.

I went on tugging at the cassette and got it halfway out, but it was jammed worse now because of the angle and I hit it back and started again, listening for voices as the gyro wound down to silence at last. The people in the search party would also be listening, guided by the sharp chittering sounds of the monkeys in the trees above the crash site.

I had to get this *bloody* thing out and take it with me: there was no choice. Take a letter, Miss Fortescue, to the Chairman of the Joint Chiefs of Staff, the Pentagon. *Dear General, the Khmer Rouge base camp is in fact located at 12°3′N, 103°10′E, as I have now established personally. A massive artillery barrage was fired as our helicopter twice made a run across the area. I trust this will leave you convinced.*

Use the sheath knife on Khay's belt, prize the bloody thing out, come on, for Christ's sake, come *on*.

I'm sorry to disturb you, sir, but this has just come in from a British intelligence agent in Cambodia.

What the hell, he trusts it'll leave me convinced? Who is this guy?

I don't know, sir, but he could have gone loco, you know, jungle fever, it's pretty hot there right now.

Get this fucking thing out, you've got one more fucking minute before they're here.

Sure. But there may be something in it. Tell him we gotta have photographs, okay? Tell him to get pictures.

Not coming out, so I kicked the side of the camera to stress the frame back to a rectangle, parallelogram now, *shit-shaped*, the sweat running off me because listen, those *bastards* are close, have to be very *close*, and I can't—I *cannot* leave here without this cassette, without the photographs for the general, Khay *died* to get me this bloody thing, *kick*, a precision kick and the cassette came out with a rush and I stuffed it inside my jumpsuit and we have to move rather quickly now, my good friend, do we not, feeling in Khay's pocket for his lighter, not finding it, try the other one, he's—he was left-handed, *I should have remembered*, wasting so much *time*, found it now and clambered onto the seats to reach the door above my head but it was stuck, the whole cabin was distorted just like that fucking camera, *hit* it with your shoulder, *harder* than that, could see a light, I could see some kind of light through the jungle, firefly, just joking, a soldier with a torch, the first of them, the nearest, *hit* it and we got it right this time and the door swung open and I clambered through and slid down the outside of the cabin, would need a fuse, the belt of the jumpsuit was all we had, so use that.

Twisted the cap of the fuel tank open and made sure none of the stuff spilled onto me, dipped the belt in and pulled it out again and flicked the wheel of the lighter and flung myself clear and hit the jungle floor and burrowed through the undergrowth as the Sikorsky blew like a sunrise, kept on burrowing through the cool darkness of the leaves, the monkeys screaming now.

I suppose I had come three or four miles, burrowing at first and then getting onto my feet and stumbling through the dark entangling undergrowth, tripping many times on creeper, going down and smelling the fibrous soil against my face, rich and moist from the recent rain.

Now I was leaning against a palm trunk, watching the glow in the distance as Khay's funeral pyre burned low. He would have wanted cremation, according to Buddhist custom, and would have enjoyed the fact that torching the Sikorsky had given them something to focus on, the men in battle dress, to hold their attention while I got clear. He would have left nothing for them in the ashes, no metal badge or insignia; he had known our sortie would perhaps bring us into direct contact with the Khmer Rouge.

Black smoke hung in a cloud above the trees, sometimes smothering the moon and then clearing again as the night air flowed, drawing out the smoke in skeins. I still listened for voices, for the clink of weaponry, but heard nothing, saw nothing of any light.

After a while I moved on again, heading east toward the nearest bullock track, and it was when I was tripped again by jungle creeper and went down with my hands spread out in front of me to break the fall that I felt a squirming beneath one of them, the left one if I remember, and then the rapid and repeated shock of the strike against my wrist, and when I hit the thing away I saw a long thin trickle of green against the jungle floor, and remembered what Gabrielle had said.

20

SKULLS

There are snakes in the river.

My spine arched again to a spasm and I lay like that, curved against the earth with my face to the sky, lay like that for I didn't know how long, the sweat pouring from me.

They swim across at night—the light attracts them, and the rats.

I slumped again like a drawn bow snapping, and the fever began. I had been expecting it.

Especially the hanuman—do you know it? The bright green one, quite small but more deadly than the cobra, even the king cobra.

Another spasm struck and I became arched, drawn taut, powerless to move, to relax the muscles. It was beginning to be difficult now to breathe, so I dragged at the air, sucked at it, but nothing happened. If the voluntary muscles were to be affected, so would the involuntary muscles, including those of the heart. I waited, with the moon swimming in the slits between my lids, and then the drawn nerves snapped again and my shoulders hit the earth.

Were there more of those things here? Did that one have a mate, and if so, how far was it from where I was lying? I couldn't do with more, with more than one. They are more deadly than the cobra.

One simply has to relax. Khay, the late Captain Khay. Western people drink whole bottle of whiskey, sometimes work. Meditation best.

187

Soon after this—hours? I didn't know—the shaking began, and the delirium.

There were nine moons when the storm came roaring into the jungle and I counted them as the trees bent low under the force of the whipping wind, nine in a circle, circling, a giddy-go-round of white-lit moons, spinning in the night as the head rolled, lolled, shaking itself, was shaken by the fever as the sweat sprang and I shouted something, shouted at the storm, shuddering, hands, fingers clawing at the soft moist fibers, bringing them to the mouth to eat, hungering for remembered motions, eating, running—staggering up and lurching and then crashing down again, singing like a drunk as the storm howled through the leaves and blew away the circle of moons and there was just the dark and I lay blinded, whirled in the deep spinning vortex of the night.

Pain was there, and this comforted me: the nerves were not yet numbed, could still serve the organism. The pain was in the left hand, wrist, arm, burning, as if I'd plunged them into fire. I got onto my feet again and flayed my arm around, filling the dark with flames, touching the trees until they too took fire and the storm sent sparks flying, seized the flames and hurled them in hot bright banners as I stood dazzled, reeling under the heat, the eyes seared, the mouth open and filled with coals, roaring like a dragon, bellowing flames.

Meditate, he, the man with the unremembered name, had said.

Crashing to the earth with the legs buckling, lying across a creeper, a long, thin—*oh Jesus Christ, I can't do with more of*—a thin, unmoving creeper, let go then, and meditate, fear nothing and fear not fear, reach for the silence, the stillness, the domain of the unified field, of universal consciousness and love, let go, let go, and drift into the void where everything is nothing, and nothing everything, let go.

But this halcyon respite has not been for long, has it, our good friend, for we are running again—running?—lurching, we mean, lurching and staggering and hitting trees, pitching down and crawling until the thought of the thin green hanuman catapults us to our feet again and we reel onward through the crashing dark, the moon down now, the nine moons down, *is this venom always lethal?* tell us, pray, are we a goner, done for, is this the Styx we're drowning in as we goad ourselves through the jungle night? Then for what purpose, for God's sake?

To find the bullock track.

A ray of sanity there, my masters, there's thought left somewhere in the fevered brain, squealing like a rat on fire for attention, the bullock track, yea, verily, in the name of the salamander: the bullock track and the road to Pouthisat and London, you must be out of your bloody mind, the veins are full of that thing's venom and the nerves are running riot, never mind the salamander, the first thing is to perpetuate life, carry this charred and ember-bright organism through the burning dark, east by the polar star glimpsed here and there through the endless canopy of leaves; listen to the thoughts still left in the smoldering consciousness and let them be thy guide, world without end as we fall again, fall down again, and this time we do not, we cannot get up, so destroyed are we in this unholy fire, a shred of blackened bone and gristle and hollow, echoing despair, God rest ye here, my most unmerry gentleman, and offer the relics of thy substance to the earth.

Skulls grinning at me, into my face as the cold light creeps through the sugar palms. Skulls, lined up in orderly rows, in serried ranks of bone-white laughter.

But these are real.

I know this.

And then there is darkness again, and in the darkness movement, a lifting, a bearing away, and in the wan light of morning a face leans over mine, smiling. An arm raises my shoulders, and a voice sounds.

"Drink."

21

KHENG

"What were those skulls?"

The monk closed his eyes, opened them. "They were my brothers."

I remembered stone columns, ancient, laced with creeper.

"It was a temple?"

"Yes."

Sometimes he spoke French, sometimes English, his language scholarly in both.

"That was a long time ago," I said, more as an exercise than anything, testing the memory, finding it sound.

"It was yesterday."

He meant it still seemed like yesterday. It would have been twenty years ago, when the Khmer Rouge were scouring the countryside, hunting for intellectuals, monks, schoolteachers, village scribes.

I finished the bowl of soup or whatever it was, perhaps herbs; it had tasted brackish, of roots.

"Did you carry me here?"

"Yes. You were in the helicopter, I assume." He had a smile like the Dalai Lama's; the sweetness of his spirit lit his eyes, humbling me, my brute calling.

"You heard it fly over?" I asked him.

"Yes."

Quick—"When?"

"The night before last."

"Today is the seventeenth?"

"By your calendar."

Two days to the deadline. Call it two minutes, then, there's no bloody difference.

"It was a hanuman?" I heard the monk asking.

"What? I think so. Green."

Gently he turned my wrist over, studying the blackened flesh. "You are a very strong man," he said. "You were already over the worst of the fever when I found you. The bite of the hanuman is usually fatal."

"You go there to pray?"

"To be with my brothers."

This was a cave we were in, draped with tapestries from the temple; a Buddha sat in a niche the monk must have carved from the rock; a small oil lamp flickered in the depths of the cave, and I saw an owl perched there, staring with bright obsidian eyes, its shadow huge against the rockface.

"You must sleep again now," the monk said.

"How far are we from Pouthisat, overland?"

"A hundred and forty kilometers."

On Pringle's topographic map it was a hundred by air. "Sleep?" My capacity to think linearly was still not back in shape. "No. I need to reach Pouthisat."

The monk hitched his threadbare robe around him, watching me with curiosity. "You flew here from Pouthisat?"

"Yes."

"I heard you disturbing the Khmer Rouge. Was that deliberate?"

"It was on the cards."

"You were accompanied?"

"Yes. My pilot didn't survive."

"He was in the conflagration?"

191

"Yes."

"We shall pray for him, my brothers and I." In a moment he said, "You were pulling the tail of the tiger. Of Saloth Sar."

"Who is he?"

"It is the real name of Pol Pot."

"He's there now, at the camp?"

"Yes. But he is ill."

Oh really. "How ill?"

"He has ceded his powers to General Kheng."

"His second-in-command?"

"So it is said."

"Who says? How do you know this?" I stood up and fell down again, knees buckling, he wasn't quick enough to catch me, hadn't expected me to do anything so bloody silly.

"You must rest," he said, his eyes amused. "You are among those who goad themselves through life. That is not the way."

"Who told you about General Kheng?" It sounded slurred.

This was perfect, wasn't it, listen, within two days I had to get this film into Pringle's hands a hundred and forty kilometers away overland and he had to get it to London for the British and American and UN brass to look at and they had to go into joint session and if they decided on an air strike the bombers would have to be airborne in time to make the hit by dawn of the nineteenth, *the day after tomorrow,* and at the moment, at this very moment when I should be kicking the whole thing into action my speech was slurred and the cerebral cortex was still deep-fried and when I stood up I fell down again, this was perfect, so what is, what is to be done, my good friend, in this rather sorry situation?

"Anger does not assist in recovery," I heard the monk saying gently. "Rather should we relax, and let our karma resolve our predicament for us."

"Right." I sat up, arms around my knees, letting my head hang loose, rolling the neck muscles. "You're damn right. Excuse me. Who told you about General Kheng?"

"It is known in the village. The peasants bring me offerings of food and the bare necessities. Look!" He held up a tin frying pan, a real work of art, copper rivets and everything. "They also bring me news of the Khmer Rouge, for what it is worth."

Do they indeed. I lifted my head and looked at him. "And what are the immediate plans of General Kheng, do they know?"

"They have not spoken of plans."

"What do they say about him?"

The monk moved, blowing on some charcoal and pouring water from a pitcher into a black iron pot. "That he is young, power-hungry, and ambitious." He took some dried herbs from a shelf, broke their stalks, and dropped them in. "He has said he will restore power to Saloth Sar when he is well again, but it would surprise me if such a thing came about."

I got onto my haunches, swaying like a drunk, pulling myself upright with my hands on the rockface for support, I am not proud, you must understand, when the need is urgent, and if there is only one way to do a thing then that is the way I will do it, so go to hell.

"No plans, then," I said. No news of the nineteenth.

"No. The peasants do not hear everything, I would think; it is simply that the soldiers talk a little to them when they come into the village for their needs." He stirred the pot with a wooden spoon, his face lit with concentration.

I wasn't surprised, as I stood with my hands away from the rockface now, that nothing about the nineteenth had been heard in the village: security on that subject would be tight. I took a few paces, needing to touch the wall only once.

"Is General Kheng at the camp now?" I asked the monk.

"I don't know."

Then I would have to find out.

"How far is the village?"

"From here?"

"Yes."

"Two kilometers, perhaps less. I will go with you." He turned his sweet smile on me. "Then when you lose consciousness again I shall be there to carry you back." He resumed his stirring, the pot beginning to steam.

"How far is the camp from the village?"

"Perhaps fifteen kilometers."

"So the soldiers use motorized vehicles all the way?"

"Yes. Usually jeeps."

I shuffled to the mouth of the cave, one hand along the wall until I could hold on to the peeling bamboo curtain, the skull of a bird watching me from the hook where it hung; it looked like an owl's, perhaps was the owl's brother. When I felt ready I made my way back, no support this time, progress.

The sun was burning its path through the palm trees toward noon when the monk said, "Seeing you were in no mood to rest, I prepared this concoction for you. It will give you strength for your journey."

It tasted of embers and sent fire through my veins, and when I'd finished it we began walking along the bullock track through the trees, none too fast in the rising heat of the day but I didn't fall down and the monk didn't help me, let me go it alone as he knew I needed to.

"Do other vehicles come to the village," I asked him, "from the road to the east?"

"Sometimes. Foreign Aid Services, some of the Catholic missions, and of course the Mine Action units." We stood in the shade of a barn on the eastern border of the village, where the huts gave way to rice fields and the road ran through a bamboo grove to the horizon.

"Where should I wait?"

"I will show you."

He took me to the house of a blind man, saying that I would be safe there for as long as I wished to stay, but soon afterward I managed to get a lift from an Australian mission truck as it was leaving the village, and by dusk I was in Pouthisat.

• • •

"I had to."

Pringle waited. I wasn't playing games, making him drag it out of me; to bring death is an intimate act and I didn't want to talk about it, that was all.

"His neck was broken," I said.

We were in the Trans-Kampuchean Air Services shed on the airfield: I'd phoned Pringle the moment I reached Pouthisat and he'd brought along a film projector and rigged it up. We hadn't run it yet: there was the debriefing to do first.

"But he was still alive," Pringle said.

"Yes. But he wouldn't have stood a chance even if I could have got him into an ambulance right away, and only a doctor could have done that, under morphine."

"And you couldn't let the Khmer Rouge find him."

"No. They would have grilled him until he was dead."

"An act of kindness, then." Pringle nodded.

"Right. Put me down for a fucking halo."

Pringle made a note. He was sitting behind the trestle table that served as a desk in here: he was like that, couldn't drop into one of the bamboo chairs, had to look like a bloody lawyer, you know Pringle by now.

"Go on," he said, "when you're ready."

How kind of him. "Pol Pot is ill," I said. "A General Kheng has taken over the army, believed to be Pol's second-in-command. Young, ambitious, power-hungry."

Pringle was watching me now, surprise in his eyes that he thought wasn't showing. "Source?"

I told him about the monk.

"Is Kheng at the camp now?"

"We don't know."

"Can you find out?"

"Probably. It'll take time."

"We don't have a great deal."

"Oh really?"

He looked away. "I was just talking to myself."

I knew what the deadline was, for Christ's sake, it was staring us in the face. Hand throbbing a lot, the arm still numb to the elbow, I should have let them see it at the hospital but I wanted to watch the film, find out if we'd got anything or if the Hartmann-Zeiss had jammed or something.

"Any other business?" Pringle asked me.

"No."

He put away his debriefing pad and I got myself some tepid Evian water from the tank while he slapped the cassette into the projector and switched off the light.

Just the jungle down there at first but good resolution, we could see some of the breaks in the trees; then we went down and there was a rush of leaves and I began looking for anything I hadn't seen live—jeeps, half-tracks, tanks—saw nothing.

"They were holding their fire?" Pringle asked me.

"They weren't even out of the sack at this point."

The image swung as we made the turn at the end of the initial run, then the first shots sounded above the beat of the chopper and the tracers started coming up and by the time Khay had turned again to make the perimeter run it was a fireworks show, God knew how we'd stayed airborne as long as we had.

"Run it again," I said, "will you?"

He rewound and started again and I watched for the lake and when it came up I said, "Hit PAUSE. No, back a bit first. I want the lake. Right. That looks like a chopper pad there, on the east bank. Some trees have been cleared at some time, what do you think?"

"I agree. And I doubt if a satellite would pick that up. You need more?"

"No."

He rewound and switched the light on again and pulled the cassette out of the projector. "Congratulations. The whole thing is rather conclusive."

"I hoped you might think so." I got some more water, still dry as a husk from the fever. "How soon can you get it to London?"

"It won't be going to London," Pringle said without looking at me, "at least until Mr. Flockhart has seen it. He arrived in Phnom Penh from Kuwait last night and he'll be here on the first plane in the morning."

22

TOYS

"Snake bites man," Leonora called across the hospital ward, "but that ain't big news around here."

I suppose she'd seen a lot of these, could recognize them from a distance. She pulled a needle from the arm of the withered European lying on the bed and dropped it into a red-tagged bag and dropped the bag into a chipped enamel bin and came over to me and lifted my hand and looked at it.

"Now *that*," she said, "is for real! Kiss of death from a genuine hanuman, yet!" She was studying my face now. "But I guess you didn't follow the instructions. How long ago?"

"I'm not really sure."

"Lot of fever, yeah, hallucinations. Jeese, you are one tough cookie! But you look like shit if you don't mind me puttin' it that way, so I'll get to you in a minute, honey, give you some magic potions, okay?"

"No drugs," I said. "Just a dressing, if you think it needs one."

"Hey, mister, the patients don't call the shots around here, they just *get* the shots"—a big grin, pleased she'd thought of it—"but maybe we can make a deal. Wanna visit with your girlfriend while you're here?"

I looked along the ward. "Where is she?"

"Back there in Outpatients—don't worry, she's fine, I just have to change her dressings. You go an' show her your trophy of the chase and I'll be right there, honey—and congratulations, any reasonable man would've been good an' dead by now."

Gabrielle was photographing a child in rags, blood on her face, three years old, four, the flash freezing her for print, her eyes wide, accepting of whatever next would happen to her.

"How did you know I was here?" Gabrielle asked me.

"I just came in for a dressing."

She looked at my hand, wanted to know how it had happened; I just said I'd been careless, trekking in the jungle. She looked thinner, I thought, even after such a short time, and there were shadows under her eyes.

"You're working too hard," I said.

She cupped the child's head against her thigh as she looked at me. "I have to catch up. I should have started sooner."

"You're losing sleep," I told her. And when she slept, her dreams would be full of the killing.

"I catch a few hours during the day." We were both studying each other as if it had been a long time, or as if we weren't going to see each other again. "Has Leonora looked at you yet?"

"Just for a minute."

"What does she say?"

"I had some fever, that's all."

Then the nurse came in and picked up the child. "Where are the parents?"

"I don't know," Gabrielle said. "I found her wandering in the street, but I don't understand Vietnamese."

"I'm going to give her to the night nurse to look after, then I'll be back real soon."

When Leonora had gone I asked Gabrielle, "Are you working tonight again?"

"Of course. Every night."

"Can I go with you?"

"Why?"

"I need some information."

•   •   •   •

Crickets were strident in the silence as we sat in the jeep, waiting. The full moon hung above the frieze of palms along the southern horizon; the air clung to the face like a web, humid after the rain; shadows were long.

We had been moving through the town for three hours, ever since midnight, stopping and starting and waiting and drawing a blank, and now Gabrielle pulled the map out of the glove compartment of the jeep again and opened it, switching on the overhead lamp.

"We could try the new school just south of here, on the road out of the town, and then perhaps the temple on the road back east to Krakor. I am not going to sleep until we find one." She switched the lamp off and put the map away. "Sometimes it is like this, and one must be patient. But it's very late now—would you like me to drop you off at your—wherever you're staying?"

I said no. When I told Flockhart about General Kheng tomorrow he'd want to know where he was: it could be crucial.

Gabrielle drove the jeep three or four blocks, passing the hotel where Slavsky was staying and turning south, rolling to a halt in the cover of a barn and cutting the engine. I could sense the tension rising in her again as she took her short-barreled Remington from the rear seat and checked it. Whether or not I got the information I wanted, she would make the kill: that had been agreed on.

"We'll give it an hour," she said softly. "Yes?"

"Whatever you decide."

She'd told me how she operated, and what she'd learned. "They always arrive in some sort of vehicle, and switch off their lights when they near the area they've chosen, slowing down. That's why they like moonlit nights, unless there are streetlamps not far away."

I remembered what she'd also said, earlier, about her childhood: *I knew I'd never want to do anything else but paint flowers, all my life long.*

"Sometimes there are two of them, but they usually work alone, perhaps to conserve manpower and place more mines. It only takes one man, after all. He is always armed, of course, and takes care not to be seen or heard: there are police patrols, and sometimes military as well if a curfew is ordered. But that applies more to Phnom Penh."

We left the jeep, walking together as far as the narrow street; then the waiting began, in the cover of bamboo, and I heard rats among the fallen leaves, disturbed by our arrival. Water was running somewhere, a cistern overflowing after the rain; its sound brought the illusion of peace to the night.

"It won't always be like this," Gabrielle said softly. "There won't always be killing."

"No. Everything will change." And come full circle, as it always did; the trick was to be somewhere else when it happened. "You should go to Paris," I said.

"When?"

"Tomorrow. Paris or anywhere. Get out of here."

"You still think something will happen on the nineteenth?"

"I think it's very likely."

Unless there was an air strike. That would be the last chance.

"I have to stay," Gabrielle said.

"And take photographs?"

"Of course. It's my job, and whatever happens will have to be recorded. But it's more than that."

I didn't answer, didn't want to think about it. If there were to be another million dead in the Killing Fields she would be one of them this time.

The rats rustled in the leaves of the bamboo.

"Will you be here," Gabrielle asked, "for a while?"

"In Cambodia?"

"Yes."

"I work under instruction. I don't know where I'll be at any given time."

There was some kind of vehicle on the move in the distance, beyond the airfield. We stood listening to it.

I was working under instruction, yes, but if I was ordered out of Cambodia before the nineteenth the reason would have to be fully urgent: I'd want to stay on to help Gabrielle, keep her from getting caught if the Khmer Rouge launched the second holocaust.

"It's going farther away," she said. The vehicle.

"Yes."

But the next one, minutes later, sounded less distant, and we stood listening again.

The moon was below the tops of the sugar palms now, throwing them into stark relief against a skein of cloud nearer the horizon. There was no other sound louder than the droning of the vehicle, still distant but nearing by degrees.

"Perhaps this one," Gabrielle said quietly. I thought it might simply be a police patrol or a merchant bringing in goods for the market, but in a moment she hitched the Remington higher and said, "Yes. This one." By now she was experienced in this kind of work, would have acquired specific instincts.

Light flowed suddenly across the wall of a building as the vehicle turned in the distance, its sound loudening; then within seconds the light went out and the engine note decreased.

We had rehearsed things already, but for the sake of security Gabrielle said again, "If there are two of them I will shoot one immediately and go for a kill. The second one I will drop without killing if I can, before he returns my fire. If I succeed, he's yours. Don't leave cover until you're sure there's only one of them still alive, because I might have to fire twice. If only one man gets out of the vehicle, he's yours until you signal me."

"Understood."

I left her and moved along the street, keeping to the cover of a dry-stone wall until I reached the school. There was an arched gateway and I went through into the playground, dropping out of sight from the road.

I could now identify the vehicle by its sound: I'd heard these things before. It was a Chinese-built jeep, bouncing over the potholes on stiff springs, the slack timing-chain sending out a distinctive clatter from the engine. It was still running blacked-out, and the only light in the street was from the moon.

I could have operated alone tonight, moving from one potential hot zone to another, but I knew only a few words of Cambodian and unless the target spoke French or English I would have drawn a blank.

The jeep neared, moaning in low gear. I couldn't see it from where I was, had only its sound to go by.

Carbon monoxide drifted on the air; tires crackled over stones; and now the canvas top of the jeep was visible, sliding beyond the dry-stone wall. Then it stopped, and the engine idled for a moment, was switched off.

There were no voices.

Smell of tobacco smoke.

Then movement, and I went on waiting. The ring of a spade as he unstrapped it from the rear of the jeep: I could see the top of his head. Only one man, then.

If only one man gets out of the vehicle, he's yours until you signal me.

The gate swung open.

He was carrying the spade and a small wooden crate. He was carrying the crate carefully.

I expected him to start digging a hollow below the archway, but perhaps people were used to that now and either put the main entrances to schools out of bounds or had them swept every morning by one of the mine-detection services, because the man was coming into the playground without stopping, and when he was four or five feet away from me I moved and closed the distance and took him down with a knee sweep and a sword hand to the carotid artery, a medium strike to stun while I looked after the crate. The spade clattered onto the ground and I left it there and checked his belt for a weapon, found none: these people were more comfortable with submachine guns and assault rifles, and he'd left his in the jeep, hadn't expected to find anyone here.

He was young, strong, snapped out of the syncope within seconds.

"*Parles-toi français?*"

He didn't answer, didn't want to stand here talking, swung a routine kindergarten-level fist and I blocked it and paralyzed his arm with a center-knuckle strike and followed with a pulled hammer-blow to the temple to get his attention. "*Parles-toi français?*" I asked him again.

Some Cambodian came out, sounded ungracious.

"Do you speak English?"

Worked on his arm, the median nerve.

More Cambodian, so I whistled twice and Gabrielle came trotting across the road with her gun and began talking to him instead.

"He's just cursing," she said.

"Then make him afraid."

She raised the Remington and held the muzzle against the middle of the man's forehead and spoke to him again, getting something out of him this time.

"He's just asking me not to shoot him."

"Then start a countdown. What does he know about Pol Pot?"

I waited. The man stank worse than the pig in the mine-detection place—garlic, tobacco smoke, and now sweat.

"He knows nothing," Gabrielle told me.

At least it was an answer, of sorts. "How far did you come down to?"

"Six."

That was quite good: he was breaking early.

"Keep going. I want to know if Pol Pot is in good health, and also where he is now." The intelligence the monk had passed on to me could have been simply rumor.

The barrel of the gun ran silver in the moonlight as she shifted it a little as a reminder, prodding the man's brow, talking to him again, her tone quiet, professional: she understood that a raised voice shows lack of confidence, would have lessened the authority of the gun.

The man was starting to shake as Gabrielle brought the count lower, perhaps as far as three; a snuffling sound was coming from him: with the muzzle of the gun against his head, against his brains, he'd started thinking of his mother. Then as she went on counting he broke into sudden, jerky speech.

"Pol Pot is a sick man," Gabrielle said.

"Is he still in command of the Khmer Rouge?"

"No."

"Who's in command?"

"He doesn't know."

"Tell him he knows, and you're going to shoot on a count of two."

She prodded with the gun.

"General Kheng is in command."

"Where is he now?"

"He doesn't know."

"On a count of one."

The man brought his hands together in prayer, shaking badly again, speech of a kind coming out of him.

"He still says he doesn't know. He's begging for mercy."

I looked at Gabrielle in the starlight, saw the sheen of sweat on her face, her narrowed eyes.

"Give him his last chance," I told her, "on a count of one."

A snuffling sound again, some words in it, his hands together.

"He swears in the name of the Lord Buddha he doesn't know where General Kheng is now."

"Ask him what's going to happen on the nineteenth."

It took time, and she had to repeat the question.

"There will be bloodshed in Phnom Penh."

"A palace coup, or what?"

She prodded with the gun. "The revolution."

"Led by General Kheng?"

"Yes."

"How will it be launched?"

He didn't know, stood shaking, his eyes squeezed shut. Gabrielle asked him again, and again he said he didn't know. I thought this was possible: security on the subject of the nineteenth would be tight, and this man had no rank, was simply a saboteur, hiding his little toys for the children to find in the sacred name of the cause.

"Try once more."

His voice became light, like a woman's, a soft scream, desperate for us to understand that he couldn't answer the question.

"That's all," I told Gabrielle.

"No more questions?"

"No."

She spoke to him tersely, made him turn round, goaded him through the archway with the gun at his spine, steered him to his jeep, made him find his flashlight. I followed them, bringing the little crate.

There were four mines, crude, flat, pressure-sensitive models, sitting there like toads. Gabrielle spoke to the man, pointing to them, asking him something, her voice low, expressionless, a monotone.

I stood off a little. He was hers now; this had been agreed on. She got some rope from the back of the jeep and lashed him to the steering wheel, dipped a rag into the fuel tank, came up with nothing, tied another one to it and pulled it out streaming.

She looked at me in the bleak, pale radiance of the flashlight.

"Will you wait for me over there?"

I walked across the road to our Rambler and got in, starting the engine. After a little while there was a single shot, too good for him, I thought, for the toy-hider, but I suppose her manners were better than mine. As she came walking slowly across the road, tripping once on a stone, the flames took hold inside the jeep, but she didn't turn round, just kept on coming. The silhouette of her slight figure against the blaze was slack with despair, and she walked with her head down as if she didn't want to know where she was going, or where she'd been. The explosions began as I turned the Rambler, and the glare fanned against the side of the barn as we drove clear with Gabrielle curled up on the seat beside me, her eyes closed and her face wet, like a child who had cried herself to sleep.

23

• •

DEADLINE

"How's London?"

"Rather pleasant," Flockhart said, "or it was when I left. The twilights are drawing out." He looked carefully round the room, the way a dog makes a couple of circles on strange ground before it will lie down.

The place was palatial by average Cambodian standards: four or five bamboo chairs and a round table, a couple of Chinese rugs, an ornate brass lamp hanging from the ceiling, a chart of the seven major chakras on the wall, but no window—this was the basement of the house, and we'd come down a flight of steps cut into the bare earth and supported with redwood boards. There was no fan either, and the early morning air was already sticky in here. But there were two telephones, a scrambler and a Grundig shortwave transceiver.

Pringle had followed us down and was standing just inside the door, hands behind his back in a posture deferential, I thought, to his master's presence. A short, wispy-bearded Cambodian stood on the other side, in a dark blue sampong and sandals.

"This is our good host," Flockhart told me, "Sophan Sann."

The man came forward and shook hands, his eyes lively in the lamplight as he appraised me; it was an honor for him to meet anyone introduced by Mr. Flockhart—this was my impression. But for a formal rendezvous like this I could have done without a stranger here, however good a host he was said to be.

Some bottles of soda on the table, a liter of Evian, and a plate of quartered lemons; incense was burning somewhere, uncharacteristically, perhaps as a gesture of welcome to Sophan's guests. A salamander clung to the plaster near a bamboo grille set high on the wall, the only means of ventilation that I could see.

"How was the flight from Kuwait?" I asked Flockhart. I wanted him to know that until we were alone he'd get nothing from me but small talk.

"Too long," he said, and took one of the bamboo chairs. "But then any flight's too long when time is of the essence, don't you agree?"

Talking about the deadline.

I sat down and Pringle followed, putting a thin, worn briefcase on the table in front of him. We were here for the executive's debriefing to Control.

"I'm told," Flockhart said, "that you suffered a snakebite."

"Yes."

"A nasty experience, I can imagine." He looked at me for the first time since we'd come down here, his eyes concerned. When I'd talked to him in the Cellar Steps his eyes had been full of rage, barely concealed. I wondered what had happened to it. "Are you still feeling any ill effects?" he asked me.

"I'm a hundred op." A hundred percent operational, which was what he really needed to know. If I had to go into anything difficult I could do it fast and successfully, given a clear field and not too much shooting.

"Splendid." He brought out a black notebook and put it carefully onto the bamboo table. "Splendid."

"If we're going to do any business," I said, "I'd rather—"

"Sann," Flockhart said straightaway, looking up at the Cambodian, "we've kept you long enough."

Sophan gave a brief bow and looked down at me. "It was a pleasure to meet you." Absolutely no accent, possibly Oxford.

"The pleasure was all mine."

His sandals flapped up the steps and we heard him close the door at the top. From habit I listened for it to open again quietly but it didn't. Call it paranoia, but when Control flies out from London without warning to debrief the executive in the field himself it means the mission has either started running very hot indeed or hit a wall, and I would have felt much easier debriefing somewhere with better security, say the top of a mountain.

"Don't worry," Flockhart said gently. "This was actually to have been your safe house. Sophan Sann affords us total security here."

"He's Bureau?"

"No. But I enjoy his unqualified loyalty. I once had the opportunity of saving his life."

"Out here?"

"During what they call the holocaust—I was observing for the British Mission at the time. He was a young man then, of course, and so was I, and together we dug out this room as a concealed chamber to shelter whole families."

The Cambodian connection. At our first meeting I'd asked Pringle what was really behind this mission: *Is it something personal, with Flockhart?* And Pringle had said, *I don't know. Perhaps he simply wants to save Cambodia.*

"But tell me," Flockhart was saying, "why didn't you accept this place as your safe house?" To Pringle: "I'm sure it was offered?"

"Of course, sir."

Control's head swung back to me.

"I didn't trust you," I said.

He nodded briefly. "So Pringle informed me, after your first contact in Phnom Penh."

"I didn't express my feelings."

"But of course not, my dear fellow—he was simply aware of the undercurrents."

I was warned by the "dear fellow" bit: Pringle had been stroking me tenderly ever since the mission had started running, and now Control had come all the way out here to help him. But there is *nothing* your control can't ask of you in perfectly plain terms, however dangerous, even suicidal, knowing that you've got the right to refuse. When he chooses to steal up on you with quiet charm instead, then you'd better make bloody sure you stay awake because once the trap springs shut you're done for.

Holmes, and I quote: *Remember that one must handle Mr. Flockhart with the tender care demanded by—shall we say—a tarantula.*

"I still don't trust you," I told him. I wasn't being offensive. If *Salamander* was running hot and we were going to try bringing it home in some kind of last-ditch operation I needed to know more than I did now. If it was classified, okay, but I didn't think so.

"I appreciate your honesty," Flockhart said, didn't fake a hurt smile, no theatrics. "It's going to be to our advantage, because events are moving apace and we need to understand each other. But tell me why I don't invite your confidence, if you will." Had avoided the word "trust," didn't like it.

"As I told Pringle at the airport, I'm out here on an operation that hasn't got official support or a signals board or any access to London through the normal channels. You're running this thing entirely on your own and I assume for your own purposes. How would you feel if you were the executive?"

"I would have felt like declining the mission in the first place."

"I'd been out of the field too long, you know that. I'd have taken anything on, you knew that too."

"And now you have regrets?"

"None whatsoever. I just want to know if we're on an official footing yet, with the Bureau informed and in charge."

A beat, but he didn't take his eyes off me. "And if I said no, the Bureau is neither informed nor in charge, would you withdraw from the mission?"

It threw me and I got up, took a turn round the room, needing time. Pringle coughed, couldn't quite take the tension. When I was ready I stood looking down at Flockhart.

"No."

"Thank you." It was said formally, carried weight. "And I must confess myself unsurprised. According to my research, you don't take kindly to officialdom."

"Look"—I sat down again, interested—"I've never done this before, that's all. I've never worked for a rogue control, if you'll forgive the term—"

"I like it."

A spark had come into his eyes and suddenly I knew why there'd been so much rage in them at the Cellar Steps. "So the Bureau turned you down?"

He looked away, looked back. "Yes."

"Why?"

"I was told that my ultimate goal would be impossible to achieve."

Very interested now, and I leaned forward. "And what is your ultimate goal?"

"To save Cambodia."

"For personal reasons?"

Flockhart shifted in his chair, looking away again, and I think I regretted pressing him at this point, but I had to. For the first time I wasn't simply the shadow executive assigned to the next mission on the books under the official aegis of the Bureau, a role I'd played throughout the whole of my career. I was working for *one man,* and responsible to him alone.

"For personal reasons," Flockhart said, "I would like to save Cambodia, yes. But few civilized people, surely, would stand by and watch the massacre of another million souls in a second potential holocaust if they could prevent it."

"But you couldn't persuade the Bureau."

"That was hardly the argument I presented."

"They're not the Salvation Army."

"Quite so. The argument I offered was geopolitical, though admittedly rather contrived. I said that if the Khmer Rouge seized power again Pol Pot might embroil North Vietnam and North Korea and bring about a resurgence of communism in the region, to the obvious advantage of China."

"Was that why the Bureau turned you down?"

"I was advised, as I say, that the goal of saving Cambodia for whatever reason would be impossible to achieve, now that the United Nations has pulled out." He looked at me, tilting his head. "So I made a direct approach to the Prime Minister, who was interested enough to contact the UN and the United States. I have since had meetings with the ambassadors to both."

"Suggesting an air strike."

"Of course. It's the only possible step, in military terms." He leaned forward, his hands flat on the table as I'd seen them on his desk in London. Take it as a gesture of frankness or leave it. "Provided, obviously, that we could locate the main forces of the Khmer Rouge with absolute certainty. And you have done that."

"You've seen the footage?"

"Yes, the moment I got off the plane from the capital. It's completely convincing, of course. The Prime Minister had told me earlier that he'd accept my word alone, so I telephoned him immediately. Meanwhile the film itself is on its way to him, with copies to the Ministry of Defense, the United Nations, and the Pentagon, time being critical."

"They can't act that fast," I said. "They're bureaucrats."

Flockhart looked down. He did it often, and I noted it. "My only hope is that by the grace of God they will." To Pringle: "Let me see your debriefing notes, will you?"

Pringle unzipped his briefcase and Flockhart studied the three sheets, sometimes brushing back his wisps of graying hair, sometimes dropping a word or two that neither of us could understand, weren't, perhaps, expected to. For the first time it occurred to me that Flockhart was a man driven by inner fires, no longer enraged by the Bureau's indifference but transferring his rage to a galvanic energy; I also sensed that he was committing himself to something conceivably beyond even his powers to achieve, and that he knew it. I couldn't see it in his square, bland face, or in his pale eyes. I could simply detect, on the subtlest level, a smell of burning.

"I congratulate you," he said at last, looking up at me, "on having made a safe return from your ordeal in the jungle. Also on having brought back the film, which of course is now the key element in this enterprise."

Stroking me. I didn't like that, didn't answer. I didn't like the word "enterprise" either, we weren't bloody buccaneers; the errand of an intelligence agent is to gather intelligence.

"Should we rely on this rumor about Pol Pot, that he's ill?"

"I got it confirmed last night," I said, "when I questioned a KR rebel. I can guarantee he was telling the truth—as far as he knows it."

"I see. And where might Pol Pot be sequestered, as an invalid?"

"I've no idea."

"Probably Bangkok," Pringle said, "under medical supervision."

"Then I wish him the least speedy of recoveries." Flockhart's tone was hushed: perhaps he was overcorrecting. I thought that if he ever found himself within touching distance of Pol Pot he would kill him with his bare hands, and not quickly. "Pringle," he said to me in a moment, "has sketched a rough map of the area embracing the Khmer Rouge camp and the village, according to your description." He spun the sheet of paper around for me. "Does it look accurate?"

"As accurate as he could make it, from what I told him."

"The village is approximately fifteen kilometers from the camp, is that correct?"

"It was the monk's estimate."

Flockhart's finger traced its way across the sketch. "The road would be more or less straight?"

"It'll be a bullock track, not really a road. But probably straight, yes—the area's just flat jungle, so it wouldn't have to go around any hills."

"A track—but it's used by motorized vehicles?" He was glancing at Pringle's notes.

"According to the monk."

"And frequently."

"Yes."

"In terms of acoustics, how close would you think one could take a motorized vehicle to the camp, with complete security?"

"In deep jungle like that I'd say a mile, coasting in neutral over the last hundred yards and depending on wind direction and the type of vehicle used, the type of engine and exhaust system."

Flockhart turned to Pringle. "Do we have anybody here who could do that?"

"Bracken's available in Phnom Penh. I could fly him here in an hour, by daylight. Another three hours from here to the village"— glancing at me—"which is the time it took you to get here, coming the other way. Is there any difference in elevation?"

"Not much. The track runs through valleys most of the time."

Flockhart got out of his chair, I thought, a little wearily. He wouldn't have slept much on the flight from London through Kuwait; this burning energy of his would have kept him restless. He began pacing, hands dug into his pockets, and on the wall the salamander trickled toward the grille.

"Do you think we should put a vehicle there, a mile or so from the camp, concealed in the jungle and manned round the clock?"

He wasn't looking at either of us, so I waited for Pringle, who gestured with a hand, giving the question to me.

"On principle," I said, "yes." Flockhart was going by the book: having located the opposition it's good practice to set up surveillance.

Control looked at Pringle—"Bracket is what, a sleeper or an a-i-p?"

"Bracken, sir. Actually he's stand-by support."

Flockhart looked down at him. "Better still. Is he married?"

I liked him for that. Doing a peep single-handed on an encampment of twelve thousand armed men was a short-fuse assignment.

"No, sir."

"He's experienced?"

"He led the support group for *Cobra* in Pakistan."

"Indeed. You did well to have him available."

"Thank you, sir." Liked being stroked. But in fact he'd done well, yes, because he'd not only had to bring the man in but he'd had to keep him from getting assigned to the next official mission to hit the signals room.

"I suggest we send Bracken out there," Flockhart told him, "as soon as we're finished here. You have a radio available?"

"Yes, sir. We can receive on this one."

"Give it to him." To me, with a swing of his head: "How are you off for sleep?"

Either it showed or he was simply assessing my resources, had something lined up for me.

"I need a few hours."

"Get them." He took another turn and came back and stood with his hands on the back of a chair. "Then as soon as you can, I want you to locate General Kheng. There can be no hope of a decision from London, obviously, until we know for certain where he is; an air strike at his forces alone could well fail if he remains at large. The moment you have any information, I can contact the Prime Minister direct on his hotline from here. Will you need any kind of backup?"

"No."

"Have you any questions?"

I looked at Pringle. "Did you mount a peep on Slavsky?"

"Yes, with a contact in support."

"I think that's it," I told Flockhart.

"Very well." He hesitated, looking at neither of us as he went on quietly, "We should keep it in mind that if in fact General Kheng intends to launch a missile attack on the capital on the nineteenth, we have only until midnight to stop him."

24

SONG

Kim woke me just before noon.

He was the man Pringle used as a contact, knew where to find me, at the house of the one-legged girl. He told me that Slavsky, the Russian, had gone to the airfield.

I drove there in the Mine Action van I'd used before: they were perfect camouflage, you saw them everywhere looking for those bloody toys.

The peep was waiting for me inside the gate to the freight area, short, round-shouldered, pointed face, bush jacket, looked like a pleasant rat, the way Disney would draw one.

"Symes," he said. Pringle had flown him in from Bangkok, said he was first-class.

We hadn't made contact before, so we exchanged code introductions and he got it wrong the first time and I had to insist before I was sure of security, I wasn't worried, it sometimes happens, you just have to check it out. Then I got him aboard the van.

"Did you signal the DIF?" I asked him.

"Yes, from the airline office." Trans-Kampuchean Air Services.

"Where's Slavsky now?"

"Over there. The three jeeps and the staff car. He's in the car."

A motorcade, looked important. Breakthrough?

We were standing off the target by a hundred yards so I got my 10 × 50's and focused, still couldn't see anything more of Slavsky than a pale blurred face behind the window.

"Where's your vehicle?" I asked Symes.

"By the gate."

Battered jeep, and I noted the number plate. "Stand off somewhere on the perimeter road," I told him, "and take up station when we move. If I lose the staff car, stay with it and contact the DIF when you can, give him the score. I'll pick it up from him as soon as I can find a phone."

"Roger." He slipped out of the van, moved at a loping walk to the nearest cover, the chain-link fence, shoulders hunched as you often see in surveillance people, the unconscious physical expression of their conscious need to hide.

I began watching the sky.

The noon heat was down, spreading a mirage across the airfield and leaving the line of sugar palms beyond the perimeter track standing in water.

We should keep it in mind that if in fact General Kheng intends to launch a missile attack on the capital on the nineteenth, we have only until midnight to stop him.

Did he think we didn't know that, for God's sake?

Chopper.

Did he think we couldn't count, read a calendar, know how to synchronize watches, manage our buttons, see the bloody *obvious* when it was staring us in the face?

Chopper, coming in low from the south, a Kamov KA-26, twin rotors, the same type, possibly the same machine, that had brought Colonel Choen here from Phnom Penh.

This was at noon plus 26 and I began noting the time because *Salamander* was obviously shifting into a new phase and it could be important for Pringle to know how things were developing, to know the time of the arrival and departure of vehicles and their travel patterns simply as a matter of keeping a moving target in the sights. This didn't mean he might not have to sit at his base for hours on end without a shred of information coming in from the field as the day drew out: it would depend on how and when we could find a telephone without breaking cover.

The Kamov was drifting in across the sugar palms toward the freight area, turning a few degrees before it touched down and blew the mirage beyond it into swirling mists.

I find-tuned the focus again.

Two men got out of the staff car: Slavsky and a Cambodian in battle dress with a Western-style army beret, officer rank. Five, six men climbed down from the helicopter, one of them leading the others across the tarmac. Salutes were exchanged, and as Slavsky came forward to shake hands I recognized the leader of the visiting group. I hadn't seen him before but he was the Khmer Rouge officer in the photographs I'd seen at the villa in Phnom Penh, standing close to Pol Pot in every shot, a younger man in jungle battle dress with epaulettes and a peaked cap, one picture with his name below it: General Kheng.

16:12.

I'd started thinking by the twenty-four-hour clock at this stage because signals were being exchanged and Pringle would be keeping an official record as they came in: I'd phoned him from an American drugstore opposite the Hôtel du Lac soon after Slavsky and General Kheng had arrived there from the airfield.

Thirty minutes later they'd come out of the hotel together, shaking hands before Slavsky had got into his rental Chevrolet and turned south, possibly back to the airfield: I wasn't curious. Kheng was now the target and he'd climbed into the staff car, moving off with one of the camouflaged jeeps ahead of him and one behind.

He was still inside the white two-story building next to the temple where I'd kept watch before, waiting for Colonel Choen. The general had been there for more than four hours now. There was no sign above the bullet-scarred doors but the building was obviously the local headquarters of the Khmer Rouge: since I'd been here I'd seen half a dozen jeeps arriving and leaving again, some carrying an officer with an escort, some with only a driver.

It was 17:23, with the late sun lowering across the skyline, when I decided it was time to take action. Flockhart had wanted to know the whereabouts of General Kheng and he now had that information, but it was beginning to look as if Kheng might have come here to stay the night at headquarters, bringing the deadline down to zero. If there was a conceivable chance of jumping ahead of him I wanted to take it, get information for Control, this time as to where Kheng would go next—back to the capital, out to the camp in the foothills here, or to the main Khmer Rouge base in the jungle. Whatever Flockhart had in his mind, this information could now be critical, conclusive, as time ran out.

I flashed my parking lights twice, and waited.

Symes came up from behind the van and put his face in the window.

"Look," I said, "there's something else I've got to do, so if I leave here at any time don't worry, just stay with the target wherever he goes. He was the leader of the group who got out of the chopper and his name is General Kheng. Signal the DIF as soon as you possibly can at every stage if he starts moving. Questions?"

"If he gets on a plane?"

"Find out where it's going and signal the DIF from the Air Services office."

"Roger."

He went back to his jeep.

It was an hour before I could make a move.

In the mirror I saw a Chinese jeep leaving the KR headquarters with an officer at the wheel, unescorted, and as it passed the end of the street I started up and took two rights and a left and saw the jeep bouncing over the potholes fifty yards ahead and took up the tail. It was following the same route as Colonel Choen had taken, but I needed to talk to this officer long before we reached the camp.

There were fewer buildings now, a few huts, then a wasteland of scrub and after a few miles a huddle of broken concrete slabs that might have been buildings once, before the revolution, its walls scarred with shrapnel and dead palm trees leaning across it. One of the buildings still stood, fissured and windowless, and I thought it looked suitable, well out of earshot from the nearest habitation and some way from the road.

The Chinese jeep was half a mile in front and it took two miles to catch up and overtake, and as I went past it I used the horn and held my hand up, asking the driver to stop, cutting in a little to reinforce the message as I hit the brakes and ran the van into the scrub and switched off the engine.

Then I left it there and trotted back to the jeep. The KR was sitting at the wheel with his right hand on the butt of his revolver, so I relaxed him a little by introducing myself.

"*Je suis un collègue de Slavsky!*"

"*Eh bien?*"

I didn't say any more because I was close enough now and used a half-fist to his carotid artery to cut off the blood to the brain for a few seconds and then caught him as he keeled over, taking him round to the passenger seat and propping him there and slipping the gun out of its holster and pushing it into my belt. He was waking up a little now and I worked on the thyroid cartilage, enough to make him fight for breath, and while he was doing that I took the jeep in a U-turn and gunned up.

He was fluent in French then, hadn't asked me to repeat what I'd said; this I would have expected in a man of his rank: he wore captain's insignia.

There was cover for the jeep under some slabs of fallen concrete and I got the captain's assault rifle and the big flashlight from the back and slapped his forehead with a slack back-fist to shock the pineal gland as he tried to throw me with a thrust to the back of the knees, been sleeping like a fox, one eye open.

"Don't do that," I told him in French, beginning tuition with the basics. "I don't want you doing things like that." He could understand, could hear me well enough, I knew that; he was just disoriented by the pineal strike: it's what we use it for.

The sun was down as I dragged him into the windowless building; the ground-floor room had possibly been intended for storage: there was just the open doorway and a floor littered with debris thrown into relief by the flashlight—broken concrete and rusted iron bars and dead birds and a small skeleton the size of a rat. The doorway faced the scrub on the other side from the road, so the light wouldn't be seen by the traffic as the night came down.

Somewhere there was a cricket singing.

"Who are you?" the captain asked. His speech was slurred.

He was heavily built for an Asian, had muscle, would be well trained, probably, but not in unarmed combat: he should have gone for the coccyx out there, not the knees, could have paralyzed me if he'd done it fast.

"I don't want any questions," I said.

"You told me you were a colleague of Slavsky's."

"No questions—and that is the last time I'm going to tell you anything twice. Kneel down over there with your back to the wall." I swung the assault rifle up. "Do it now."

The weapon seemed to impress him and he backed off against the wall but didn't kneel, stood watching me like a jungle cat, furious, a man of pride, what the shrink we use in training at Norfolk would categorize as strong, excitatory. Pride was something I could use, work on, given enough time.

I backed away too, as far as the opposite wall, and dropped the assault rifle and the revolver onto the floor, then moved toward the captain again until I was within striking distance.

"There are things you've got to understand," I said. "You're quite an educated man, and can probably think well, so it won't be difficult. You need to understand that you're my captive, and that there's nothing you can do, nothing at all, to free yourself. You must also understand that the only time I shall injure you is when you ask for it. Only then."

He went on watching me. I'd put the flashlight on the floor to one side, its beam directed toward him. It shadowed his face, making it look like a mask lit obliquely to give it drama; the light was reflected in his narrowed, amber eyes. It would take days to break a man like this one physically. It could be done; it can always be done; but I hadn't got days, only a few hours. The quickest way would be to destroy him from the inside, reduce his persona, his creaturehood, to nothing.

"I told you to kneel," I said, "and this is the second time." He tried to block it but wasn't fast enough and the strike rocked his head back and it hit the wall and for a moment I thought I'd misjudged things, used too much force, but he didn't go out, he just stood watching me, surprise in his eyes, I'd started to make him think. There wasn't any blood: it had just been a hammer-fist to the forehead.

"Remember," I told him, "you'll be injured only when you ask for it. Kneel."

I gave him a few seconds but he didn't move, watched me with the anger coming back into his eyes now that he could think straight again, so I went across to the opposite wall to fetch the assault rifle, turning my back to him, already hunched over to the correct degree so that as he made his run I went straight into a basic aikido roll that flung him against the wall, then caught him as he came down so that he didn't land anywhere near the two guns.

"Don't do things like that," I told him. "I don't want you to do things like that. You need to *think* more, with your brain instead of your gut. This is an intellectual exercise we're doing together, can't you see that by now?"

He didn't answer, mainly because he'd hit the wall with quite a lot of impact and it had left him disoriented.

The man who teaches interrogation techniques at Norfolk is a Chinese, Yang Taifang. The Chief of Signals had him pulled out of a prison in the province of Fukien when no one was looking, because the first two or three years of his thirteen-year sentence had been spent under intensive interrogation, so he knows which end the flint goes in. "Must remember," he says, "not much good talking to subject when fully conscious. Must first disorientate, and this easy. Save excellent amount of time this way." He can't speak too clearly because of what they did to his face: some of the motor nerves are gone; but mentally he's still very bright and his memory is sharp. "First, disorientate," he says, using his own verbal spelling. "Then humiliate, especially if subject proud man, like soldier."

When the captain could stand up I pushed him across the room and turned him round to face me. "Do you remember," I asked him, "what happens when you make me tell you twice to do something?"

He was trying to watch me but his eyes couldn't quite focus.

"Yes."

Breakthrough.

"Kneel."

I don't think he went down onto his knees with any conscious intent; it was just that he was aching a lot and felt like letting his body collapse.

"That's good," I said, and ripped the linen name tab off his battle dress and gave it to him. "Eat that."

I waited, listening to the cricket singing.

"Is that your name?" I asked him.

"Yes."

"I want you to eat it, and if I have to ask you a second time you know what's going to happen."

His eyes still couldn't focus very well: he'd hit his head when we went through the aikido roll, and it had affected the occipital area. He looked at the name tab, then at me.

"Eat?"

"Yes."

He put it into his mouth.

"Just chew it a bit, then swallow. Don't choke."

Faint light swept the open doorway as something went past on the road. The heat of the day had been trapped in here, and sweat had started running on the man in front of me, this now temporary man, the captain.

Then he spat the name tab into my face and I drove one finger into the trigeminal nerve between the neck and the point of the jawbone and he screamed because pain in that area is instant and agonizing.

I wiped my face and picked up the name tab and held it out for him.

"Take it," I said.

Tears streamed on his face, and for the first time I had to think of the girl with one leg, who was sore under her arms because she still wasn't used to her new crutches.

"I don't want to tell you what to do," I said, "more than once."

Two seconds, three seconds, four, five, then he put the name tab into his mouth. He wasn't watching me anymore, was looking down.

"Don't waste my time," I told him, two seconds, three, then he swallowed.

"Was that your name?"

"Yes."

"What did you do with your name?"

He looked up at me now, head a little on one side.

"What?" he asked me.

"Can you hear me all right?"

It took time. "This side."

"All right. Keep your head turned like that." Perhaps he'd burst an eardrum somewhere along the line, and I didn't want to make any punitive strikes if he hadn't heard the command; it wouldn't get us anywhere.

"I'm going to ask you again," I said, "because you might not have heard me the first time. What did you do with your name?"

"Swallow it."

The left hemisphere a little dulled, I'd have to be careful: I didn't want to impair his memory, because that was what I was here to listen to when the time came. The time wasn't now: he wasn't ready yet, would clam up, whatever I did to him, *finito*.

I looked at my watch. We'd been working for thirty-four minutes. Outside the building, dark was down: I could see it through the doorway. The flashlight was still bright but I didn't know how long the battery would last: we'd only just started, and it would be another two hours, perhaps three, before I could ask the first question, and even then I would have to do it with extreme care.

"You swallowed your name?"

"*Bat.*"

"In French. Stick to French. You swallowed your name?"

"Yes."

"You ate it?"

"Yes."

"Who are you, then? Give me your rank and name."

"I am Captain Saloth."

The same as Pol Pot's real name: perhaps this man had adopted it, was full of borrowed pride.

"No," I said, "you're nothing now. You have eaten your name, so now you are nothing. What are you?"

"I am Captain—"

"You're not listening. When I tell you something, it's always right. If you contradict me, you know what will happen to you. Now, what are you?"

"I am Captain—"

Screamed again because I worked on the same nerve.

I waited, listening to the cricket's song. The nothing was silent now, its eyes shut and the tears dripping from its face, its knees folding at last as I knew they would.

"Don't do that. Kneel upright. Knees straight. Can you hear me?"

The nothing said nothing. I had to think of the former Captain Saloth in that way now to create the reality. What was real in my mind must be made real in his.

"Can you hear me?"

"Yes."

"Then straighten your knees." Waited. "Good. Now, I've told you what you are, remember? You are nothing. Listen carefully to the question. What are you?"

The song of the cricket had stopped.

The nothing was swaying slightly from side to side. The agony of the last strike would still be burning through the nerves; it would last for some time, perhaps for days, would be tender for weeks, months. I know this: it was a month before I could even shave there after I came out of the underground cell in Zagreb.

"Are you going to make me ask you the same question twice?"

It flinched. "No."

"Do you remember the question?"

Its face looked at me, the eyes flickering with pain, the head held slightly to one side, the tears drying on the blotchy skin. I thought of the other girl, the one in the photograph on the wall of the mine-clearing office, smiling, radiant, used to her crutches by now, no problem, held in a bear hug by the two grinning men.

It said something in Khmer.

"French. Always speak French."

"What question?"

"Listen," I said, "you're not paying enough attention. I'm going to tell you what you are, and then you're going to answer my question. Now listen carefully. This is what you are: you are *nothing*." I waited, watching it to see if it understood. I thought it did: there was still intelligence in the eyes and the swaying had stopped. "So here comes the question. *What are you?*"

It was silent. It didn't move. It looked like the remains of a wood carving half-destroyed by time, the head angled on the neck, the eyes splintered, the mouth half-open and askew. But I could hear it breathing, and in the sound of its breathing there was a faint musical note, a kind of mewing that loudened suddenly into speech.

"Nothing."

I look at my watch, the last chance I shall get because the battery of the flashlight is running low.

The time is 21:39.

We have been here for two and a half hours, something like that.

It seems longer, much longer.

I watch its face as the light grows dim. It's still alive, and still conscious. There wasn't very much more to do since it recognized itself as nothing: that was the breakthrough. But we needed more time between the questions and the answers, because sometimes it remembered its pride and did silly things, and there is now a gash on my face and I can feel the blood caked there, itching as it dries, a trophy won by inattention, but then I'm tired too, and I feel some of its pain. All men are brothers, however divided by their lunatic ideologies.

The cricket is singing again, and in the rectangle of the doorway there is moonlight.

"Who are you?"

"Nobody. Nothing."

"You are my prisoner. What are you?"

"I am your prisoner."

"Your life is in my hands. Do you want to live?"

"My life is—"

"Listen to the question. Do you want to live?"

"Pain. Want end of pain."

The light is very dim now, just a glow.

It is still kneeling, immediately in front of me. I can smell its sweat. It reeks. It can smell mine. I reek. I can smell its blood. It can smell mine. All men are pigs.

The light goes out.

"Your pain will end if you're very careful."

I think it is swaying, in the pale light from the doorway, from the moon. I think I am swaying too. It's getting late. I didn't sleep last night. I slept for a few hours today but this has been tiring for the psyche, which is exhausted by the endless need to withhold compassion even from this thing, this child-crippler, this hero of the holocaust to come.

"What did I tell you?"

"My pain end if I care, take care."

I think there's just enough consciousness, just enough memory, to have made it worthwhile, worth coming here, worth talking with my brother pig.

"How will you take care?"

"Take care, yes."

"You will take care by answering my questions truthfully. I shall know if you are lying."

Blind suddenly, my eyes closing.

I open them again.

I must take care too.

"Shall I know if you lie to me?"

"Lie."

"Listen to the question. Shall I know if you lie to me?"

"Yes."

"Then we'll begin. But the pain will only end if you take care not to lie. Do you understand what I'm saying?"

"Yes."

Harken ye then to the cricket's song.

"How long will General Kheng remain at headquarters?"

25

ALTERNATIVE

I turned into the side street where I'd been parked before in the Mine Action van, watching the white two-story building. I could see the jeep in the distance. Symes hadn't move.

He got out of his vehicle when I flicked my lights a couple of times, but walked slowly, warily, because in the moonlight he could see only a Chinese jeep with two people in it. When he was near enough to hear my voice I called out the code name for the mission, and he quickened his step.

"He's still in there," he said when he recognized me. He meant General Kheng.

"I know. He'll be there until morning. There's no need for you to stay."

He looked at my passenger. "People been talking?"

"Yes. I want you to take him over, look after him somewhere. He's a bit switched off at the moment but put him under restraint in case he wakes up to things."

"Roger."

He went back to his jeep and brought it alongside, and I helped him with the prisoner. Then I drove to the little bullet-scarred post office and used the telephone outside.

Pringle picked up on the second ring, hadn't gone to bed: Control was in the field and the executive had made contact with the target and the mission was running hot.

"I brought in a prisoner," I said. "Symes is looking after him."

"Is he for interrogation?"

"No. But I need to debrief."

"To Control?"

"Yes."

"I'll make him aware."

"I was hoping you'd make contact," Flockhart said.

He'd put a coat over his bush shirt, though the night was still warm. We were in the dugout room, in the house of Sophan Sann. Pringle was here too, looked underslept.

I waited.

"We have received a reply," Flockhart went on heavily, "from London." He hadn't slept much either; the blanket on the settee was still smooth, and there was steam clinging to the glass of the coffee percolator.

"When?" I asked him.

"Nearly three hours ago. And the decision of those concerned is that there is to be no air strike against the forces of the Khmer Rouge."

In a moment I said, "Did that surprise you?"

He looked at me, his smile acid. "No."

Pringle cleared his throat; he didn't easily handle tension.

"You mind if I sit down?" I asked Flockhart.

"What? Oh, my dear fellow, please."

Still his dear fellow: beware. I dropped into one of the bamboo chairs. I'd been on my feet half the bloody night with that gallant young captain in front of me, hero of the new holocaust that no one in London or Washington or anywhere else could think how to stop. Or wanted to.

"What were your expectations?" I asked Flockhart. "From the bureaucrats?"

He didn't want to sit down, watched me with something shadowing his eyes, pain, I could believe. "Extremely low," he said. "But you knew that, didn't you?"

"It was such a long shot, and so late in the day." I didn't look at him, didn't want to watch his suffering. "At one time, I thought you were simply playing me along for some reason, not signaling London at all."

"Did you now."

I gave it a beat. "Were you?"

He looked at me in surprise, and then remembered. "Of course, you don't trust me, do you? But no, I was in fact conducting a rather desperate bid for military intervention, and I did indeed hold out some slight hope of success. The Prime Minister was not entirely unsanguine."

"My condolences."

I wasn't being sarcastic. He'd just lost something he loved: Cambodia. Nor was I myself unaffected: Gabrielle had come immediately into my mind again when he told me the news. Whatever happened I wouldn't be leaving here without her, or without making sure she'd be safe.

"Thank you." Flockhart said.

Pringle sat down and pulled the pad out of his briefcase and got a ballpoint ready. "Is it urgent?" he asked me.

My need to debrief. "I don't really know. It's probably academic at this stage." I looked at Flockhart. "For what it's worth, I've got the schedule of events planned by the Khmer Rouge."

He looked suddenly alert, which surprised me: he'd led me to believe that to his mind all was lost. "Have you indeed?"

I'd forgotten that neither he nor Pringle had known I'd mounted any kind of operation during the night. My last signal had been to the effect that I was simply keeping surveillance on General Kheng.

"There's a new deadline," I told them. "It's for sundown tomorrow, and this is the schedule: General Kheng is to fly at first light to the base camp in the jungle, where he'll complete preparations for the missile attack on the capital at six this evening. Armored troop transports and six medium tanks will start rolling soon afterward, at nightfall, heading for the city. They should arrive before midnight. At the same time, the troops based here in the foothills will also be moved into the capital to assist in taking over the government, seizing King Sihanouk and rounding up the civilian population for immediate transport to labor camps."

Pringle was making notes, and I had the chilling sense that reason had slipped away, that since there was to be no air strike we were like actors still walking the stage with the play over and the curtain down and the audience long gone home.

"There's to be no ultimatum?"

"No ultimatum."

Control still wouldn't sit down, paced steadily as I filled in the few details I'd managed to get from my source.

"How certain are you," Flockhart asked me at last, "that these facts are correct?"

"My informant was beyond knowing how to lie."

End pain, he'd kept saying when I pushed him for more answers, more facts, pushed him to the brink, *no more pain*, but it had been his own bloody fault, for Christ's sake, I'd told him that.

"Is he still alive?" This from Pringle.

"Technically. Symes is looking after him."

Flockhart had been giving me his whole attention up to this point, but now he looked away. I don't think it was anything to do with the fate of my "informant"—Control was familiar enough with interrogation techniques and would have been quite happy to hear I'd used thumbscrews on any member of the Khmer Rouge.

"You did rather well," he told me at last.

I didn't say anything.

I wanted sleep now, to get the face of that bloody thing out of my mind, the nothing thing, you gotta do whatcha gotta do, right, but you also gotta live with it until it's had time to silt over like the rest of the rotten by-products of this bloody trade.

Pringle asked me some things he needed to know, would have to take action on: where could the van be picked up and had I got the ignition key, had I told Symes to get medical attention for my informant and had there been significant loss of blood, things like that. Then Control put some questions, did I know the troop strengths of the Khmer Rouge base and the camp in the foothills near Pouthisat, how many missiles were to be fired on the capital, would General Kheng lead the ground assault or fly ahead of his forces to confront Sihanouk and demand his surrender?

I didn't have information on things like that, or I would have told him already, debriefing is debriefing, you don't leave anything out, he should know that, *knew* that. He still wasn't looking at me, just listening with his head half-turned as he kept up his *bloody* pacing, getting on my nerves.

Then he stopped, as if he'd picked it up, and stood with his back to the plaster wall, moving his shoulder blades against it rhythmically, unconsciously, like a bear scratching itself.

Pringle looked up to ask him something but didn't, changed his mind, saw something in Flockhart's eyes, perhaps, I don't know, all I wanted was sleep, get in a few hours so that tomorrow I'd be fit for whatever had to be done, a long tussle with Gabrielle, for one thing—she'd want to hold out here, shoot as many KR's as she could before the capital went up in flames and the survivors were driven into the killing grounds, she herself among them if I didn't make absolutely sure she listened to reason, run like hell and fight again another day, and so forth, make sure she was on the last flight out of Phnom Penh before the whole thing blew.

My eyes closing, opened them again, wondered how much time had gone by, Pringle still sitting there with the pad in front of him, Flockhart still scratching himself on the wall, probably not that exactly, more like thinking things out, trying to get his mind to accept that there was nothing else he could do, anyone could do, or trying, like a well-seasoned control in a trade where we accept nothing we don't like until we're actually dead, to find a way out, dream up a last-ditch eleventh-hour *nil-desperandum sauve-qui-peut* circus act that in the final analysis would count as a success of sorts because it would at least leave the battlefield strewn with the corpses of the well-intentioned, never say die and all that, go down with banners flying, I think—I've thought more than once, you know—that your Mr. Flockhart is that kind of clown, a closet romantic beneath the trappings of the steely espion.

Sleep, listen, get me some sleep now.

"Is there an airstrip at the base camp?"

Is there a *what?*

"I didn't see one. There's nothing on the film. Only a chopper pad."

My eyes fully open again because here we are, the control and the DIF and the executive in the field convened for debriefing, a time to keep awake if only for the sake of appearances.

"A helicopter pad?" Flockhart.

"Yes."

"General Kheng, then"—his shoulders coming away from the wall, his head swinging to look down at me— "will fly there by helicopter. Is that so?"

"The only way," I said, "without a strip."

He looked at Pringle, their eyes holding for a moment before Pringle looked down.

"I did in fact have in mind," Flockhart said, "an alternative move, if there was to be no air strike."

What did I tell you? Here was his last-ditch *sauve-qui-peut* trick coming out of the bag before your very eyes.

"It would succeed," he was saying, "only if you were prepared to take the ultimate risk, to achieve the ultimate goal."

Pringle was staring down at the table, thin shoulders hunched a little as if he expected fallout from somewhere.

I got out of my chair, fed up now, I didn't want to hear about it, I was going, been a hard day last night.

I was halfway to the steps when I heard Flockhart saying from behind me, "I am asking you to assassinate General Kheng."

26

SAKO

"What the hell do you take me for, a hired gun?"

Pringle was on his feet too, couldn't sit still. This was the fall-out he'd been expecting: he'd known what Flockhart was going to ask, known what I would answer.

"*You mean you refuse?*" Flockhart, pale suddenly with rage.

"Of *course* I refuse."

He stared at me, his eyes murderous, swung away and showed me his back, shoulders lifting as he took a deep shudder-ing breath and got some of his fury under control before he turned again and faced me, his voice icy, the sibilants honed. "I know your principles on this subject, of course; they are well documented. But you were prepared to kill once, were you not? In Bangkok?"

"I was. The man I was trying to protect was close to the queen."

"That's right. I rather admired you for that. For once you chose to set aside your principles." The word came whittled from his tongue.

"You haven't much time," I said, "for principles?"

"Of course. But wouldn't there be a place somewhere in yours for the consideration that if you were to fire one shot you could save a million people?"

"There's no—"

"Or is it that they haven't the privilege of being close to the queen?"

Watching me, his eyes frozen.

"You should have given this," I said in a moment, "a lot more thought."

"I gave it six weeks."

I began listening carefully. "Six weeks?"

"Ever since you got back from *Meridian*. The Chief of Signals had two new missions for you during that time, but I asked him to keep you on stand-by. I didn't tell him why. I just assured him it was important."

"You kept me off two missions?" Prowling those *bloody* corridors with my nerves losing their tune while this bastard was pushing me around the board behind the scenes.

"I wanted," Flockhart said, "to line things up over here. I also wanted to bring you to the point where you were ready to take on anything. Anything at all."

Bastard. "Then you were wasting your time."

He shrugged. "There was also that man in the train, wasn't there, in London? The Soviet."

"He'd gone back on his word and killed a woman, one of my couriers."

"How romantic."

"That was the *only* time I've ever killed except in self-defense, you know that, you've done your research. And if I ever do it again it'll be on my own decision, not because I was conned into it."

"Shall we rather say coerced?"

"All other things apart," I said, "I do this—even if it's possible— and then what? You send me after Saddam Hussein? Qaddafi? Zhirinovsky? I'm an intelligence officer, not a hit man."

"Your records show—"

"My records show everything but the man himself. And that's what you're up against now."

"As an intelligence officer you are of course first-class. The information you brought in tonight is without price." His head went low and his voice was so quiet that I only just caught what he said. "Could be without price."

His rapid switch of mood made me think of an instant of manic-depression as stillness settled into the room. Pringle hadn't moved for a long time, was standing with his arms folded and his eyes nowhere.

In a moment I said, "Flockhart, what got you into this Cambodia thing?"

His head came up and he looked at me with a flash of hate. I think he just didn't like the way I'd put it, and perhaps he had a point, *mea culpa.*

"I became involved in the fate of the Cambodian people," he said in a low voice, "when I was here in the late seventies, during the holocaust. I was here as a clandestine observer for the Bureau. Even at that time there was the feeling in London that someone should do something to stop the bloodshed." He moved suddenly, as if wanting to free himself of memories. "To have been here during that time was to be changed by it, if one had any feeling at all for one's fellow humans, whatever the color of their skin or the language they spoke."

That was understandable, but I thought there must be more: a more personal motive for turning himself into a rogue control, for mounting a rogue mission.

Then intuition flashed, and I paid immediate attention. "When I went into your office," I said, "in London, you made a point of hiding a photograph on your desk."

He looked away. "I did."

The room was quiet again. Perhaps I shouldn't have asked him about it, but I needed to know. "Whose is it?"

It took him time but I waited, not pushing, and at last he gave me the answer.

"It is a photograph," he said, "of my daughter Gabrielle."

There was the faint sound of music coming from the top of the steps, a thin Chinese voice, a woman's, singing to a stringed instrument. I listened to it, letting the mind explore what had just been said.

Then I said, "She told me her father was the French consul here."

"Yes." Flockhart spoke in a monotone, his back to the wall again, perhaps symbolically. "He was a good friend of mine. Two days after his wife was reported missing he was hit by a stray shot, and died in my arms. I was in his house at the time, and so was his five-year-old child, Gabrielle."

"You adopted her?"

"Of course. I took a young Cambodian woman out of the country to care for her, and later saw that she was educated in Paris, as her father would have wished."

"I'm glad."

He turned his head. "You've been seeing her, she tells me. She's rather fond of you."

"We've been thrown together, you could say."

"I didn't expect you to feel anything for the people of this country, so my hope was to arouse your compassion through Gabrielle. Your record in the archives does in point of fact reveal a little of the man. You are stated not to be uncompassionate, and to have a high regard for women." I didn't say anything. "Don't blame her"—he took a step toward me—"for what she told you when you arrived in Phnom Penh. I briefed her to say what she did."

"Of course I don't blame her. She wants to save this country too. She'd also make a first-class intelligence officer."

"I think so, yes, though it's hardly a pursuit I'd wish for her."

"At the moment she's playing with fire, did you know?"

He closed his eyes for a moment. "Yes. And of course I've tried to dissuade her, but she knows her own mind. Let us hope—" He shrugged.

"Amen." I took a turn, needing to think, needing more answers. "What was Fane doing in Paris?"

He was the man getting blown up on the steps of the hotel when Gabrielle had been shooting footage.

"I was lining things up at that time," Flockhart said, "as I mentioned. Fane was to have directed you in the field here, but there was a leak in security." A beat. "I imagine you enjoyed the film." Knew about Murmansk.

"Not really." All men are brothers. I took another turn. "You didn't give me the final objective for *Salamander* in London for the simple reason that you knew I wouldn't touch it. Isn't that right?"

"Perfectly."

Moving his shoulders against the wall again, restive as a caged bear, nothing but his veiled rage to thrive on, his rage against General Kheng and the shadow executive who refused to put him in the cross-hairs. "So what makes you think I'll touch it now?"

"I rather think we've discussed that. It concerned compassion."

"All right, I feel compassion for these people—anyone would. But that doesn't override my principles—and they're not only mine. Who else in the Bureau would have taken this on? Wellman? Locke? Thorne? They'd have turned it down flat and you know that. We're not hired guns, any of us, we don't kill in cold blood. And who, anyway, would take the risk?"

Flockhart turned his head. "Of firing a single shot?"

"Of firing the shot and getting it wrong, of being shot himself before he could get clear. I told Pringle that for a single executive in the field to take on the Khmer Rouge is a suicide run, one man against an army of twelve thousand. How could *anyone* go in there—"

"No," Flockhart said, and came away from the wall and stood in front of me, hands in motion, chopping the air—"No, it's not like that. You don't have to engage twelve thousand men. You have to destroy only one, and from a distance, and with a gun."

"Where?"

"Wherever you can reach him."

"He'd have to be isolated."

"Isolated, then." Staring at me, fire in his eyes.

"Then find someone to do it for you. Ask Bracken. Ask Symes. Ask one of the agents-in-place in Phnom Penh, or one of the sleepers."

"Oh come, they're not marksmen. You brought home the Queen's Prize two years ago at Bisley."

"That was another reason, was it, why you picked me out for this one?"

"But of course."

"You knew it'd come down to one final shot if all else failed?"

"I believed so. Destroy the leader of a rebel army and the ranks will be left in total disarray. History is clear on this point." Head on one side: "I thought perhaps it might tempt you, in the last hours of your mission, to be offered a task that even the United Nations is powerless to take on, for whatever reason."

He waited, sweat beading his face, his eyes locked on mine.

"An appeal to my vanity," I said. "That's in my records too?"

"You're known for undertaking operations that others might well refuse because of the difficulties. Rather, I would call it pride."

"Bullshit."

But he was right: he'd given this thing a lot of thought. I'd been the perfect candidate—a single man with no one and nothing to lose and a feeling for women and a streak of vanity that'd come close to getting me killed a dozen times, be this admitted. But Flockhart was finally trying to goad me into an operation I couldn't take on because of the one personal factor he hadn't believed would make any difference.

He turned away and I saw Pringle look up, look down again. Then he swung back to me—"Having refused to complete the mission, would you at least set up the end phase, in case we can find someone else to bring it home?"

"Not if you put it like that."

Anger flashed again in the cold blue eyes. He was a major control, very high in the echelon, and I, a lowly ferret in the field, wasn't expected to speak my mind in so forthright a fashion. Our good Pringle, yonder, was clearing his throat again.

"How, then," Flockhart asked, his voice hushed with control, "should I put it?"

"I'm not refusing the mission. I'm refusing to kill in cold blood."

"Even for the most urgent and compelling reasons."

"They're yours, not mine. You'd have to give me a reason I could call my own." I looked across at Pringle. "Have you got that map you made?"

While he was getting it from his briefcase I told Flockhart, "You wouldn't have a chance of hitting Kheng at the airfield here in Pouthisat when he takes off at first light"—I looked at my watch— "in four hours from now, four hours and nineteen minutes. There's no cover, only the freight sheds, and nowhere to run clear except into the six-foot chain-link perimeter fence, make a perfect target. Your only hope is to get Kheng when his chopper lands on the pad you saw in the film—if that's actually what it is—and shows himself in the doorway. I imagine there'll be a big welcome from the troops because this is D-Day, so he'll do his photo-op pose in the doorway, giving your man five seconds or more to line up his sights. Be an oblique shot, partly across the lake—Kheng won't be seen face on, but he'll present a full enough target profile for a body shot."

Flockhart had moved to the bamboo table, stood looking down at Pringle's map. "Where would he be?"

"The sniper? I'd put him here, at the edge of deep jungle, perfect cover. You said you were going to send Bracken out there on surveillance. Did you?"

"He signaled an hour ago," Pringle said, "from the village."

"By radio?"

"Yes."

"What kind of reception?"

"Adequate, some squelch but no actual breaks."

I looked at the map again. "All right, this is the way it could go. Assuming you could find a chopper from somewhere, you'd have—"

"I'm sorry," Flockhart cut in, and looked at Pringle. "My compliments to the officer commanding, Phnom Penh, and would he dispatch a helicopter to Pouthisat immediately, highest priority. If there's any problem, contact General Yang, the king's military aide. Apologize for waking him and ask him to expedite matters if necessary—again, this is red alert. Then signal Symes to meet the aircraft and have him ask the pilot to stand by for further orders, with the likelihood of immediate takeoff at any time, carrying a passenger." He turned back to me. "Please excuse the interruption."

Pringle picked up the red telephone and I told Flockhart, "All right, you'd fly your sniper out there at least one hour before first light, and the pilot would be told to put down somewhere here, two kilometers east of the village. Bracken would guide him in with lights or flares or whatever he's got available."

Pringle was talking on the telephone behind me. Control had hotline access, then, to King Sihanouk and his army commanders, presumably through the good offices of the British Prime Minister. I would have expected that.

"The pilot," I went on, "would stand by at the landing point while Bracken drove the sniper—by this track here—to within a mile of his attack position. He would cover that mile on foot and by moonlight—"

"Following the shot," Flockhart said, "he'll have to run back over that mile, to—"

"No. When Bracken hears Kheng's chopper coming in he can use its sound cover to move his vehicle right up to the sniper's position and turn it round, leaving the engine running. It's deep jungle here, but the track runs through it to the camp." I shrugged. "It's not perfect, but I've cut down on the risk factors all I can."

In a moment, "This is how you would proceed?"

"Give or take a few changes according to how things were going."

"Excuse me, sir." Pringle.

Flockhart turned to him.

"Compliments of the officer commanding, Phnom Penh. The helicopter is lined up and the ETA Pouthisat is forty-five minutes from now."

"Thank you." Flockhart looked at his watch. In profile his face showed the stress that he managed to blank out when he looked at people.

"The deadline you've got to work with now," I told him, "is 04:00 hours. Your aircraft will have to take off at that time, one hour before first light, to give the sniper time to reach his position."

Flockhart nodded, not looking at me, didn't want me to see the frustration in his eyes, the anger. He'd flown out from London to push this mission personally into the end phase and the objective was attainable, almost in his hands, except for this obstinate bloody executive who valued his principles more than the lives of a million people, I could see his point, could feel for him, the man was a saint, could be a savior if he could only find the instrument he lacked: a man with a gun and the will to fire it.

"Why not ask the army for a sniper?" I asked him.

Impatiently—"That's out of the question."

I just thought he might have taken a chance, that was all. It's perfectly clear in the book of books in London: *No person, civilian or military, shall be entrusted with the ultimate sanction in any operation of any kind directed by an officer of this organization unless he is himself an accredited officer of the same organization with a specific assignment in the field.* Flockhart was running a rogue mission but he was still an officer of the Bureau and it must have been tempting for him to break the rules at this stage with so much on the line. But perhaps he too had his principles.

"And the risks?" I heard him ask.

"The risks are about what you'd expect: the chopper could make a bad night landing; there could be mechanical trouble with the jeep; the sniper could miss the target first time and have to put more shots in and give his position away. Nothing's going to be certain on this one, or easy."

"But you deem it viable."

"Technically."

He began prowling again. "And the weapon?"

"You can't use any kind of missile or mortar because the noise and the smoke would expose the sniper and bring immediate return fire. The range for this setup is close to a hundred yards, so you'll need something like a Finnish-made bolt-action Sako TRG-21 with a—"

"Excuse me," Flockhart said, and looked at Pringle. "Can you put this on tape?"

I had to wait for him to set up the Sony but it gave me more time to think. "All right, something like a Finnish-made bolt-action Sako TRG-21 with a ten-round box magazine. Ideally you'd want a 168-grain hollow-point boat-tail bullet, ideally a Matchking. And try for a Bausch and Lomb 10 × 40 tactical scope with a Mil-dot reticle—he'll be sighting in early morning light."

Pringle left the recorder running.

Flockhart asked, "Can we find a weapon like that?"

"There are two people in the black market here," Pringle told him, "who trade in guns. If I gave them this one as a model, maybe they could come close."

"The moment we finish here."

"Yes, sir." He shut down the Sony.

This was at 01:13.

"I need sleep," I said.

"But of course." Courteous to the last, though he had nothing but hate for me. "You should know that in view of the information you brought in tonight I intend to contact the Prime Minister and suggest he advise King Sihanouk to order the capital evacuated as soon as possible, to prevent at least some loss of life when the missiles are fired. Meanwhile we shall set up your operation and try to find someone to take it on." He took a step toward me. "However, if at some time before the deadline is reached you should for any reason change your mind . . . " He left it.

There was nothing I could say that hadn't been said.

As I turned toward the steps I noticed that the little salamander had gone from the wall.

I slept, on and off, lying uncovered on my bed in the stifling warmth of the night, the bed with the young girl's hair still caught in the split bamboo.

Sometimes shots woke me from the distant streets; sometimes I woke to the thin plaintive song of the Chinese woman, thinking I could still hear it. And then, soon after three o'clock, the sound of footsteps brought me out of my sleep and I heard an urgent knocking at the door of the house and then the voice of my host, demanding to know who was there.

It was Flockhart, and he gave me the news.

27

REQUIEM

The air was still, here at the edge of the jungle.

The helicopter turned through forty degrees, forty-five, then settled on the pad across the lake. The power was shut down and the rotors began slowing.

As I lifted the gun I saw Flockhart for an instant in my mind as I'd seen him earlier, his face drained and his eyes burning as he gave me the news and at last a reason I could call my own.

Then the memory was gone and I sighted through the scope as the door of the helicopter came open and a man stood there in battle dress, and as he thrust his arm above his head with his fist clenched a shout went up from the rebel soldiers who were there to welcome their leader.

I centered the target in the cross-hairs—*Pour toi, Gabrielle*—and colored the morning with the blood of General Kheng.

DATE DUE